Search of the Moon King's Daughter

Search of the

Moon King's

Daughter

A novel by

LINDA HOLEMAN

Tundra Books

Copyright © 2002 by Linda Holeman
First Paperback Edition 2003

Published in Canada by Tundra Books,
481 University Avenue, Toronto, Ontario M5G 2E9

Published in the United States by Tundra Books of Northern New York,
P.O. Box 1030, Plattsburgh, New York 12901

Library of Congress Control Number: 2002101150

National Library of Canada Cataloguing in Publication

Holeman, Linda
Search of the moon king's daughter

ISBN 0-88776-592-0 (bound).–ISBN 0-88776-609-9 (pbk.)

I. Title.

PS8565.06225S39 2002   jC813'.54   C2002-900775-5
                          PZ7

We acknowledge the financial support of the Government of Canada through
the Book Publishing Industry Development Program (BPIDP) and that of the
Government of Ontario through the Ontario Media Development Corporation's
Ontario Book Initiative. We further acknowledge the support of the Canada
Council for the Arts and the Ontario Arts Council for our publishing program.

Design: Terri Nimmo

Printed and bound in Canada

This book is printed on acid-free paper that is 100% recycled,
ancient-forest friendly (40% post-consumer recycled).

4 5 6 7   08 07 06 05 04

For Daniel, Leila, Rebecca,
Alexis and Zoé

CONTENTS

I

Tibbing, near Manchester
1836

mmaline's life changed in the moment her needle finished the last golden loop of the embroidered apple on the cuff of a blue watered-silk gown. All she was thinking of was the oatcake, the sweet taste of it flooding her mouth. . . .

It was February 2 – Candlemas – although the day of festivity was like any other for Emmaline. She had promised Tommy she'd buy oatcakes on her way home from work, a small treat to mark the day of celebration. But long before finishing time, Fanny Shoesmith arrived with her message: "Emmaline! Emmaline, you're to come quickly."

Emmaline stood, the dress in her lap falling into a heap on the floor. The scrawny girl panted in the doorway of the sewing room, while a heavyset woman, her arms crossed over her broad chest, stood beside her.

"What is it, Fanny?" Emmaline asked, staring at the girl. "Is it our Tommy? Has something happened?"

"No. 'Tis Cat, Emmy. Your mother's been hurt bad." The words came out in gasps as Fanny tried to catch her breath. "I've been sent from the mill to fetch you. The overlooker wants your mother out and she can't walk on her own and she's calling for you. She won't let anyone else near her."

As Emmaline approached the door, the woman gripped Emmaline's forearm. The movement made the nest of keys hanging from her thick waist jingle cheerily, the sound a sharp contrast to the scowl on her face.

"You get back to work," she said, gesturing with her chin toward the pool of blue silk on the floor. "You're not going anywhere. Not until your day's work is done."

Emmaline wrenched her arm from the woman's grasp, sending the keys dancing. She grabbed her shawl from the hook beside the door. "I'm sorry, Mrs. Brill, but I've got to go to my mother. You heard. She's been hurt."

Mrs. Brill's heavy eyelids lowered, and she gave a sniff. "How do I know this to be true?"

Fanny bobbed at the woman. Her tongue – gray and slightly furry – darted out to lick her dry lips. There was the beginning of a sore at the corner of her mouth. "Beggin' your pardon, Missus, but it's true. I seen it with me own eyes. Terrible, 'tis. Blood everywhere." There was an unmistakable gleam of excitement in her eyes. "An' her hand – oh, it's crushed to near a pulp, so 'tis, as it were caught in the machine. I seen it with me own eyes," she said again, the word "pulp" coming out louder than necessary. Fanny licked her lips a second time and pressed her own narrow hand to her throat.

As Emmaline brushed past Fanny, color flushed high on Mrs. Brill's doughy cheeks. "Emmaline," she called, striding after her.

"You come back here. I haven't given you permission to leave. Emmaline! I'll tell your aunt!" But Emmaline was gone, running along the dim hall, away from the sewing room.

Mrs. Brill's lips tightened. She looked down at Fanny, and then gave the girl a sudden thump on the side of the head with her knuckle.

"Ow," Fanny whined, pulling her head away. "Weren't my fault, Missus. I were only doing what I were told."

"Be off with you," Mrs. Brill said. "Go on back to the mill, you filthy urchin."

"Yes, Missus," Fanny answered, and turned and ran in the same direction as Emmaline. Something made her look back. Mrs. Brill stood in the doorway, watching her. "Pursy cow!" she said, making sure her voice was low enough that Mrs. Brill couldn't hear.

And then Fanny ran on, away from the house, glad to be out in the fresh air. It had been raining earlier, but a weak sun now floated over the factory stacks. The February wind was cold, blowing through her patched dress. She hadn't had time to grab her shawl when the overlooker had sent her to fetch Emmaline. She inhaled deeply, creating a frosty tingle in her nostrils, then blew a long steaming breath into the wintry air. For this unexpected moment life was good, away from the clattering din of the cotton mill for a brief time. She rubbed her head as she ran, partly to soothe the sharp stinging from Mrs. Brill's knobbed knuckle, but also to will away the sound of Cat Roke's quick, high, animal shrieks above the constant *thrum* of the spinning machines.

Poor Emmaline, Fanny thought. She liked Emmaline, for when she saw the older girl on the street outside the mill waiting for her mother, Emmaline always had time for her. Sometimes she told her wonderful stories from the books she read. No one had ever told Fanny a story before, and usually Fanny envied Emmaline, for not only could she read, she also had a home and family.

But now, for these few moments, and maybe the first time in her short life, Fanny was glad she lived in the mill dormitories, with only herself to fend for, and nothing but shadowy, confusing memories of family. Emmaline had a family, all right, but what a family: a mother who was more trouble than help and a scrawny little brother who couldn't hear nor speak. And then there was the snobby aunt who allowed her own niece to be treated as little more than a drudge by that awful housekeeper, Mrs. Brill. Even though Emmaline, at fifteen, was two years older than Fanny, she had told Fanny that she was still paid as one of the lowest in the house, when by now she should be receiving wages as an assistant seamstress. And, she had confided to Fanny only the week before, she doubted that this would ever change.

Poor Emmaline, Fanny thought one more time, then slowed to a walk, allowing herself to be lost in the thought that there was someone with more cares than she had.

"Mother! Mother, what's happened?" Emmaline gasped, rushing into the overlooker's office, not even bothering to knock: something that might get her mother's wages docked if the overlooker had a mind to punish her. She glanced at him, seeing anger on his thin sallow face. His oily hair brushed his collar, and he nervously fingered the polished button on his waistcoat.

But his anger wasn't for Emmaline. It was for Cat Roke, for along with crushing her hand she'd done damage to the machine.

He'd have to report it to Mr. Slater, and it would be on his head. As for the Roke woman, well, she wouldn't be good for the mill any longer, he'd realized, after one look at her injury. She'd lose the hand, surely. Maybe even her life, if the wounds turned poisonous.

"Fool," he'd muttered, shaking his head at the gray-faced woman sitting on the low stool in front of him, her mouth twisted in agony and her eyes tight shut. All they needed, these mill workers, was to keep their eyes on their machines and their minds on the job. Any accidents were, he knew with certainty, purely the fault of lack of concentration on the task at hand. The mangled object that had once been this woman's right hand was now just a spongy mass of crushed bone and torn flesh cradled in a pool of blood in the folds of her skirt.

Emmaline's mouth opened in shock as she looked at what rested in her mother's lap. She knelt beside her then, stroking dark strands of hair back from the woman's forehead. "Mother," she murmured, "oh, Mother. What have you done this time? What will we do now?"

The overlooker answered. "You'll get her away from here, that's what you'll do, and you'll keep that," he nodded in the direction of Cat's hand, "hidden from the others. We don't want them turned from their labors. There's nowhere near enough work done here as it is."

Emmaline pulled her light shawl off her shoulders. At her first attempt to wrap it around her mother's hand, the woman gave a cry so piercing that Emmaline jerked involuntarily, dropping the shawl onto the greasy thread- and lint-covered floor. "Come, Mother, you must let me help you," she said, hardening her tone. "Open your eyes, and look at me."

Her mother's eyelids lifted, the deep brown eyes filmed with pain.

"I know it hurts terribly," Emmaline said, "but we've got to get you home. We have to wrap it. Your hand," she added, because her mother was now staring into Emmaline's face with shocked confusion.

"That's it, that's right," Emmaline muttered, getting the shawl wound around the damaged hand. Blood immediately seeped through the wool. Her mother was whimpering now, a low mewling sound.

"Come. Stand. I'll help you." Emmaline put her arm around her mother's waist and half pulled her to her feet. She supported the wrapped bulk of her mother's injury with her own free hand.

"I can't," her mother whispered. "I can't walk, Emmy."

"Yes, you can," Emmaline answered. "You can, Mother. You have to. We'll get you home, and then see what we can do for your hand. Everything will be fine."

As she spoke, loudly and clearly, Emmaline knew her words were false. All she had to concentrate on, for now, was getting her mother down the narrow stairs and along the winding streets, to their home.

Near to the row of back-to-back houses in the foul-smelling court that had been their home for the last five years, Emmaline dragged her mother past a ragged group of children chasing each other about the shadowed cobbled street. The oldest one, a small boy, let out a rough, braying laugh. "Has yer muvver bin out on the town all night, then, Emmaline?" he jeered.

Emmaline held her mother up, and the woman's feet stumbled and dragged on the cobbles. The stones were greasy from the earlier cold rain, and more than once Emmaline felt the worn soles of her boots slipping sideways. It was a struggle to keep both herself and her mother upright.

Emmaline said nothing, pushing past eight-year-old Justy Dilton, the skinny boy with a mouthful of crowded, protruding teeth. Her mother's weight was heavy against her.

"My ma says Cat Roke needs takin' down a notch or two, her with her fancy men," the boy went on, hopping alongside Emmaline, his head coming only to her elbow.

Emmaline ignored him, finally getting her mother to their doorway. Then she turned back to Justy, instructing, "Run and get our Tommy from Bethany's. And be quick about it."

Whether it was that Justy caught a glimpse of the blood-soaked shawl around Cat's hand, or perhaps it was the hollow sound of Emmaline's voice, but in the next instant the mocking expression fell from the boy's face, and he made an attempt to close his lips over his mess of teeth. He gave one quick nod, then turned and ran.

Mama sick? Tommy signed to Emmaline as he burst through the door and took in his mother's form, sprawled across the flock-filled mattress, his sister crouched beside her. He stepped back, his feet on the threshold, the door still open behind him, one hand holding its edge. His cornflower blue eyes were huge, his hair, white-gold: a wild halo, standing out around his head and lit from behind by the feeble light that managed to make its way down into the dark courtyard. His bony legs hardly seemed strong enough to hold his slight frame. He was shivering; he wore all he had – a thin jacket over an even thinner shirt, pants that were too short, and his bare feet stuck into cast-off worn shoes so big that Emmaline had stuffed crumpled paper into the toes to keep them from falling off. He had had his fifth birthday three months earlier.

Not sick. Hurt. Emmaline answered him with her own fingers. *Her hand is hurt.* In the few minutes it had taken to get her mother onto the bed, the blood had completely soaked the shawl. In the puny gleam of the candle Emmaline had lit, she saw how white Cat's lips were. *Bloodless,* she thought, as if all the blood in her mother was being pulled downward, draining into the hand and out through the wounds. As Emmaline realized she had to stop this rapid flow of blood – for she knew a body could not stay alive with too much blood gone – the woman gave one sudden shake, as if stricken with palsy, and then began trembling violently.

Emmaline grabbed the thin coverlet from the bed and tucked it over her mother. Then, with hand gestures, she indicated to Tommy that he was to shut the door and bring both his own small blanket and Emmaline's from the pallet they shared. When he held them out to her, his eyes huge and wet, Emmaline snatched them and wrapped both tightly around their mother.

"Mother? Can you hear me?" she asked. "Mother?" But her mother's eyes were rolling back in her head now, and her teeth chattering with a terrible, involuntary dance. Emmaline ran to the bucket in the corner and scooped a tin cup of the murky water.

"Try to drink, Mother," she said, holding the cup to the woman's lips. "I'll get a fire started in a moment." But as Emmaline tipped the cup, the water rolled down her mother's chin, gathering like glistening beads along the grimy line that ringed her throat.

The shaking stopped as quickly as it had started, and suddenly Cat lay motionless.

There was a touch on Emmaline's shoulder.

"Tommy," Emmaline said, and put her arm around her brother. His body was trembling almost as much as their mother's had been seconds earlier. Emmaline hugged him tightly, his body reminding her of a small terrified animal.

Emmaline make Mama better, he signed. *Fix Mama.*

Emmaline nodded. She knew her mother had fallen into unconsciousness from pain and shock, and if she was going to be able to do anything to her mother's hand, it was now. She would never take her to the Tibbing Infirmary – more died there from other diseases caught in the fetid filth and squalor before they could be cured or mended. And there was no point in going for a surgeon; they couldn't afford what he would demand. It was up to her to do whatever could be done.

She pulled the bundle of rags out of the one small glassless window beside the door, for more light, then moved the candle from the table to the wooden crate beside the pallet. Holding her breath, she slowly unwrapped her mother's hand. At the sight, she gagged, but swallowed hard. Then, wetting a soft clean cloth, she gently bathed the hand, washing away blood – both the congealing and the fresh – so she could inspect the damage. The back of the hand had deep open wounds exposing muscle and bone, where stitching would be necessary. She took one of the needles she had stuck through the waistband of her apron in the sewing room that morning – one threaded with the finest silk – and began to stitch the ragged flaps of skin together. The thin sharp needle punched through the torn flesh as easily as if it were piercing satin, but a draft came through the window, causing the flame of the candle to leap and pull, creating twisting shadows that made the stitching difficult.

Emmaline kept glancing at her mother's face as she worked, but the woman's eyelids remained half closed, and her lips moved, but no words came. She grew aware of a small keen from across the room. Tommy, his arms hugging himself, was perched on the edge of the stool in front of the cold fireplace. He was rocking back and forth, crying.

"It will be all right, Tommy," she said, glancing up, although she knew he couldn't hear her. But he could see her face, and she tried to smile at him, to reassure him, even though her mouth wouldn't obey. The tiny exposed bones of her mother's hand had been so white. Gleaming.

When Emmaline finished, she tied off the thread and snipped it with her teeth, then tightly wrapped the hand with strips of cloth from the rag bag that hung from the door handle. She straightened her back and eased her shoulders, realizing her neck and the front of her dress were damp with perspiration. Her mother opened her eyes, and croaked out a single word: "Hurt."

"I know. I know," Emmaline said, holding the cup of water to her mother's lips again. This time the woman managed to swallow a few drops. "This is the worst time, Mother. The next few hours. Try to hold on."

"Can't," Cat whispered. "I can't stand it, Em."

"You can. You're strong." Emmaline motioned for Tommy to come closer. "Look, here's Tommy home from work. Tommy will sit with you while I start the fire." She pushed Tommy by the shoulders so that he was sitting beside their mother, then ran to the fireplace. Using the flint and scraps of paper, she created a quick blaze, then added enough coal from the bucket beside the fireplace to ensure a strong fire.

As the small room warmed, Cat's head tossed restlessly. "Talk to me, Emmaline. Talk to me."

"Shall I tell you about the shop? Remember the shop, Mother?"

"Yes. Tell me about the shop. Tell me."

Emmaline lowered herself onto the pallet, one arm holding Tommy, the other hand stroking her mother's hair back from her forehead. "Listen for the tinkling of the bell over the door," she said. "Remember how the bell would dance and sing with each new customer? Remember the sun coming in through the windows at the front, and how Father had me wash the glass, inside and out, every single day, so that the customers could see the fine bolts of linen and cotton and the spools of bright ribbons?"

Tommy watched her face, his own relaxing as he saw the beginning of pleasure creep across Emmaline's features.

"Do you remember, Mama?" Emmaline asked, softly.

"I remember," Cat said, her pupils seeming to pulsate with each beat of her heart, and Emmaline knew that her mother's hand would be matching each heartbeat, throbbing with pain.

"The lovely shop in Maidenfern," Emmaline said, even softer, seemingly hypnotized by her mother's eyes. "Our lovely shop. . . ."

II

Maidenfern, Lancashire County
1830–31

But listen yet, I have a tale to tell,
It is of younger years, when life was sweet,
Long ere you came into this land to dwell,
I lived a happy child in Muslin Street;
And where thou standest now, I've gathered flowers,
And spent my sweetest, purest – childhood hours.

> – Ellen Johnston
> from "John Street, Bridgeton"

OUR LOVELY SHOP

t was both the village shop and their home, owned by a landlord from a neighboring town. He paid Jasper, Emmaline's father, to run the shop, extracting the rent he charged for the cottage at the back from Jasper's salary.

Emmaline loved their cottage home: the way the thatched roof wrapped round like a blanket of warmth, and how sparrows twittered in the overhanging eaves, flitting down to light in the garden and then fly back up, their tiny gray-brown bodies puffed with importance over the seed or insect in their pointed beaks.

Inside, the one big room had been separated into two: one for cooking and eating and sitting, the other for sleeping. There were scarlet geraniums on the deep windowsills and colorful handmade rugs on the floor of the bigger room, which had a simple fireplace. Bulging sacks of flour and oats hung from the beams, and always, always, a cauldron of something rich and warm bubbled over the flames of the fire. The yeasty smell of fresh bread daily scented the room. On the mantel over the fireplace sat a few heavy earthenware painted plates, as well as a Staffordshire pottery figure of a shepherdess. Jasper had won the shepherdess – first prize – with his pot of superior sweet basil in the annual village flower show the year Emmaline was eight. Now, at almost ten, she often stood on tiptoe to run her fingertips gently over the delicately turned rosy skirt and the tiny white hands holding a crook. One small shy sheep peeped out from the folds of the skirt. Emmaline loved the shepherdess. Her mother wouldn't allow her to take it down and dust it every week; she did that herself, tenderly wiping away the dark layer that grew on the figure from the smoke in the hearth below.

Along one wall there was a dresser, with heavy pots placed in the open bottom shelf. The top shelves were laden with rows of pewter vessels, as well as crockery, while the one drawer held her father's fruitwood writing box. In the middle of the room was a solid deal table, always graced with a jug of garden flowers. The table was surrounded by three rush-bottomed chairs and her father's old Windsor chair, made of elm and stained to resemble mahogany. On the walls hung spoon racks and boxes for salt and dried herbs, as well as a calendar from *The Churchman's Almanac*.

In order to get into the shop facing the street, the family had to go through the garden at the rear of the cottage. Most of the exterior back wall was hidden with ivy and woodbine growing in thick profusion, while near the door was a cabbage rosebush. In the vegetable patch, Emmaline and her mother grew beans, onions, carrots, parsnips, and leeks, with extra rows of potatoes and cabbages. They kept one corner for the spreading rhubarb, and another for Jasper's beloved herbs: basil and thyme and sage for cooking; rosemary to flavor the homemade lard; lavender to scent their clothes; tansy and meadowsweet to sprinkle on the floors to keep away pests; and chamomile, peppermint, and balm for tea.

The herb garden was separated from the vegetables by a border of cotton lavender, its silver-gray filigree foliage shimmering softly when the sun caught it just after midday. And then there were the flowers, which Jasper fussed over endlessly – the pinks, larkspurs, stocks, and carnations being regulars, with Jasper experimenting and adding new plants each year. The year before he had obtained a moonflower – a tender climber that clung and twisted round the fence railing along one side of the garden.

The village shop itself made up the rest of Emmaline's world. It was half timbered, with a roof of slate-colored tiles. Its windows looked out onto the wide street, with its row of merchants and craftsmen: the carpenter, the blacksmith, the baker, the shoemaker, and the butcher. At the end of the street was the Blue Horse, the public house. Occasionally a fancy barouche would pass through the village, and every third day, the mail coach would stop to pick up and deliver mail. Most traffic, though, was made up of dogcarts, wagons, men, women, and children; cows, horses, pigs, and dogs.

The hard-packed dirt road was long and straggling, yellow with dust in summer and muddy in winter, deep with ruts worn down by many years of feet, wheeled carts, and hooves. It snaked its way through the village, past the shops and clusters of cottages with their tile or thatched roofs, winding upwards to the common – a huge square of green used by the village for the children to play on and as a gathering place during times of celebration. Across from the common was St. Martin's, the quiet parish church, with its Gothic tower and decorated lych-gate leading into the churchyard, where generations of villagers were buried. The common had a long boundary of woodland. Beyond the last of the cottages, past the church and common, the winding uphill road with its borders of turf and hedgerows disappeared.

Emmaline had never been past the rise in the road. She knew this, and only this: the village and common, her cottage home, and the shop.

Inside the shop all was orderly and predictable. Her father kept the food counter – of cheeses and nuts and gingerbread and jams and chutneys – spotless. Many of the shop goods were purchased from itinerant traders passing through regularly: the eggler who brought fresh eggs from local farmers; the chandler, selling candles and soap; and the tinsmith, with his selections of pie pans and utensils. There was one corner where the villagers could post letters and pick up any that were sent to them. There were dry goods as well: bolts of dress fabrics – gingham and muslin and wool – and spools of ribbons of every color and baskets of thread. In the last month Jasper had put Emmaline's pillow lace on display, and so far she had sold two pieces: one for a collar and another for a wedding purse. She had been making lace since she was six years old, taught – like all the other village girls – by Mrs. Goodrow. While the other girls learned the art, none were able to keep up to Emmaline's speed with her pins and bobbins and thread. When her father examined the yard of lace it had taken Emmaline over a month to make, he decided it was fine enough to sell. "Perhaps you've a future in lace-making or sewing, Emmaline," he told her, smiling kindly, and Emmaline's heart had leapt at his approval.

"Working a village shop is the best way to live," her father said, as he often had, one warm October day, while he and Emmaline stood side by side in the empty shop, looking out at the quiet street. "In the middle of the countryside, with its beauty and peace and open sky, and yet not depending on the whims of weather, as farmers must. To own your own shop is freedom," Jasper said. "Nobody breathing down your neck, nobody standing over you with a stick or a threat. Oh, yes. My dream would be to someday own my shop outright."

Emmaline admired her father, handsome in his patterned waistcoat, his blue eyes crinkling at the corners as he smiled at the street outside the gleaming windows. *Yes,* she agreed, inwardly. *I wish to stay here, always and forever. I'm never going to leave.*

"City life holds no comparison," he went on, placing his hand on her shoulder. "I never found contentment in Tibbing, even though it was my home till I was grown. And the times I journeyed into London were —" he thought for a moment, "almost impossible to describe. The noise was deafening, and the sheer number of people and the filth, in many places, well," he stopped to take his clay pipe out of his waistcoat pocket, running his thumb over the smoothness of the bowl, "the less said of that the better. And I saw few proper shops, like ours. Instead, there were the hawking stands, with their owners pulling and shouting at those they wanted for customers. There was little fairness in their prices. It always seemed to me that those who cheated were the best sellers, while those customers who held out the longest were the best buyers. It wasn't for me, Emmaline. I knew I always wanted a simpler life, even if it vexed my family no end when I made my decision to move here, to Maidenfern." He suddenly squeezed her shoulder. "The day is too fine to be inside – summer weather, and yet here it is past Michaelmas, already into October.

And business is slow. Let's close the shop and get your mother and take a picnic to the common."

Emmaline fingered the smooth sheen of the green ribbon on its spool. "Are you sure, Father? It's just after midday; there will be customers who need –"

"They can wait," he interrupted. "Your mother needs her spirits lifted. Go and fetch her. And bring along the Scott book – *Ivanhoe*. We'll finish that chapter we started last night."

Emmaline hurried around the back of the shop to the house. A picnic in the middle of the afternoon, when they should be working. Sitting in the village green, reading. Those wanting to buy something at the shop would be angry to find its door closed. She had realized, for the last year now, that her mother and father were different than the other villagers in a number of ways. It seemed to her that her father looked on their lives as a perpetual holiday. The owner of the shop was frequently displeased with him. Emmaline had heard him asking her father why the sales tally was often lower than expected, and Jasper just shook his head and said he couldn't understand it; it was a fine little shop, yet it didn't seem to ever make a profit. Emmaline knew it was because her father thought nothing of shutting the door, like today, to enjoy fair weather. And also because he had a soft heart, and often asked less from those who didn't have enough of a jingle in their pockets to pay full price. He looked especially kindly on old Binny Elwood, tiny and frail and with no family to provide for her. Many of the villagers viewed Binny with suspicion because of her suspected witchcraft, but Emmaline saw a gentle light in the old woman's faded gray eyes, and knew her father did, too. Once a week he packed a basket of eggs and cheese and gingerbread and other small treats and took it to her, or sent Emmaline with it, never charging Binny a penny.

Emmaline's mother, Cat, had grown up near the village, the only daughter in a pack of burly farmer sons. But – as it was with Binny Elwood – being known by the villagers all her life didn't mean she was accepted. Or even liked.

Emmaline had been about seven or eight when she first noticed the way the other women around the pump and in the street eyed her mother, and whispered behind their hands about her. Many didn't include Cat in their conversations, and others pointedly stepped around her in wide circles as they passed. But Emmaline also saw how her mother didn't seem to care, and was more interested in talking and laughing with the women's husbands.

With her thick dark hair that she was so careful to keep clean and groomed, and her large dark eyes and clear smooth skin, her mother was beautiful in a way the other women weren't, and when she was younger Emmaline had thought that perhaps the women of Maidenfern didn't like Cat Roke for that reason alone. But in the last year Emmaline had started to understand more. She saw how her mother sometimes drank too much ale. Emmaline knew now that Cat snuck in the back door of the Blue Horse, where only the men went to drink, and drank pint after pint, out of sight in a dark corner, and Jasper would have to go and bring her home. Emmaline also saw how Cat's laughter, when a certain man might come into the shop, was just a little too loud. She saw how her mother's eyes grew wider than usual as she served particular men, sparkling with almost a greedy glitter, and how her face lit with a strange look of pleasure that Emmaline couldn't yet name.

THE CATHERINE WHEEL

mmaline tried not to watch her mother as they ate their picnic lunch under the spreading boughs of a wide larch on the common. Cat had taken a few bites of cheese and eaten two damsons, but wasn't interested in listening to Emmaline and her father take turns reading. Instead, she hauled herself up from the soft grass and heavily ran to join a group of children playing blindman's bluff in the center of the green.

"My turn," she cried, clapping her hands. Then she reached for the scarf and covered her eyes with it, tying it at the back of her head.

Emmaline glanced at her father. He was watching Cat with an indulgent smile. "You see how this has cheered her up? She's nervous about the child."

There had been other babies, carried to full term but born silent and blue-tinged, never drawing a breath. This baby was due in another month. While she was glad to see her mother carefree, she was also ashamed, and hoped no one would pass by and see her mother with her belly huge behind her apron, her face flushed and full, her hair falling loosely as she lumbered among the little children. Blindfolded and laughing, her hands clawed the air as she attempted to catch one of the five-year-olds who danced around her skirt. The children shrieked with excitement at an adult joining their game.

"I love to see your mother like this," Jasper went on. "I've told you about the first time I saw a Catherine wheel, haven't I?"

Emmaline nodded, but her father wasn't watching her. He was still watching Cat. Emmaline had heard the story dozens of times, about how her mother, whose name was Catherine – shortened to Cat when she was a child – had won her father's love.

"It was in London, on New Year's Eve," he said, his voice smooth and practised at telling the old story. "The fireworks at Vauxhall were astounding, exploding overhead while the crowds below roared their approval. And the Catherine wheel was my favorite, spinning off sparks in a huge spiral of color, like arrows shot into the air. Every time I saw a Catherine wheel, I felt my chest swell with those same colorful explosions. And then only months later I was riding through Maidenfern on an errand, up from Tibbing, and I met your mother. All I could think about was the Catherine wheel, sending out brilliance and color. My own Catherine wheel." His voice faltered. "I was expected to stay in Tibbing and work my way up in the world, as my father had done, and as my sister was doing with her husband." He stopped for a moment, and when he spoke again, his voice had recovered its usual jovial tone. "But there's no better life like that in a village, where one can see the sky."

Emmaline looked overhead, at the clear blue with faint brush strokes of white.

"Aye, Emmy," her father went on, "you'll never go wrong as long as you can look up at night and see the whole of the sky, instead of a city's stingy strip of darkness – the stars bleached by the false light thrown by the stinking oil of the streetlights. And the moon out here! Its slow, changing dance is, I swear –"

Emmaline stood, putting the last damson into her apron pocket. Although she loved the night sky as much as her father, she wasn't in the mood to hear him start in on his beloved moon poetry. "I'm going to gather some nuts," she said.

"Why?" Jasper asked, looking up in surprise. "Stay here with me. We're not done reading." He half lifted the book from his lap.

But Emmaline shook her head and headed to the woodland that bordered the common. It was filled with elms dazzling golden and beeches burning crimson in the afternoon sun. She knew the hazel and sweet chestnut trees were ripening, and she planned to fill her apron with their offerings. At the edge of the woods, she glanced back. Her mother pulled off the blindfold and ran, as best as she could, back to Jasper, leaning down and throwing her arms around his neck and kissing him on the cheek in plain view. Although Emmaline was too far off to make out her father's expression, she knew his face would be wreathed in a foolish grin.

Emmaline was glad she was in the shadows of the trees, where no one could see the flush that rose to her cheeks. Yes, Cat could be loving, and full of excitement, but her moods were really like the beautiful burning wheel her father described. They changed from moment to moment – sometimes soft, yellow as spring's earliest buttercups; other times, a loud and gaudy red. And there were the dark moods, too, these mysterious and deepest blue as the heart of a fire, and they most often surfaced after too many pints of ale. Jasper tolerated Cat's lapses, forgiving her time and time again, explaining away her drunken exhibitions as sorrow over the lost babies, or the heaviness of the winter rain, or whatever excuse came to him most readily.

In a sudden small burst of autumn breeze, the leaves around Emmaline rattled crisply. She took the plumlike fruit from her pocket and bit into it, expecting the sweet juice to flood her mouth and take her mind away from her mother and the empty looseness of her face after a bout of drinking. But the damson had secretly spoiled, for although its dark purple skin was firm, the meat inside was mealy and soft, overripe.

Emmaline spit the pulpy mouthful onto the mossy ground, and then hurled the rotten fruit into the underbrush. And even though she gathered saliva and spit again and again, she could not get rid of the aftertaste of decay.

MOONFLOWERS

hree weeks later Tommy was born, warm and pink and squalling. Jasper shut the shop for two days, buying drinks for the villagers in the Blue Horse to celebrate his son's healthy appearance. He also sent a message to Tibbing, to let his sister Phoebe know of the safe arrival.

With Tommy's birth came the end of the long, unseasonably warm weather. It felt, to Emmaline, that whatever force had pushed her tiny brother into the world had pulled the warmth and sunshine away with it. The last truly beautiful night, a few hours after Tommy's birth, was magnificent. The dark warm air caressed Emmaline's skin as she followed her father out into the garden, leaving Cat and the new baby sleeping peacefully. They sat on the rough bench leaning against the back of the cottage. Bullfrogs boasted in the marshy land behind the garden, and the sky was strewn with a seemingly random network of stars. The moon was full and soft, hanging low in the sky, as if its own weight were drawing it closer to the earth. It cast its subdued white light onto the dying garden, illuminating the withered plants and throwing exaggerated shadows.

"Look at my moonflowers," Jasper said, leaning toward the flowers on their twining vines that covered the railing of the fence. "What a wonderful plant, waiting until evening to open, and then showing its blooms all night, until touched by the first morning brightness. Moon worshippers, they must be."

Emmaline took in the large white flowers with their rounded leaves and heart-shaped bases. Their faces seemed to glow in the light from above.

"They've done so well because I planted them when the moon was new. It was Binny who instructed me."

Emmaline watched as a night-flying moth settled on the soft petals of one of the flowers, and held its wings very still.

Her father suddenly stood and pulled at a vine. Startled, the moth fluttered into the dark sky. Jasper worked with the vine for a moment, fashioning a circle of moonflowers that he placed on his head like a crown. Then, turning his face upward, he made the sound in his throat that signaled to Emmaline that he was about to change to his quoting voice.

What is there in thee, Moon! that thou
shouldst move

he started, and Emmaline let out a sigh of pleasure. Keats. She loved Keats, and quoted the next lines:

My heart so potently? When yet a child

she said. And then her father joined her, their voices blending seamlessly:

> *I oft have dried my tears when thou hast smil'd.*
> *Thou seem'dst my sister: hand in hand we*
> > *went*
> *From eve to morn across the firmament.*

"That's one of my favorites," she said, watching her father light his pipe. The crown of moonflowers shone on his hair.

"Yes. *Endymion*." Jasper puffed slowly, and Emmaline breathed in the fragrance.

"You are the Moon King," she said, smiling at her silly lovely father in his flower crown.

Jasper removed the crown, and sitting beside Emmaline once more, placed it on her dark blonde head. "And you, the Moon King's daughter," he said.

From the open window came soft newborn whimpers, soothed by Cat's murmuring.

Emmaline closed her eyes, then opened them and looked at the full face of the moon. She smelled the sweet fragrance of the moonflowers that circled her head. *That thou shouldst move my heart so potently*, she thought, and relaxed fully against the solid warmth of her father's arm.

COMING OF WINTER

t had been raining for most of the week – a steady, arrogant rain that heralded winter, turning each day mournful and gray. There was a crackling fire of fir cones and animal dung mixed with straw in the shop's fireplace, but still, the damp seeped in. It hung in the very air, so that the fine thread running through Emmaline's fingers felt clingy and resistant as she wound it around each pin in the lace-making pillow. She was trying to create a new pattern for the lace that would adorn the hem of Tommy's christening gown, the same gown she herself had worn over ten years ago.

She glanced down at her brother, sleeping peacefully. Cat had gone out earlier, complaining that it had been almost three weeks since Tommy's birth, and she could no longer sit about. "I'm feeling fine," she had told Jasper, putting the basket with the baby at Emmaline's feet. "Emmaline can keep an eye on him while she works; he's just been fed, and is clean and dry. I'll be back in an hour."

"But it's such a wet day," Jasper argued gently, setting down the cloth he had been using to polish the countertop. "Do you think it's best for you to –"

Cat tossed her hand in the air. "I need a bit of a walk and some air. The rain's never stopped me before." She wound her shawl over her head, blew a kiss at the three of them, and before there could be any further discussion, was out the door, sending the bell jumping.

Emmaline pretended to concentrate on the intricacy of her lace pattern, so that she didn't have to see the mournful expression on her father's face as he watched Cat disappearing. Finally he went back to his polishing, heavy frown lines marring his forehead.

"Can we start our next book – the one by Maria Edgeworth?" she asked, hoping to cheer him. She set down the pillow with its pattern of pins, and picked up the copy of *Castle Rackrent* she'd brought with her into the shop. It was the latest of the books her father had rented from a circulating library.

"If you like," Jasper said, smiling in a distracted way, but the lines didn't leave his forehead. When he didn't say any more, Emmaline put down the book and went back to her lace.

The next hour passed with Jasper serving a few customers and Emmaline working on her lace. The sudden sound of horses' hooves made both of them turn to the window. A handsome barouche, pulled by two gleaming black horses, stopped outside the shop. A driver hurried down from his seat to open the door.

"Who is it?" Emmaline asked, peering through the rain-streaked glass. Few carriages as fine as this one passed through the village, and fewer still stopped at their shop.

Jasper rushed to the shop door, flinging it open. "Phoebe!" he called, his voice loud and hearty. "Phoebe. How wonderful to see you!" He put out his arms, and the woman returned his embrace. Then, stepping back and shaking her thick wool cloak so that droplets of rain flew like a ring about her, she looked around the shop.

"You're on your own, then?" she asked.

"Well, just myself and Emmaline. And the baby," Jasper said. "If you're asking about Cat, she's stepped out for a few minutes."

Phoebe's face brightened as she turned to her driver and took a pile of packages from his arms. She dismissed him with a slight lift of her chin. "I had to come to see my new nephew," she said, then, and turning to Emmaline, added, "and my very favorite young lady."

Emmaline smiled shyly at her Aunt Phoebe. Although she didn't come often to visit, when she did, she always brought a bottle of fine wine for Jasper, and a bag of fancy sweets for Emmaline. Sometimes she tried to imagine Aunt Phoebe's house in Tibbing. According to her father, it was very grand.

"Why don't we ever go there – to visit Aunt Phoebe?" Emmaline had asked her father as she watched him compose the letter to his sister about Tommy two weeks earlier.

"Your mother and my sister are two very different women," he told her, setting down his nibbed pen on the table and leaning closer, although Cat was asleep with the baby in the other room. "Phoebe is very strong-willed, used to getting her own way. And your mother, just as strong-willed in her own way, has it in her head that Phoebe looks down on her because of her upbringing in the country – because she didn't learn to read and write, and isn't used to city ways. Your mother said she'd never go back to Phoebe and Nathan's after our last visit, when you were just a little older than Tommy. She wasn't comfortable, not at all, in Phoebe's fine house with all the servants."

He'd told her something else that day, too. "And perhaps it's because she knows that Phoebe thought I should have done more with my life than be a shopkeeper in a small village," he said, carefully blotting the ink. "She thought I should have . . ." He stopped, shrugging, studying the letter. "Well, she thought I made the wrong choices."

Emmaline wanted to ask him what wrong choices, but she suspected she knew – an uneasy feeling she had whenever she had seen her mother and Phoebe together. Cat would take on a sulky expression, and say very little.

Now Phoebe put her hands on her hips and shook her head. "You're looking pale, brother," she said. "Are you not being fed properly? You know how easily you fell victim to the fever when you were younger. You haven't had any of those fevers lately, have you?" She reached out a slender hand and touched her brother's cheek.

Jasper laughed, covering Phoebe's hand with his, and then taking the straw-wrapped bottle Phoebe held out. "Thank you for the wine. I'm in excellent health."

"Well, all the same, you must take good care of yourself." She smiled then, and the smile lit up her delicate features and took away the pinched look that Emmaline had noticed around her lips and nostrils.

"And as for you, Emmaline, well, I must say you're looking quite grown-up. I've brought something for you."

Emmaline smiled. The last time there had been sugarpaste mice and colored marzipan in fruit shapes.

"Since you're almost grown, I thought you would appreciate some real finery," Phoebe said, handing Emmaline a paper-wrapped parcel. "No more childish sweeties. This is for a young lady."

Emmaline unwrapped the package. Inside was a small drawstring bag, its base made of papier-mâché and the silky netted fabric top a soft cream. "It's beautiful," she breathed, running her fingers over the bag. "I've never had a reticule."

"I'm afraid it's not suitable for carrying about *this* muddy street," her aunt said. "But when you come to Tibbing –" She stopped as Jasper cleared his throat, loudly.

"We're going to Tibbing?" Emmaline asked, her mouth open.

"Phoebe had invited you and me for a visit, some time ago," Jasper said. "I didn't get around to telling you about it, Emmaline. And now with the baby, and your mother needing extra help. . . ."

Emmaline saw Phoebe's eyebrows lift, punctuating her smooth forehead. "It was for more than a visit," Phoebe said. "She's old enough to be told, Jasper." Ignoring her brother, Phoebe turned to Emmaline. "I suggested you come to Tibbing for schooling," she said. "You could live with me, and be educated. *Properly*. I know your father has taught you well, and that you attend the Sunday School at the parish for further instruction, and you read ably," she went on with an almost weary acknowledgment, glancing at the copy of *Castle Rackrent* next to Emmaline's lace. "To say nothing of your proficiency with the needle. But there are so many other things to learn, and so many opportunities for a girl like you in the city. There's nothing, absolutely nothing, for you here."

Emmaline glanced at her father. His expression had grown dark. "But . . . but do you mean, go to Tibbing without Father and Mother? Without Tommy?"

"Yes. I did say to live with me, did I not? We could have a fine time, you and I. There are so many empty rooms in our home, and your Uncle Nathan has approved of the idea. Surely you –"

"I think this is too much for Emmaline to take in," Jasper interrupted. "Please, Phoebe. Leave it for now."

"But I think we must –"

"No! I said not now, Phoebe!"

Emmaline had never heard her father raise his voice in anger. Her breathing quickened uncomfortably. She set the reticule on the counter.

Phoebe didn't seem offended. "Fine, fine," she said, lightly. "All right, now, let's see the baby. I've brought him a christening dress of fine Chinese silk, with Belgian lace trim. Put it somewhere safe, Jasper," she added, handing him the last wrapped package, "where nothing can happen to it."

What could happen to it? Emmaline wondered. And what about her old gown that she'd thought Tommy would wear, trimmed with the new lace she was making?

Phoebe leaned over the basket. "Oh, my," she said. "Oh, dear."

Emmaline crowded beside her aunt to see what she found distressing. Tommy looked as he always did when he was sleeping: his long, almost white eyelashes against his warm cheeks, one hand curled up beside his ear, and his white-gold hair a sweet-smelling cap on his small round head. No other children in the village had hair like Tommy. Emmaline reached down to touch it.

"He looks . . . ," Phoebe said, leaning closer, "well, he doesn't look at all like Emmaline did. Or like you or I. And certainly Cat is darker than most."

"Why should he look like anyone in particular, Phoebe? And you're fair, and our Emmaline's hair is the color of yours. Fresh honey," he said, with a smile at Emmaline.

"Fair, yes. But this . . . well, surely he's got the hair of a Swede, or a Dane. Do any pass through here?"

Emmaline looked at her father. His smile had faded.

Jasper thumped his fist on the counter, the unexpectedness of it making Emmaline jump.

"You'll not come here and make accusations against my wife," he said, his voice a low growl. "We've been through this, Phoebe, and I'll not stand for it again. You know nothing of our lives here."

"I know more than enough," Phoebe said, pulling her cloak around her, as if suddenly cold.

"Do you want to hold the baby?" Emmaline asked, loudly, wanting to stop the argument. She'd never seen her father like this.

"I don't think so," Phoebe said. "Not at present. Why don't you show me what you're working on?"

Relief flooded through Emmaline as Jasper turned away. She picked up the pillow. "It's a new pattern," she said, touching the threads twisted around the pins and across one another in an intricate design. "There are sixty-two twists for each width of my fingernail," she added, proudly.

"Quite fine," Phoebe said, smiling at Emmaline.

The front door burst open, the bell crashing. "I saw the carriage out front, and knew we must have a visitor of great *importance*," Cat said, too loudly, looking straight into Phoebe's face.

Emmaline closed her eyes for a second. She knew that tone too well. *Not today*, she prayed. *Not in front of Aunt Phoebe.*

"Jasper, my love," Cat said, walking toward him. As she passed, Emmaline smelled the stink of ale. Her mother's clothes were soaked through, and her hair hung in dripping strands over her shoulders. "I've had a lovely walk about town, and it's cleared my head ever so much," Cat said to Jasper, then raised herself on her toes and pressed her mouth to his. "Your lips are so warm, my sweet, on such a blustery day."

Emmaline heard Phoebe suck in her breath.

Jasper put his hands on Cat's shoulders, gently pushing her away. "Have you not said hello to Phoebe? She's come all the way to see Tommy, and brought lovely gifts for the children."

Cat stepped away from Jasper, straightening her bodice as she turned back to Phoebe. "Yes, I see that you've lowered yourself to come to Maidenfern," Cat said, her voice slurred. "I hope you haven't muddied your fine skirts in doing so."

Phoebe said nothing.

"Have you seen our new boy, then?" Cat asked. "Isn't he just the loveliest child?" She went to the cradle, stumbling a bit, and picked Tommy up roughly. Startled from his sleep, Tommy gave a loud wail. "It must be the most terrible curse to never feel a child of your own in your arms," she said.

Phoebe's face drained. Her eyes stood out large and dark against the ivory of her skin.

"Cat, no," Jasper said.

"I must be going," Phoebe said, raising her voice over Tommy's crying.

"Phoebe – you haven't even had tea, please, stay. I'm sorry for all of this. I –" Jasper said, taking hold of her arm.

"It was fine to see you, as always, Jasper," Phoebe told him, regaining her composure and speaking quietly. "And you, too, Emmaline." She stepped away from Jasper, not looking at Cat. "Remember what I said about Emmaline, Jasper," she added. "The invitation is always open."

Jasper shook his head. "You know that's impossible, Phoebe."

"What invitation?" Cat asked.

But Phoebe acted as if the other woman hadn't spoken. "Good day, then." She turned and went through the door, attempting to slam it. But the little bell caught with a sad choking sound, and the door swung open again.

Jasper turned to Cat.

"It wasn't my fault," Cat said, even though he hadn't said a word. She jiggled the howling baby against her rain-soaked shoulder.

Jasper ran out after his sister.

Tommy's cries grew weaker, dwindling to short whimpers as his mother swayed with him.

"What's that?" Cat asked, her eyes focused on the counter where Emmaline's new reticule sat.

"Aunt Phoebe brought it for me."

Cat shifted Tommy and reached for it. "Nothing but a piece of cheap frippery," she announced. "It doesn't suit you." And then with one swift movement, she tossed the reticule into the fire.

Emmaline's mouth opened in protest, but before she could get a word out, Cat shouted at her: "She's nothing but a barren prissy cow, that Phoebe Slater." Her shrill voice started Tommy howling again. "And you'll never have anything to do with her. Do you understand me, Emmaline? You'll have naught to do with her, ever, no matter what your father says."

Emmaline felt heat rush into her face, and as she clenched her fists, a sudden sharp pain made her look down at her hand, still holding the lacing pillow. Two of the pins had punctured her palm, and tiny pinpricks of blood leached onto the lace she'd worked on so diligently. As she watched, the minute dots of blood widened, creating two small rings of brilliant red against the snowiness of the lace, and she knew it was ruined.

Her mother sat on a stool behind the cheese counter to feed Tommy, putting an abrupt end to his screaming. Now there was only silence in the shop, except for the baby's rhythmic nursing and the tiny popping of the beautiful netted handbag shriveling and curling in on itself as the flames devoured it in greedy bites. Emmaline could see her father and Phoebe through the window. By the look on their faces, they were arguing. Then Phoebe climbed into the carriage and the driver slapped the reins against the horses' backs.

Jasper stood in the steady rain, his spine rigid, watching until the carriage disappeared over the hill. He continued to stay there, staring at the slick ruts in the empty road until Emmaline thought she could bear it no longer.

A drenched dog, its dun-colored hair standing in thin tufts from its skinny ribs, slunk out from between two buildings, looked at the motionless man, and gave one feeble bark. The sound stirred

Jasper from his reverie, and he shook himself, finally turning back to the shop.

Later, when Emmaline realized that her father and Phoebe's last good-bye was that suspended time in the empty wet street, she wondered if, somehow, her father had sensed this as he stood for so long, staring up the road where the carriage was no more.

WE CAN CARRY NOTHING OUT

t was only two months afterward that Cholera passed by, traveling by road on the carts and by sea on the colliers. It made a brief stop in Maidenfern and the surrounding countryside before it continued on its journey, northward into Scotland and southward toward London, killing hundreds of thousands by the time it burned itself out.

It was a bleak January day – midmorning – when Jasper complained of sudden pains in his limbs, and then muscle cramps in his legs. Earlier that morning, as she had walked to the shop with her father, Emmaline had seen frost on a holly spray that hung near the garden, and smelled leaves decaying in the sad winter air.

Unable to stand, Jasper took to his bed at noon, and all that afternoon Emmaline stayed in the cottage with him while her mother tended shop. As she carried a brimming mug of tea to the bed, Jasper cried out, doubling over and clutching his stomach, retching dryly. By early evening the tremors had begun, and by the next morning he was almost unrecognizable, his features shrunken by dehydration from bouts of vomiting and diarrhea, his lips and skin taking on a blue-gray hue.

He was dead as the afternoon shadows began to lengthen, less than thirty hours after the first symptoms.

It had happened so quickly that for the next few days Emmaline kept thinking she'd awaken, that it was only a terrible nightmare. But her father's sheet-draped body on the deal table and her mother's steady sobbing drove the truth home.

Reverend Lewis came the evening Jasper died, to offer his condolences and recite from the *Book of Common Prayer*. "We brought nothing into this world, it is certain we can carry nothing out," he said, his pouched eyes closed. "The Lord gives, and the Lord also takes; blessed be the Lord's name." Then he put his arthritic hand on the side of Tommy's cradle. "And it is a blessing from our Lord that you and your brother have not succumbed to the terrible pestilence, Emmaline. 'Tis a bit of a miracle, after all. So often it's the wee babes and children who fall the fastest."

As he spoke, Emmaline watched his lips move within his beard as if they were two senseless worms in a white nest. *Blessing? Miracle?* How dare he use these words when her father's body lay so still and cold in front of them!

Jasper Roke's funeral was small and quiet, and had followed two others that day. After he'd been buried in the churchyard of St. Martin's, most of the villagers had stopped by the cottage to stand silently and nibble on barley cakes provided by the women of the parish. Emmaline stayed in the garden of winter flowers: the silver laminum, hebe, and the rich purple buds of the rhododendron. A feeble sun made a brief appearance, creating a lavender lacework of silhouettes on the hard ground dusted with snow.

When the last mourner had left, Emmaline went inside, her toes and fingers nipping with cold. Cat set Jasper's writing box on the table. "Now you must write a letter to your Aunt Phoebe, Emmaline. No matter what has passed between us, it's only right she should know." She looked as if she were about to say more, but suddenly covered her trembling mouth with her hand and went into the sleeping-room.

Sitting in her father's Windsor chair, Emmaline ran her fingers over the polished top of the brass-edged writing box. The fruitwood surface was French polished, enhancing the beauty of the dark striations within the wood. One inlaid flower, of mother-of-pearl, was set in the center. Emmaline caressed the cool smooth petals, reminded of her father's beloved moonflowers.

"I am the Moon King's daughter," she said aloud in the room, silent except for the brittle black branches of the cabbage rose-bush, limned with frost, rattling and clicking against the window.

"What's that?" her mother called dully from the other room. "Have you finished?"

Not answering, Emmaline opened the lid of the writing box. Very carefully she scraped flakes off the dry cube of lampblack and gum, and mixed them with water in a small cup. She set out a sheet of light paper and picked up the straight pen with its split nib, feeling the familiar smoothness between her fingers. Then she dipped the nib into the India ink. She thought a long time about what she would write, but there seemed to be no other words than the most simple.

Dear Aunt Phoebe, she finally wrote. *Father died. He was taken with cholera. Your loving niece, Emmaline Roke.* As she reread what she had written, one droplet of ink fell from the nib onto the *g* in the word *loving*, making a small dark orb, marring the perfection of the page.

Phoebe had done very well for herself. Through the right circles she had met Nigel Slater, who had risen to a higher position by using his inheritance as eldest son to purchase a cotton mill. He had married Phoebe and she had worked hard to make herself into the grand lady she always knew she could be. She entertained the society of Tibbing in their large fine house on Mosely Road. She had painstakingly decorated it, and outfitted it with a large staff to keep things running smoothly.

The day after Emmaline had sent off the letter, a tall wiry man – a messenger from the owner of the shop – arrived at their cottage door to tell them that they would have to vacate by the next quarter day.

"But that's in less than two months' time. Where will we go?" Cat had asked. "I've the children, and –"

"No concern of mine, Missus," the man replied. "This cottage is for them what works the shop. Or, of course, them what owns the shop. I don't suppose you've a mind to buy the shop outright, have you?"

Cat's lips tightened. "No, although it was my husband's plan. But it's out of our means."

Emmaline came to stand beside her mother. "We can keep on running the shop, Sir. I've helped my father, always, and my mother knows how to serve as well. And I can read and write, and keep track of the accounts. I'm well past ten, and I can work every bit as well as –"

But the man cut her off. "You should be teaching your girl to control her tongue, Missus Roke. I'll have no chit speak up to me so. And it's a man needed for a man's work in the shop. Somebody new has already been taken on, and with the job comes this cottage. I'm sending him in to take over the shop tomorry; folks need their goods, and I see you haven't opened the shop's door since your loss." He shifted his weight and turned his hat in his hands. "My master has long suspected that more was given away than sold, and I've just had a look at last year's records. They do show that Jasper owes money, a goodly sum, for the food he's been supplying to his family and who knows else. So it will be the few bits and bobs of furniture and the like you have here in payment. You'll be getting off easy, for I can see your belongings aren't worth much."

Aren't worth much? Emmaline thought. *Father brought most of these pieces from Tibbing. They're all we have left of him.*

"But out of respect for them what's passed on," the man continued, "I've been instructed to allow you to stay on in the cottage for the next little while. I'll thank you to not frequent the shop any longer, unless it's to purchase supplies with coin, like any other. And at the next quarter day, the new man and his own family moves in here, and you're out."

"But we have hardly any money. What will we do?" Cat asked, as she had so often asked of Jasper when there was even a minor problem. Her voice was small, and she looked up at the man from under her dark winged eyebrows. Emmaline knew that look had always made her father smile, and he would tell Cat not to worry, that he would look after everything.

But this man wasn't Jasper.

"Find yourself work as itinerants," he told her, the tiniest hint of sympathy weeding through his words. "Farms along the roads always need temporary hands, and now, with the cholera taking so many, there'll be plenty of work going for hard workers come spring planting. And you yourself, Missus Roke, are used to the ways of the land, are you not?"

"But I've the baby," Cat said. "They'll not want to take on anyone with a babe in arms. And it's been years since I've worked the fields. Can you not . . . ," Cat went on, but the man simply shook his head, put on his hat, and strode through the tangled winter garden.

"Could we go to live with one of your brothers?" Emmaline finally asked.

Her mother shook her head and covered her face with her hands, lowering herself into a chair. She wept quietly. "Last I heard from someone coming through town, they're just barely hanging on with their own families. They couldn't take on even one more mouth to feed, let alone two and a baby. One of them might take us in for perhaps a week, but that would be all. I can't think about it now, Emmy. Not now," she said.

And the next day, there was a strange man behind the counter in the shop. Through the front window Emmaline saw him standing where her father had stood, laughing and talking to the villagers as if he were an old friend. And even while she was inside the cottage, Emmaline heard, through the wall connecting the cottage to the shop, the tinkling of the bell as customers came and went, but it seemed that even the bell sounded differently, subdued, as if it, too, missed Jasper.

A PROPOSITION

nd then Phoebe arrived, in the same barouche with the same fine team of horses, the same driver sitting straight in the seat, staring ahead as if his eyes were fixed on some distant spot on the horizon.

It was a surprisingly fair day for late January, and Emmaline was in the garden with Tommy when she heard the muffled clomping of the horses' hooves in the frozen mud in front of the shop. She went out to the street and saw her aunt emerging from the carriage.

"Oh, my child," Phoebe said, tears spilling from her eyes. She put her arms around Emmaline, also enclosing Tommy. Emmaline could hear the frenzied beat of her aunt's heart through the sweet-smelling wool of her dress.

"I can't believe Jasper is gone," Phoebe said, composing herself, delicately wiping at her eyes with a lacy bit of linen. "I've already visited the churchyard." She stifled a low sob. "Where is your mother?"

"In the cottage, having a lie-down," Emmaline said.

"Come," Phoebe said. "We'll go and speak to her."

Emmaline was ashamed at the state of the cottage. The fire had gone out, and the big room felt cold and dim. There were no winter flowers on the table, no soft friendly sigh of the kettle or warm smells of food cooking.

Emmaline hurried to lay Tommy in his cradle. He kicked his chubby legs and let out a series of soft gurgles. "Mother's let the fire go out. I'll just light it," she said. "Would you like me to fix you a cup of tea?"

Phoebe gave a small sad smile, looking around the darkened room. "That would be nice, Emmaline." She lowered herself into the Windsor chair as Emmaline poured water into the kettle hanging over the hearth. "Are you doing most of the work here – looking after the baby, as well as your mother?"

Emmaline kept her back to her aunt as she fussed with the kindling. "I'm sure it won't be long until Mother is herself again. And I don't mind looking after Tommy. Not for a minute." She lit the kindling from the flint kept on the mantel, and immediately a small flare rose and the room brightened. Wiping her hands on her apron, Emmaline went to the cradle and put her finger against the baby's palm. His padded fingers immediately closed around it, and he spluttered excitedly, his mouth opening into a wide gummy smile. Emmaline smiled back at him. "He's a very good baby, is our Tommy."

Phoebe didn't respond, not even glancing at the cradle.

"Shall I fetch Mother, then?"

Phoebe nodded, closing her eyes.

Emmaline went into the other room and roused her mother. As Cat sat up, rubbing at her eyes, Emmaline smoothed the woman's hair and straightened the collar of her dress. "Be polite, Mother," she whispered. "Maybe she's come to help us. I'm sure that's why she's come – not only to visit Father's grave, but to help us. Now we won't have to worry about what to do." She could hear Tommy fussing with small plaintive sounds.

Cat kept her eyes lowered as she went into the main room. "Good day, Phoebe," she said, her voice husky. Tommy's fussing was getting louder, but Phoebe hadn't stirred. Cat sat at the table, across from her sister-in-law. She studied the tabletop.

Emmaline picked up Tommy, patting his back and humming against his temple. He quieted immediately. She saw that her aunt's eyes were wet again.

"What will you do?" Phoebe asked, wasting not even a sentence on condolences. "I see there's someone else running the shop. Will you be staying on here?"

Cat shook her head. "We must be out by quarter day."

"Has Jasper left some provision for you?"

Again Cat shook her head. "No."

"Jasper left nothing." It wasn't a question. "He managed to spend all he had, and not even put aside a small saving." Phoebe's voice didn't hold any surprise.

Cat lifted her hand to the table. She traced the cuts and grooves in the fir planks with her index finger. "He was a generous man. We wanted for nothing while he was alive. But all we have is enough to get us through the next short while. We can't even sell our furnishings. They're being kept, to pay off our debt in the shop."

Phoebe's features tightened, her eyes dry now.

Tommy's head was warm and soft under Emmaline's lips.

"And?" Phoebe said. "Where will you go? Home to your family?"

For the third time Cat shook her head, but said nothing this time. Her finger hadn't stopped its restless tracing of the markings on the table.

"So you have no plan? No money, and nowhere to live?"

Cat remained silent. The slow hiss of the kettle coming to a boil was the only sound in the room now.

"Then it falls on me to help my brother's family," Phoebe finally said, and Emmaline saw her shoulders straighten. A strange look crossed her face as she glanced at Emmaline.

Emmaline wondered why her mother still did not lift her eyes, or at least show some gratitude toward Phoebe.

"You won't have to worry, Catherine," Phoebe said. "I will see to it that you are looked after. You and the child."

"The child?" Cat echoed, finally meeting Phoebe's gaze.

"The baby," Phoebe said. "You and the baby will be provided for."

Cat looked at Emmaline.

"As for Emmaline," Phoebe said, "she will come and live with me."

The kettle let out a puffing squeal as it came to a full boil. Emmaline jerked at the sound.

"No," Cat said. "No. She'll not. I'll not let her go. Not ever."

Phoebe stood, pursing her lips. "Don't be a fool, Cat. There's no future for her here. If you give her to me, I'll see to it that you and —"

"I said no, Phoebe." Cat stood as well. "You can't make a trade for her, as if she's no more than a donkey or a pig. No, we don't need your help that badly, and we never will. Never!" Her face flushed as her voice grew shrill. Emmaline recognized a dangerous glint in her dark eyes.

Tommy struggled in Emmaline's arms, and she realized she had been holding him tighter and tighter.

"You're a foolish woman," Phoebe spat back, her fine-boned features contorted with anger and frustration. "You always were. My brother had a good heart, but no sense at all. Instead of building up a business of his own in Tibbing, he gave it all up to marry beneath him and live out his life in this forsaken little village. And now you dare to pretend that you don't need my help – that you can really manage on your own!"

Cat didn't move. "Get out," she said, her voice almost a growl. "Get out, and never bother us again. My daughter is not for sale. Do you understand me?"

Phoebe raised her chin. "Perfectly, Catherine. I understand you perfectly." She cast one more glance at Emmaline. "And I think you do, too, Emmaline. You've inherited a good measure of intelligence from your father; that much is obvious. And perhaps you've a touch more sense. Perhaps you don't want to throw your life away, as he did. So it may be that you'll think about what has happened here today."

And with that, she turned and left.

The kettle continued to boil, but neither Emmaline nor her mother paid it any heed. When she could stand the silence no longer, Emmaline whispered, "I never want to leave here, Mother. And I'll never leave you and Tommy."

Cat sat down, laying her cheek on her arms on the table. Eventually the fire beneath the kettle flickered, gave one hopeful surge in a sudden small breeze that blew in from under the door, but with no fresh kindling added, slowly smoldered until it was dead.

BRAIN FEVER

fter they'd eaten a cold silent supper, Cat announced she was going for a turn around the common. When she wasn't home after an hour, Emmaline knew she had gone only as far as the Blue Horse, and no further. Although the villagers had been kind those first few days after Jasper's death – the women bringing food and the men murmuring condolences as they crushed their hats between their fingers – Cat had no real friends, and Emmaline knew she wouldn't have stopped at anyone's home.

Cat didn't come home until the publican sent the last customers away, and Tommy was fussing for a feeding. After Emmaline put the baby in her arms, her mother took Tommy to her bed, and within minutes was snoring heavily, with Tommy still latched to her breast.

That first night set a pattern. From then on, Cat didn't even wait for evening to fall, but started to frequent the Blue Horse in the late afternoon. She wouldn't listen to Emmaline, no matter how she cried and begged her mother not to go, accusing her of using the few coins they had for food on ale.

And one terrible night, less than three weeks after Phoebe's visit, another tragedy struck the Roke cottage.

Tommy had been fussing all afternoon, and no matter what Emmaline did for him, he remained fretful. Emmaline noticed, when she changed him, that his skin was blotchy and his tiny body too hot. She knew he needed feeding, and that her mother might not be home for hours. So she took Tommy to her mother, where she sat in a dark corner of the Blue Horse, a tankard of thick, foaming drink on the table in front of her. Emmaline begged Cat to come home and feed him, but Cat wouldn't. Laughing too loudly, lightly slapping Emmaline away, Cat called for another drink and turned her attention to a stranger – a tall thin man Emmaline didn't recognize.

Emmaline, holding the wailing baby tightly, ran down the road to Gemma Wellington's cottage. Gemma had a daughter only a month older than Tommy, and Emmaline had asked her to feed Tommy once before, when her mother had got herself into a similar state. The good-natured woman had taken the baby and nursed him along with her own child, and Emmaline hoped she would do the same this night. But when she arrived the house was empty, and a neighbor told Emmaline that the family had gone off to a nearby village to visit Gemma's mother, and would be home the morrow.

Emmaline then went to the Hoopers, for they had a milch cow. Mrs. Hooper took pity on the girl and the baby, although Emmaline didn't tell her the truth about Cat. She told Mrs. Hooper her mother was sick, and couldn't feed Tommy. Mrs. Hooper nodded, her lips tight, and Emmaline lowered her head in shame, for she knew she wasn't fooling Mrs. Hooper for one moment. Mrs. Hooper looked at Tommy, lying stiffly in Emmaline's arms. She picked up one of his hands, and Emmaline saw that he moved it jerkily.

"The baby's sickening for something," Mrs. Hooper said, shaking her head. "I hope you're not bringing a fever onto my family with him here."

"No, Mrs. Hooper, I'm sure he's only hungry. He hasn't been fed for hours now."

"Looks ill to me," Mrs. Hooper said, touching the baby's cheek with a roughened finger. "Wait on now, and I'll get you a cup of milk." She went to the cow tethered beside the cottage, and milked warm frothy strings into the bottom of a deep, narrow tin flask, and gave it to Emmaline. Carefully Emmaline carried both the flask and the baby, whose cries had grown unfamiliar and high-pitched. When they got home, she made a twist out of a clean rag. Dipping it into the milk, she put the rag into the baby's mouth. Tommy stopped howling and greedily sucked on it for a moment, but then turned his face away and refused to feed.

"What is it, Tommy?" Emmaline whispered to the child, holding him close and lowering her face onto his silky white hair. Under her lips she felt the soft spot on the top of his head, felt it pulsing, but it appeared to bulge abnormally with each heartbeat. She knew, now, that he was truly sick, and didn't know what else to do but wrap him tightly and hold him against her as she lay on her own pallet. Eventually his cries stopped, and Emmaline thought he had fallen asleep, although his eyes were half-open, and his body, which had been stiff earlier, grew floppy.

Although she wanted to stay awake and watch Tommy, as darkness fell Emmaline felt herself giving way to sleep.

Some time later Cat stumbled in, falling against the empty cradle, knocking it over with a crash. Tommy gave a wail of fright.

"Shut him up," Cat slurred, collapsing onto her pallet. The baby made a soft, moaning sound.

"Please, Mama," Emmaline said, bringing Tommy across the dark room to her mother, who lay on her back. "Please. I tried to feed him with a twist, earlier, but he wouldn't take it. He seems ill, Mama. Could you not –"

Cat threw up her hand unexpectedly, catching the baby underneath and knocking him from where he lay loosely in the crook of Emmaline's arm. In horror, Emmaline felt the tiny body fly away from her. There was a sickening thud, and then quiet.

Whenever Emmaline thought about that instant, she convinced herself that her mother didn't know what she was doing, that she hadn't meant to strike at her or at Tommy, and that the powerful swing of her hand was simply a drunken reflex, much like the slapping motion she had made at Emmaline earlier that evening. She couldn't bear to think that her mother would ever intentionally hurt Tommy.

The only light in the room was a chalk mark of moonlight coming in through the window. All Emmaline could make out was the tiny form on the floor. As she felt for Tommy, her fingers told her that the side of his head was pushed tight against the over-turned cradle. Emmaline snatched him up and hurried into the outer room, and with a shaking hand, lit a rushlight from the fireplace embers. When it flared up, she held it close to Tommy, examining his face.

"Tommy? Come on, little Tom Tom, come on," she said. The baby's eyes were shut, his head loose on his neck, and when she gently turned his head this way, and then that, she was horrified to see a trickle of blood coming from a cut on his temple.

She wiped away the blood, crying quietly, and then held him through the rest of the night, sitting on the edge of her pallet while her mother made deep snuffling sounds in her sleep. The only thing that assured Emmaline that Tommy wasn't dead was that his motionless little body stayed warm. Eventually the sun came up and Tommy stirred, making strange, whining sounds deep in his throat.

Emmaline looked at the sleeping form of her mother, and then down at the baby. Something cold turned over in her, and lying the baby down, she went to Cat.

"Wake up," she said, shaking her mother's shoulder. As the woman grumbled and pulled away, Emmaline shook her more roughly, finally slapping her mother's cheeks.

"What is it?" Cat said at last, sitting up and holding her head. "What are you on about?"

"Are you awake?" Emmaline asked.

Cat pulled herself into a sitting position, licking her lips. "Get me a drink of water, would you, love? I'm parched."

Emmaline fetched a tin cup of water from the pail by the door, then watched as her mother drank. When Cat let the empty cup drop onto the pallet beside her, Emmaline picked up Tommy and carried him to her mother.

"Feed him," she demanded. "Now."

Silently her mother fumbled with her dress, then took the still baby. "He's quiet this morning," she said. "Are you mother's good boy?" she murmured through dry lips, looking down at Tommy. He looked back at her, his eyes wide yet dazed, the pupils too big, making his eyes glow like heated coal. "You're a good baby, aren't you? Are you not hungry, littleun?"

Emmaline watched her mother trying to get Tommy to nurse. "You hurt him last night. You don't remember, do you?"

Her mother raised her head, wincing at the pain of sudden movement. "I hurt him? No. I'd never hurt my own baby."

"You did. You knocked him to the floor. Look here." She pointed to Tommy's temple – a dark flowering of purple, so visible on the pale skin threaded with delicate blue veins. In the middle of the purple was a jagged line beaded with congealed blood.

Cat's face grew pale. She unwrapped the blanket from around the baby and pressed his arms and legs, his stomach and back. "But he's all right. He's all right, isn't he? He's got a bit of a rash, but that's nothing."

"He's not himself, even before – before his head was hurt, Mother. He wouldn't smile or make any proper sounds like he usually does. He's not even crying, although he hasn't been fed properly since yesterday morning. He's sick, Mama. Really sick. Mrs. Hooper said –"

"When did Mrs. Hooper see him?" Cat interrupted.

"Last night. I got milk from her cow, and she said he looked as if he were sickening. And he is. Look at him, Mama. He's not moving."

Cat closed her eyes and pressed her lips against the bruise, so softly, Emmaline saw, that it was more as if she were breathing. She didn't say anything, but when she finally opened her eyes Emmaline saw the glint of tears.

Tommy stayed the same – motionless, unwilling to feed – for the next few hours. Finally Emmaline convinced Cat that they must take him to old Binny Elwood. Her father had said she was a wonder with herbs and advice, and the elderly woman had given Jasper many of her own plants to start his herb garden.

The old woman unwrapped the limp silent baby and shook her head. "'Tisn't the cholera, nor the pox, of that it's clear. He would be dead by now if it had been the cholera, and covered with blisters if it were pox." Her eyes narrowed as she looked at the fresh bruise on Tommy's temple. Then she moved his neck, tentatively, gently pressing on the back of his head, trying to push it forward. Emmaline saw that her brother's neck appeared rigid.

Binny's fingers were like gnarled twigs, the nails dark yellow, split and hoary, as she pressed on the blotchy surface of Tommy's small chest. The rash whitened under the pressure, then resumed its scarlet appearance when she removed her fingers. "Have you given him pennyroyal in hot water?"

Emmaline nodded. "And I tried horehound, but it was too bitter, and he wouldn't take it."

"That's only for the cough, anyway. Has he the cough?"

Emmaline shook her head.

"Has he been throwing fits?"

"No," Emmaline and her mother said together.

"Seems to me it's brain fever. He might be taken with fits. It's to be expected."

"Brain fever?" Emmaline said, looking anxiously at her mother and then back to Binny.

"Aye." Binny folded the blanket back around the child. "Take him home. There's nothing to be done. If he lives, he lives. It's in God's hands."

"It's a fever, then?" Cat asked, one eye twitching slightly at the outside corner.

"Of sorts. Seen it before in littleuns. The heat of the body, the rashes and limpness, the stiffness in the neck. Usually takes them within a few days. Or if they do recover, oftentimes they're never right in the mind." She tapped her own temple with a crooked finger.

"So . . . ," Cat hesitated, and Emmaline knew what she was thinking. "So it isn't caused by an injury? Like a blow to the head."

Binny Elwood's keen old eyes studied Cat's face. "Nay. But surely a blow to the head would do no good to a babe, ailing or not."

"No, no, I just . . ." Cat fell silent, and Emmaline took Tommy from Binny.

"Just try to feed him, if he'll take nourishment," Binny called, as Cat and Emmaline, with Tommy in her arms, filed down the narrow path through tall thistles that led away from the low sloping cottage. "And pray to the Almighty, for there's naught else to do."

ommy was sick for some days, his tiny body warm with fever, although he never had one of the fits Binny Elwood had predicted. He would nurse and sleep restlessly. Emmaline fussed over him, wrapping and unwrapping him, singing to him and soothing him. Eventually his body lost the unnatural heat and his eyes grew more focused, and then one afternoon he showed interest when Emmaline dangled a little straw doll over him. After that he began to feed more regularly, and finally smiled at Emmaline as she gently tickled his tummy. But soon Emmaline realized that he could no longer hear her, or any sound. Emmaline did everything she could to try and prove that her suspicions were wrong. She'd wait until Tommy was playing with some small object, then clap her hands loudly, right behind him. He wouldn't even blink. Nor would he look toward the window when there was the whinny of a horse or a shout nearby.

"Tommy can't hear, Mother," she finally told Cat, who had grown silent and thin, paying little attention to either of her children as she sat, day after day, at the table, staring into the fire or at the window. She hadn't been back to the Blue Horse since the night she'd knocked Tommy to the floor, but she also had withdrawn, and sometimes didn't answer Emmaline when the girl spoke to her.

Now Cat gazed at the little boy on Emmaline's lap. "He can't hear?"

"No. Is it like Binny said? Is it something wrong with his brain, from the fever?"

Her mother didn't answer, still watching Tommy as he waved his fingers in front of his face and smiled. Then she stood, and took her shawl from the nail on the back of the door.

"Mama? Where are you going? You're not going to the Blue Horse, are you?"

Cat looked down at Emmaline. "Nay, child. I'm only going out to walk up the road and back."

"Don't go, Mama. Please."

"I can't think properly. I must clear my head and think about what to do. We'll be turned out in ten days. Our time is almost up."

Emmaline's stomach lurched.

"It's late, love," Cat said. She smiled at Emmaline, and Emmaline wanted her to say, *It's all right. I'll look after everything. You mustn't worry*, as her father had always said. But Cat's smile dropped away as quickly as it had risen on her lips, and all she said, as she put her hand on the door latch, was, "Go to bed, now."

Emmaline put Tommy to bed, but stayed in the big room as the spring sounds of evening unfolded. She heard the beautiful song of a linnet and tried to count the twenty-four different tones as her father had taught her.

Finally she went to her pallet, her head aching with worry. She hugged Tommy close to her; too long for his cradle now, he slept with her, nestled between her and the wall, safe from rolling off the low bed. The slow even rhythm of his breathing was a comforting pattern, and Emmaline breathed along with him. She felt it working, matching her breathing to his, and relaxed as she drifted, letting a welcome fuzziness soften her thoughts.

Suddenly she felt her mother's hand on her shoulder.

"Come, Emmaline, wake up."

Emmaline frowned. "What is it?" she murmured.

"Get up, girl. Come with me."

Emmaline rose, shivering as she followed her mother to the other room. The fire was blazing, and on the table was a sheet of paper, the pen, and a small cup. Her mother had already mixed the ink.

"Sit down. There's no way but one."

"What is it?" Emmaline sat in front of the paper, staring at it dully.

"You'll write to your aunt."

All trace of sleep left Emmaline, and she stared up at her mother. "What?"

"You heard me. You'll write to Phoebe and tell her we need her help. Tell her . . . tell her we'll do anything she asks. Anything but . . . but what she wants most." She didn't look at Emmaline, but out the window, into the blackness. Her voice was sharp. "Don't just sit there. Get on with it."

Emmaline dipped the nib into the ink. *My dearest Aunt Phoebe,* she wrote, in her neatest script, and then stopped. The nib refused to write smoothly this time, producing letters that were alternately faint or blotchy. "What should I say?" she asked.

"Tell her that although you cannot be given to her, as she wishes, that we will accept anything she can offer. Tell her . . . tell her we are *begging* for help. That as her brother's family, we have nowhere to turn, and if she is a good and godly woman, she will help us."

"Should I tell her you're sorry?" Emmaline studied the dark glow of the ink in the bottom of the cup.

"Sorry? I have nothing to be sorry for." Cat whirled from the window, crossing her arms over her chest. "I do not speak out of turn, Emmaline. I simply speak the truth. Isn't that so?"

Emmaline didn't answer, but lowered her head over the paper and began writing again. *Mother and Tommy and I are not doing well. Tommy nearly died, and now he cannot hear. We are begging you for help, and are at your mercy. And Mother wants you to know she is very sorry for the way she acted when you have come to visit. She says she will not ever behave in such a way again. Please write back soon, Aunt Phoebe. We have only ten days left in the cottage.*

She stopped. She didn't want to just sign her name. She thought for a moment about one of the books she and her father had read together – *Sense and Sensibility* – remembering how John Willoughby had closed his letter to Marianne Dashwood, and wrote what he had, changing only a few words. *I am, dear Aunt Phoebe, your most obedient humble Servant, Emmaline Roke.* She blew on the ink to speed its drying.

"Did you write what I told you?" Cat demanded.

Emmaline nodded. She busied herself with folding the letter into its nine sections and gluing the final fold with sealing wax that she melted in a spoon over the candle in front of her.

She wrote Phoebe's name and copied her address on the section in the folded center of the letter, never raising her head as she worked, unable to meet her mother's eyes.

. . . AND THE REPLY

he reply came nine days later. Written on fine parchment and smelling faintly of lilacs, it was addressed to Emmaline. The new shopkeeper brought it to their door, looking around Emmaline into the main room.

"You'll be out by tomorrow night, I'm told," he said. "My family will be arriving day after tomorrow, and they must have a decent place to live."

Emmaline saw his eyes settle on the Windsor chair, and then move to the mantel, where the china shepherdess sat in its usual place of honor. She followed his gaze to the deep window casement where the geraniums still bloomed, bright flames against the whitewashed walls.

"I can't expect them to move into my room over the inn, after all. They're used to a real home. And I've been promised that all that is here will remain, although, in truth, our own belongings are so much finer than these. Of course, our last home was much grander than this, and I'm sure my wife won't be overly pleased when she views —"

"We'll be out," Cat said, coming to stand behind Emmaline. "Don't worry yourself over it." She pulled Emmaline back and slammed the door in his face with one swift movement.

Emmaline took the envelope close to the fire. "Mother? What if Aunt Phoebe won't help us? What will we do?"

"Open it," Cat said, her voice harsh, and Emmaline fumbled with the letter, slightly tearing the paper around the wax seal.

"*Dearest Emmaline,*" Emmaline read aloud in the quiet cottage. "*I have spoken at length to Mr. Slater with regards to your circumstances. He agrees that it is our Christian duty to see to it that my brother's family must not starve, nor be turned away from shelter. To that end, he has fulfilled his duty by assuring Catherine a job in his cotton mill. There is lodging in Milk Court for those who work in the factory. Ask directions to the Slater factory workers' cottages when you reach the city limits. Number Three is currently vacated.*"

Emmaline looked at her mother. Cat's face was lined and wavery in the flickering glow of the flame. It looked different to Emmaline — not just older, but something else. She didn't know that what she was seeing on her mother's face was defeat.

"Is that all?" Cat asked.

Emmaline nodded, reading the last line: "*Yours with affection, Phoebe Slater.*"

"She doesn't talk of what you're to do. But we'll soon sort that out."

Emmaline touched the edge of the paper. "You're to work in a mill? Oh, Mother, you said you could never, ever work in a mill," she said quietly, remembering hearing her parents talk about all the textile factories springing up the length and breadth of the country.

You could never get me inside a mill, in the steamy, stifling heat, she remembered Cat had said. *The air filling my lungs with dust and lint, and my ears hearing nothing but the constant thump and clatter of machines – that would be sure death to me.*

"Mother? You said you'd never work in a mill," Emmaline repeated. "I heard you tell Father. You said –"

"Hush now, Emmaline. I'm weary," Cat said. "I'm going to bed. We'll have a lot to do tomorrow, and then the journey to Tibbing. At least we've still enough money to hire a tumbrel to take us there." She walked from the room, her shoulders sloped, and Emmaline heard the straw of her mother's mattress rustle.

Emmaline stayed by the fire, the letter lying in her lap. Eventually she picked it up and put it to her nose, breathing in the sweet, slightly musty odor that lingered in the fine paper.

III

Tibbing, near Manchester
1831–1836

Work-work-work!
From weary chime to chime,
Work-work-work –
As prisoners work for crime!
Band, and gusset, and seam,
Seam, and gusset, and band,
Till the heart is sick, and the brain benumb'd
As well as the weary hand.

Work-work-work!
My labour never flags;
And what are its wages? A bed of straw,
A crust of bread – and rags.
That shatter'd roof – and this naked floor –

A table – a broken chair –
And a wall so blank, my shadow I thank
For sometimes falling there.

Oh! but to breathe the breath
Of the cowslip and primrose sweet –
With the sky above my head,
And the grass beneath my feet,
For only one short hour
To feel as I used to feel,
Before I knew the woes of want
And the walk that costs a meal!

– Thomas Hood
from "The Song of the Shirt"

MILK COURT

n that first evening as she walked through the streets of Tibbing, Emmaline had known exactly what her father had hated.

They had ridden all afternoon from Maidenfern in a small cart, the donkey driven by a man with a slight hump on his back and one shoulder higher than the other. Emmaline didn't cry, but sat facing what lay behind them. She had watched as the tumbrel passed the church cemetery; she had gone to her father's grave the evening before, placing a handful of lily of the valley on the new grass growing there. Now she waved in the direction of the churchyard – a small half-flutter of her fingers.

Maidenfern became smaller as they went over the hill, and although she stood on her toes for one last glimpse, the road suddenly dipped, and all she could see was a faint haze from the sweet-smelling smoke that wafted from the cottage chimneys.

They lurched along for hours, the small donkey trudging, head down. They crossed the Ribble River and continued on the seemingly endless road, white with dust. The only sounds, for most of the journey, were the creaks and groans of the weathered boards of the cart. Even Tommy remained quiet, lulled by the monotonous rumble of the tumbrel's wooden wheels.

Toward late afternoon, Emmaline saw a dark cloud smearing the horizon. As they drew nearer, she became aware of a continual booming – an unnatural, trembling sound – and then smokestacks appeared. The smokestacks belonged to factories, too many to count. Each factory was five or six or seven storeys high, and each great smokestack belched an endless stream of dark heavy breath into the scudding layer overhead. She felt as if the sky had suddenly lowered, and was pressing down on the city and people.

The driver let them off at the outskirts. Even though her mother had told Emmaline that Tibbing wasn't that big, it felt huge and frightening. "'Tis only a small city, girl, although to hear Phoebe talk of it you'd think it were London itself," Cat said, after she'd asked directions to Milk Court.

Still, used to only the village, it was all confusing to Emmaline. So many people on the streets, so much noise and bustle. Her head began to throb, while the soles of her feet, accustomed to only earth, had an unfamiliar ache from the cobbles. Her arms quivered with the weight of the unwieldy bundle of bedding she carried. Tucked inside the blankets were her father's writing box and her lace-working pillow. Tightly tied around her waist was an old shawl, and in it was the china shepherdess. Cat had told Emmaline to take it, as well as some other things: the writing box and the cooking pot and kettle and a few dishes and utensils.

"But I thought we were told to leave –"

"I know what we were told." Cat interrupted. "And we're leaving all of the furniture, and most everything else," Cat had said, her mouth twisted into a bitter line. "Your father won that shepherdess, and the writing box was dear to him. No, I'll not leave them for some greedy cow to get her hands on."

Emmaline shifted her hips, trying to get comfortable. Tommy was tied to her back with a blanket sling. Her mother led the way, loaded down with a heavy sack on her back and, like Emmaline, more bundles in her arms, some containing the last of their bread and salt and root vegetables. A light spring rain was falling, ashy and dirty as it wet Emmaline's face.

They wound their way through narrower and narrower streets to the very center of Tibbing, where rows of blackened brick houses sat in moldering disrepair. Emmaline could see that once the brick had been red, but now there were only small traces of the original color, as everything was hidden by a thick layer of soot.

Cat stopped to look at a building, or the picture on a sign outside a shop, now and then, finally coming to a low slanting row of attached houses in a courtyard, the dwellings dark and squat in the shadow of higher buildings around them. The houses were only one room deep, and each one-roomed home in the narrow court had another identical house attached to the back of it.

"This is it. Milk Court," Cat said.

Emmaline saw a washhouse, an ash-pit, and a privy at the end of the court where they stood. Down the center of the court was a gutter, running with scummy water and vegetable parings.

At the third crooked door, Cat said, "We're at Number Three." She pushed at the bowed door. It squeaked on its hinges, and the bottom scraped on the mud floor, forcing Cat to give it a shove with her hip.

Emmaline followed her mother, standing in the doorway until her eyes adjusted to the darkness. When Cat pulled the rag out of the small window beside the door, enough dim light filtered in so that Emmaline could see the room. It was hardly bigger than the storage cupboard at the back of the shop in Maidenfern. Emmaline judged it to be eleven or twelve paces long and the same wide. It was bare except for a pile of dirty straw in the corner, some broken crockery in the recess of the window, a small rough table, and two rickety stools. There was a tiny fireplace with a splintered board for a mantel. A pile of cold and blackened ash sat in the fireplace, but there were still a few gnarled sticks of wood and two lumps of coal tossed to one side. The floor was damp, the hard-packed mud sticky from the unheated air.

Just as Emmaline opened her mouth, her mother spoke. "It'll be the same as all back-to-backs for the millworkers. Just be grateful there's only the three of us. Were we six or seven or even eight, we'd have the same size place," she said, her voice daring Emmaline to complain. "We're lucky enough not to have to share the space with a lodger, as it is. Although, who knows? It may come to that."

Emmaline closed her mouth and wiped the rain from her face with the edge of her shawl. As they'd walked through Tibbing, she'd seen dark shapes in doorways. At first she thought they were piles of rubbish, or heaps of rags, and then, to her horror, realized they were people – mainly women with children. Some had skeletal hands outstretched, begging in a listless, instinctive gesture. They huddled for shelter against the rain, and Emmaline saw that many of the babies were too weak to cry, their eyes glassy and enormous in their shrunken faces. She realized, with a growing horror, that these poor wretches had no homes to go to, no jobs to bring in a few coppers for bread or tea.

Thinking of them as she watched her mother light a fire and spread a blanket over the straw, she pulled Tommy out of the sling and hugged him. "We'll be all right here, Tommy," she whispered. "You'll be all right, with Mama and me."

Tommy watched her mouth, and then put his fingers on her lips.

She kissed the warm dimpled fingers, and he smiled a slow sweet smile.

An hour later, after their meager supper of hard bread soaked in salted hot water, there was a quiet knock on the door. Cat opened it to a boy, a little older than Emmaline. He silently handed her a folded paper, then left.

Cat gave the paper to Emmaline.

"It's from Aunt Phoebe," Emmaline said, after reading it. "She wants you to bring me to her house before you report to the Slater mill tomorrow."

Cat nodded, and then put on her shawl and went out to the court. She was back within fifteen minutes to report that there was a family a few doors down with a girl too young to go into the mills. "Her name is Alma, and she looks after her own sisters and brothers and three other littleuns while her ma is at the mill," Cat said. "For twopence a week, her mother said she'll let Alma take on Tommy as well."

"But . . . but I can look after Tommy, like I did at home."

"Girls your age are all in the mill, here in Tibbing," her mother said. "You'll be finding a job, as well. That's probably why your aunt wants to see you. And I don't want you dragging Tommy there. It may set her off. Now get to bed."

Emmaline rolled herself into the blankets beside Tommy on the pile of straw. She closed her eyes, but how could anyone sleep amid such noise? Busy footsteps, the heavy rumble of carts, the shriek of steam from boilers, the beating of the looms.

She pulled the blankets over her head and whispered her bedtime prayers over and over, concentrating on the soothing words, until, finally, exhaustion won over the cacophony outside Number Three Milk Court.

A BEAUTIFUL BED

t six o'clock the next morning, after leaving Tommy, still asleep, with Alma, Emmaline and Cat stood at the back door of Phoebe's fine house. They had walked to the outskirts of the city, where large homes with gardens sat at a distance from each other. Here the air was cleaner, the noise muted.

"We don't know what she wants of you," Cat told Emmaline, looking at the plain, sturdy door. She hadn't wanted to go to the imposing front door, with its gleaming brass knob and knocker and leaded glass windows on either side. "But she knows you're not to stay, from the letter you sent. You wouldn't want to stay here, would you? Isn't that right, love?" There was a slight tremble in her voice. "And of course Tommy will be crying for you by bedtime," she added.

Emmaline was not able to look at her mother. "I don't want to stay with Aunt Phoebe."

"That's my girl," Cat said. "And you remember your way back to Milk Court from here?"

Emmaline raised her head to answer yes, and Cat gave her a tremulous smile, the old one Emmaline hadn't seen for a long,

long time. It made unexpected tears burn under Emmaline's eyelids. Why couldn't her mother always smile at her, and have that look on her face – the one that said she loved her and would care for her? Emmaline wanted to wrap her arms around her mother's waist and bury her head against her shoulder, but the door swung open before she had the chance.

Cat immediately stepped back into the shadows.

"You're Emmaline Roke, then?" said the woman who stood in the open doorway.

"Aye," Emmaline said.

"The niece," the woman added, unnecessarily.

"That I am," Emmaline answered.

The woman's bushy eyebrows raised. "Well, I can see there'll be work to be done with you," she said, looking at Emmaline's hair, then her face, her neck, and all the way to her boots. Her gaze came back to Emmaline's hands and rested there.

Emmaline looked the woman square in the face, putting her hands under her apron. The woman had a high bulging forehead and deep pouches under her eyes. Her dull brown hair was so thin that her scalp showed through, a skinned pink-gray that reminded Emmaline of newborn mice.

"Well, come in then," the woman said. "I'm Mrs. Brill, and I run the house for the mistress. She's not up yet, but you can sit in the kitchen until she's ready to receive you."

Emmaline turned to say good-bye to her mother, but all she saw was a flash of dark brown – the edge of Cat's skirt as she slipped around the corner.

"Hello, my dear," Phoebe said, setting her china cup in its saucer with the tiniest clink. She was wearing a morning dress of mauve mousseline, and had gleaming tortoiseshell combs holding her thick, dark blonde hair off her slender neck. She rose gracefully and hurried across the sitting room to embrace Emmaline.

Emmaline guardedly put her arms around her aunt, aware of the faint odor of chocolate from her aunt's breakfast cocoa, and the fresh, powdery hint of lilac that clung to everything her aunt touched. Emmaline breathed deeply, wanting to swallow the delicious scents.

"Well," Aunt Phoebe said. "Here you are." She smiled broadly.

Emmaline returned the smile, although hers was distracted. Even though she had often read about houses like this one, to be inside was another matter.

First there had been the back stairs up from the kitchen, and then the second flight to Aunt Phoebe's sitting room. She had kept her eyes fixed on Mrs. Brill's broad back as she lifted one foot after another on each narrow step from the kitchen. As Mrs. Brill led her out into the main foyer and up the second flight of stairs to Aunt Phoebe's room, Emmaline grasped the smooth balustrade tightly so she wouldn't stumble. She caught a glimpse of a parlor with serpentine mahogany chests and a rosewood piano and so many chairs and settees that Emmaline thought half of Maidenfern could have a place to sit. The wall of the stairway to the second floor was lined with oil paintings of grand proportions, all elaborately framed. Aunt Phoebe's personal sitting room held more gleaming wood furniture.

By the time Aunt Phoebe had stopped hugging Emmaline, Emmaline's head had a peculiar ache that made her feel both exhilarated and dizzy. On the wall hung a full-length cheval glass, and in it she saw her whole body reflected for the first time. She noticed the mud crusting her scuffed boots, the limpness of her dress, and the bits of straw clinging to her hair.

"First, I'll show you your room. Then I think you might like to bathe. Mrs. Brill, instruct Mollie to prepare water for my niece, and I'll choose a new frock from the ones I've had made these last few days. I'm not sure if they'll fit – you seem thinner than when I last saw you – but Mrs. Stanley can easily alter them if need be. Come, my dear." Then Phoebe took Emmaline by the hand and pulled her down a long hall. She pushed open the carved door.

"This is it," Phoebe trilled. "The windows face east, so you'll have plenty of morning sun. This is my favorite room, after my own bedchamber. The furnishings came from London and Paris, of course. Emmaline? Don't just stand there. You may touch anything you like. It is yours, after all."

Emmaline stared at the bed. She had never seen a bed so wide, and so high. Her mother and Tommy and she would all have fit on one-half of it, with plenty of room to spare. There was a canopy with a fringe of pale green wool, and the cords and tassels were green and gold.

"Do you like the bed? The head- and footboard are specially designed papier-mâché. It's all the rage in France, you know. Quite lovely, isn't it?"

"It's so . . . big," Emmaline whispered.

"There's a little footstool – where is that now? Probably on the other side – that you use to climb into it. And there are curtains –

see, there? – that you can pull around if you want. Do you like it? Emmaline?"

But Emmaline had shut her eyes.

"Emmaline? What is it?" Phoebe put her hand on Emmaline's shoulder.

"Aunt Phoebe, I . . . I . . ." Emmaline blinked, fingering the edge of her apron. "I can't stay," she finally said, still whispering.

"I beg your pardon?" Phoebe took her hand away from Emmaline's shoulder.

"Thank you for my mother's job, and for Milk Court," Emmaline said, her voice so low Phoebe had to lean forward. "But – I promised my mother – I can't live here, with you."

Phoebe's face tightened. "You wrote to me, Emmaline. Begging for help."

"I know," Emmaline answered. "I know, Aunt Phoebe. And we're ever so grateful for your help, my mother and I. But I never meant that I would come and stay with you. I didn't say . . ."

Phoebe felt behind her for the chair at the dressing table. It was a small padded chair, covered in velvet, the same spring green as the canopy. She sat on it, carefully, as if it were made of some rare fragile material, even though Emmaline could see its sturdy oak legs.

"I thought perhaps I could get a job at the mill, too. Could you not ask Uncle Nathan if I could work alongside my mother –"

"No!" Phoebe cut her off. She picked up a silver hairbrush that lay on the dressing table, and rubbed its soft bristles over her palm. "I'll *never* see you working in that place. Not you. Never." She turned her face toward Emmaline. It was paler than usual. "Please, child. Look at this room. And I could hire a governess. You could study all sorts of wonderful things. Learn to play the piano."

Emmaline had never seen a piano before the one in Aunt Phoebe's parlor. She tried to imagine what those smooth ivory keys would feel like under her fingertips.

"I can't leave Tommy. Or my mother. I can't live here without them, Aunt Phoebe." She looked at the bed again. It would be so soft, and so warm. She took a deep breath. "There's room for us all, isn't there, Aunt Phoebe? We wouldn't be any trouble. Really. My father wouldn't want me to leave Tommy, or my mother. He'd never want that."

At the mention of Jasper, Phoebe looked away. "Your Uncle Nathan is very . . . careful – with his accounts, and with the decisions he makes. It was very difficult for me to persuade him to take on your mother at the mill. He was willing to let you live here, for my sake. It would be impossible to even consider a woman such as your mo –" She stopped.

Emmaline waited. The silence in the room stretched. Aunt Phoebe studied the bristles of the brush. "And besides, if you stay with your mother at Milk Court, she'd never be able to clothe and feed all three of you on her mill wages," she argued. "Herself and the baby, yes. But not a growing girl as well."

Emmaline had been thinking while she waited for her aunt to speak. "Is there anything I could do here, Aunt Phoebe? I'm a hard worker. I would do anything you asked, here in the house, and then go home at night."

Phoebe put down the hairbrush and straightened her shoulders. "I don't know," she said. She sighed, her features sagging.

"You've seen my lace. And I can sew, as well."

"I have a seamstress."

"I could help her."

"Mrs. Stanley doesn't need . . ." Phoebe stopped. "Well, I've not been completely pleased with some of her detailing lately. Perhaps," she said, nodding to herself. "Well, perhaps." She stood. "I suppose so," she said reluctantly. "But only for a while. We'll see how long it takes you to come to your senses, Emmaline. For now, you can help Mrs. Stanley in the sewing room. But I'm sure it won't be long before you realize you don't need to be there. When you could be here," she added.

Emmaline looked at the bed one more time, and then tore her eyes away.

WHAT WAITS UPSTAIRS

mmaline didn't see her aunt for the next five days. She reported for work at the back door on Mosely Road at seven every morning, and then scurried through the long lower-floor hallway to the sewing room. She was given a small dinner shortly after one o'clock – with the other servants, in the kitchen – and left at seven in the evening.

On the sixth day, Aunt Phoebe swept into the small sewing room. Mrs. Stanley immediately rose, pins bristling between her lips. She bobbed a knee and lowered her head, then pinched the back of Emmaline's arm. The girl stood and copied Mrs. Stanley's knee-bob, although she didn't dip her head.

"I'm told you've done well," Phoebe said. "Mrs. Stanley has reported that you've a straight eye, and clever hands. Your seams are tight as a dead man's fist. High praise, coming from Mrs. Stanley." She pursed her mouth. "Well? Are you ready to come upstairs now?"

"Upstairs?" Emmaline repeated.

Phoebe snicked her tongue in annoyance. "Surely you've had your fill of that horrid mill row where you're living, and can see sense. I've given you most of a week to live with your initial, foolish decision. It's unthinkable that you'd chose life in Milk Court and this," she lifted one hand to indicate the sewing room, "over what waits for you upstairs, with me." The silver hairbrush. The rosewood piano. The bed.

Silence filled the small room. Emmaline could hear Mrs. Stanley's shallow breathing. The dream of the huge, glorious bed was replaced by an image of the narrow, lumpy, straw-filled pallet she shared with Tommy. Tommy took up so little room, and yet the warmth of his baby body seemed to fill the whole space, keeping Emmaline warm.

"Well?" Phoebe finally said.

Emmaline swallowed. "No, Aunt Phoebe. I must be with my mother, and with Tommy."

Her aunt's nostrils tightened. "Do you really not understand what I'm offering, child? Who wouldn't trade what you have now for the life I'm willing to give you?"

From the corner of her eye Emmaline caught a movement from Mrs. Stanley, and Aunt Phoebe's neck swiveled in the woman's direction, but when Emmaline looked she saw Mrs. Stanley standing in the same position, her eyes lowered.

Emmaline blinked rapidly, but returned her aunt's stare. "I do understand." She fought to keep her voice firm, to will herself not to think of the bed. "No, thank you, Aunt Phoebe."

Pink bloomed through the white powder on Phoebe's cheeks. "Are you quite mad, girl? You're mistaking pigheadedness for loyalty. You're every bit as stubborn as your father was. Fine, then." Her voice rose. "You can stay in that airless hovel for as long as you want, and you can stay here, as well, in the sewing room, for the rest of your life!" A fine line of froth shone on her bottom lip. She licked it away, and when she spoke again, her voice had lost its edge. "Look," she said slowly, "I'll leave you be for now. I know you'll eventually be reasonable. And when you are, you're welcome upstairs. Is that clear? The offer will always be open." Then she turned so abruptly that her full skirt surged like a boat on a wave, knocking a pile of cambric handkerchiefs waiting to be embroidered with her initial to the floor.

When Phoebe had swept out of the sewing room, Emmaline picked up the handkerchiefs. Although her hands shook slightly, she carefully refolded and set each back into a tidy pile.

"She doesn't like to be made a fool of, the Mistress," Mrs. Stanley said quietly.

Emmaline didn't know what to say, and she and Mrs. Stanley got back to work. Emmaline felt the woman's eyes on her as she stitched a ruffled lace cuff onto the sleeve of Phoebe's muslin dress. Mrs. Stanley's fingers never stopped moving, the needle flying through the delicate fabric like a tiny swooping swallow, but there was something different in her expression.

Emmaline wasn't sure whether Mrs. Stanley thought she was brave for standing up to her aunt, or whether she thought she was an idiot for choosing to stay in the dim, chilly sewing room under the stairs.

"EM"

s Tommy grew older, his smile grew brighter, and his light eyes shone with understanding. He had lovely thick curly hair, still a brilliant white-gold, which Emmaline washed and combed through every week. She knew Tommy suffered less from head vermin than other small children. Emmaline washed her own hair at the same time, even though it was vanity. She liked the feel of her hair smooth and clean-smelling from the ash and lye soap. It meant a long weary hour or more after work, standing in the pump queue in the somber half-light at the far end of Milk Court for two extra buckets of water each week, but Emmaline didn't mind.

She had worked out an elaborate set of finger and hand signals to communicate with Tommy. Little by little he grew to understand her, and learned the same signs to make back to her. She had tried to teach him to speak, for he hadn't lost his ability to make sound, but all he produced were strings of strangled babbling. He tried so hard when Emmaline took his face between her hands and said simple words over and over. He moved his lips and tongue in an attempt to mimic hers, but it didn't work. When he was angry he'd make garbled, growling noises, but when he was happy – oh, how Emmaline loved to hear him laugh. His laughter was free and pure, bouncing off the walls of their one room as if it were shafts of golden sun or silver moon, bringing light to the persistent gloom.

Cat tried, but she always had to depend on Emmaline. When the warning shrieks of the factory whistles woke her, Emmaline would rise in the cold dark hours before dawn. She would sometimes have to slap her mother's hands and pinch her cheeks to get her to drag herself from her pallet. While her mother was rousing herself, Emmaline would carry Tommy, still sleeping, to Alma, and tuck him in beside the four children crowded on a dank flock pallet. Sometimes he woke and cried when she left him, clinging tightly to her neck; other times he didn't stir.

When Tommy was about three, Emmaline realized he was afraid of the dark. He'd shake his head *no no no* when Emmaline blew out the rushlight at night, and she'd hold him close, humming against his temple. The vibration of her lips against his scalp seemed to calm him, although she knew he couldn't hear the melody.

Some nights the moon would be almost visible through the ceaseless thick smoke belched out of the high factory chimneys, although its light couldn't reach down into the knotted maze of narrow courts. But on those nights, if it wasn't too cold, Emmaline would take the little boy outside.

"Look, Tommy," she'd say, pointing at the round orb that would appear and then disappear in the perpetually murky sky over the city. "Our father was the Moon King." She'd touch her chin, then make a circle around the moon with her hands and move the circle onto her head. Touching her chin meant *Father* to Tommy. "Moon King," she'd repeat, and Tommy would make the same motions with his small hands.

"You're my smart boy," she'd say, and then whisper about their father and what it had been like to live in a village; how one day she'd take him back and they'd live together in a lovely cottage and look up at the moon every night. "The moon will shine so brightly over Mama and you and me – when we go back home. To a real home, one in the countryside, Tommy. This," she gestured to the stinking street, "this will never be home." She knew Tommy couldn't understand, but he liked to watch her mouth and eyes as she talked, and she knew she was smiling when she talked about their dreamed future because Tommy always smiled back, smiled and pointed at the moon for her.

And one day he learned to say her name, or the first syllable, which was enough for Emmaline. She had coaxed it out of him, pressing his lips together and squeezing his throat. The first time the sound came out *Em*, she nodded and clapped her hands, and Tommy clapped his, making the *Em* sound over and over.

Shortly before he turned four, Tommy started doing piecework, along with the other children a few doors down. The mother of the house brought in the work for her own children too young to be in the factories. Alma had joined the endless snaking lines of children who plodded daily to the mills for nine hours of work a day; as they grew older they would work twelve hours and more. Now it was Alma's younger sister, Bethany, who was responsible for Tommy. His job was to glue matchboxes together, and this he did for hours each day. Occasionally, when they ran out of glue before the end of the day, he would follow the others out to the cramped courtyard and imitate them in their play, jumping over the stinking, flowing gutters or throwing pebbles against a wall.

He earned a halfpence at the end of every sixth day, and would proudly give it to his mother.

Cat took the ha'penny from his small fingers, patting his cheek absently. She worked at the mill for up to fourteen hours a day, six days a week, but still found the energy to go out on a Saturday night every few weeks. She'd be taken out by men who worked with her at the factory, men who bought her a meal and often a trinket, and maybe made her feel – for a few hours at least – the way she'd felt back in Maidenfern.

When she returned, in the early hours of the morning, Cat would empty her pockets and give whatever she had to Emmaline and Tommy. Sometimes it was food – soft buns or chunks of well-cooked beef or sweet cakes – she'd saved from her own plate. Other times it was a bright ribbon, or small piece of gaudy jewelry. Emmaline had never seen any of the men, and never smelled alcohol on her mother. Cat hadn't taken a drink since the terrible time she'd struck Tommy.

At night, when her mother didn't come home, Emmaline allowed herself to think about the bedroom at Aunt Phoebe's. She saw herself waking in the high clean bed, the sun's first rays streaming in through sparkling glass.

But in the morning, when her mother came through the door, Emmaline wondered if this was all there would ever be. Her in the sewing room, ruining her eyes, eventually, like Mrs. Stanley. Her mother standing in front of a spinning machine, dulled by monotony and despair. Tommy hunched over a table, breathing in the fumes of cheap glue. All of them working just to keep a roof over their heads and have enough to stop their stomachs from aching.

There had to be a better way, some way to escape the narrowness of this life, that Emmaline felt more and more strongly as she turned twelve, and then thirteen and fourteen. It was as if the narrowness were squeezing tighter and tighter between her shoulder blades and across her chest and around her ribs, as if the whalebone stays she sometimes sewed into her Aunt Phoebe's fine dresses were clamped around her like a vice, holding her in one place, unable to go forward or backward. She knew she needed more space – not just a bigger space than the sewing room at Aunt Phoebe's, or at the house in Milk Court – but more space inside her head, where even her dreams were starting to feel stingy and mean.

FIVE YEARS

mmaline passed her fifteenth birthday, and worried more and more for Tommy. He continued to work at the matchboxes. There was no schooling for poor children in Tibbing, no kindly parish minister to teach them their letters. Here in Tibbing, there was only work in the factories. Tommy had been kept out of the mill this far by the Factory Act, passed two years after the Rokes arrived in the city. It forbade employment of children below the age of nine in the mills. So Tommy had a little more than three years before he joined his mother in the clattering, rattling swish of thrusting levers. When the time came, Emmaline knew he would start as a scavenger: still small enough to slip under the spinning machines with their thousands of whirling spindles that slid forward and back, while cotton became yarn and yarn changed to weaving material. He would crawl on his belly to pick up the fluff that had become loosened. The fluffy material was then respun to avoid waste. As he grew bigger he would move on to piecing at the long rows of huge spinning-frames. If the threads on the spindles broke as they were

92

stretched and twisted and spun, it would be Tommy's job, as a piecer, to instantly and nimbly tie them together. He would have to learn ways to avoid beatings the overlooker deemed necessary to keep him alert when he swayed with exhaustion. He would learn to never lean against anything in case he drowsed, for if he did, he would be grabbed and held upside down and dunked into the huge cold water cistern at one end of the room, to wake him up and teach him a lesson for falling asleep on the job.

Five years, Emmaline thought, now, *five years in the sewing room at the Slater House.* Mrs. Stanley had shown Emmaline how to create delicate finishing and ruching and embroidery. Over the years she had mastered the more complicated stitches, and her embroidery was delicate, each stitch tight and symmetrical. The needle seemed to listen to Emmaline's fingers; at times, they knew what to do before her mind instructed them. She made the lace for Aunt Phoebe's clothes and household linens, and she still did lacework for herself. On warm summer nights, when there was an hour's light at the end of the workday, she'd stand outside in the courtyard, leaning against Number Three, and form lace collars. These she was able to sell in the market for a few shillings.

Emmaline knew she had surpassed Mrs. Stanley in her sewing, but her quarter-pay packets never held anything extra.

More and more Mrs. Stanley had Emmaline do all the fine work, as she rubbed her eyes with her fists and often had to set down her sewing and press a wet cloth to her temple. Emmaline knew this was a secret between her and the older woman: that Mrs. Stanley was having trouble with her eyes after a lifetime of straining them over tiny stitches in poor lighting, and now she relied on Emmaline to cover for her growing inability to see well enough to do the smallest work.

Mrs. Stanley was kind to Emmaline, bringing her books – small ragged volumes – novels and poetry that Mrs. Stanley's own daughter, a governess with another family, gave to her once the books were in such disrepair that she was instructed to throw them out. Emmaline read them by a candle stub at night, even though usually she could barely keep her burning eyes open. She kept the books safe from mildew and mold in a tin box, well hidden behind her pallet. Her father's writing box was in another hidden tin box, along with the china shepherdess, both wrapped carefully in clean rags. Milk Court was not a place to display anything of value.

Emmaline didn't know if her aunt was aware of how much of the sewing she was doing; Phoebe didn't come to the sewing room any longer. She had paid a regular visit to Emmaline every few months for the first few years. She would always ask the same question, whether Emmaline would come to live upstairs. She never asked about Cat or Tommy. And Emmaline always had the same answer, a simple *no*.

The last time Phoebe had asked the question, she had entered the sewing room carrying a plate of tarts. She wore a navy crepe dress, tight-waisted, the skirt very full. Her hair was plaited over the crown of her head in an elaborate wickerwork fashion. "I thought you might like a treat," she'd said, holding the plate under Emmaline's nose. Emmaline stood, glancing at Mrs. Stanley, but the woman's head was bent over her work.

"Go ahead," Phoebe said. "Cook made them this morning."

Emmaline took one, putting it onto the palm of her left hand.

"Christmas is coming. We'll have a lovely party," Phoebe said then, smiling pleasantly. "You could have a new frock, and I could have Mollie dress your hair."

Emmaline looked at the tart. Raisins and nuts and bits of candied fruit glistened in the heavy syrup. It looked delicious, but suddenly her mouth was dry.

"And when the party is over you can sleep in the canopied bed. You'd like that, wouldn't you? I suppose Milk Court is quite chilly at this time of year."

Emmaline gently set the tart back on the plate.

Phoebe stayed very still, and then put the plate on the table beside Mrs. Stanley. Unexpectedly, she grabbed Emmaline by the shoulders and shook her, shook her so hard that Emmaline felt her neck snapping painfully.

Phoebe let go of her abruptly. She brushed her hands together, as if wiping them clean, and then picked up the plate of tarts. Very carefully, as if she was worried about dropping the tarts, she left the sewing room, her back rigid. The door closed behind her with a small final click.

She had never come to the sewing room again, and now Emmaline saw her only when she accompanied Mrs. Stanley to her aunt's bedroom to fit her for each season's new wardrobe.

Sometimes Emmaline still thought of the bed and the rosewood piano, but they had faded to pale, grainy images in her memory. Instead, as she was falling asleep to the familiar endless thudding from the factories, she thought she heard the distant tinkling of a bell, like the one over the door of the shop. Snuggling against Tommy, she could almost believe she smelled, briefly, in his clean hair, the scent of a pinecone fire in their cottage home. But she knew these sounds and smells weren't real.

What *was* real was Tommy's face at the end of the day. Through each long day she thought of him: of seeing his dear little face light up, and of hearing his laugh.

As long as she had Tommy near her, and knew he was safe, she would carry on.

MAGIC IN THE BOTTLE

can't go on," Cat moaned now, her face contorted in agony. Emmaline's throat was sore; she'd told her mother stories about Maidenfern for a whole hour. But no matter how wonderful and nostalgic these stories about their old life might be, they couldn't stop Cat's misery. Emmaline knew the pain in her mother's injured hand was terrible.

"You must get me something, Em. Something to stop this. I can't go on, I can't," she repeated, her voice rising. "Ale. Get me ale, and lots of it."

Emmaline shook her head. "No. I'll go to the chemist. I'll get you some Godfrey's." She moved a loose stone from the hearth and scooped out a few coins from their small savings.

Looking at the money in her hand, the enormity of her mother's injury and what it would mean to them filled Emmaline's head. Cat wouldn't be working again for a long time. She tried to push the thought away, to concentrate on what she must do right now. She pulled Tommy to her. Tears had made salty paths down the dust of his cheeks. Emmaline wiped them away with her thumbs.

"I'm going to the chemist, Tom-Tom," she signed. "For medicine for Mama. You sit with her." She led him to the side of the pallet, pushing him down gently. Tommy reached out his small hand and stroked his mother's forehead.

"That's right, our Tom," Emmaline said. And then she ran out, the door banging shut behind her.

Neither Tommy nor his mother moved at the sound.

The laudanum eased the pain. Emmaline had bought a bottle of Godfrey's Cordial, wondering why she hadn't thought of it sooner, and had given her mother a large dose. It was a mixture of treacle, water, spices, and opium.

She'd hurried through the steep streets and narrow passageways to the cobbled market square. "I need something for pain," she told the chemist, when it was finally her turn, after waiting behind six others crowded into the tiny shop.

He leaned his elbows on the counter and studied her. "Well, you can take your pick," he told her. "We've got Steedman's Powder, or Godfrey's Cordial. Both do the job. Good for aches and pains. What sort of pain might you be in, young lady? Mill fever? Or is it for your babe?" He winked at her. "We've got Atkinson's Royal Infant's Preservative. Now that's a real favorite, for the quietness. Sends them off to sleep right nice."

"No," Emmaline said, studying the dark bottles and jars on rows behind the counter. "No, it's for my mother."

"Your mother, is it? Well," he said, when Emmaline didn't elaborate, "a quick dose of Steedman's or Godfrey's does the job for whatever ails you, whether it's mill fever or just soothing away the day. Cheaper 'n ale, too."

"Give me the Godfrey's, then," she said, putting her money into the chemist's fleshy palm. "And quickly, please."

"Haven't seen you in here before," he said, keeping his hand on the bottle a little too long, so that she had to tug at it slightly.

"No," she said, turning to leave.

"I'm sure I'll be seeing you again, now," he called after her, but Emmaline didn't answer, pushing her way through those still waiting.

"Do you have it?" Cat asked, before Emmaline was even through the door. She tried to lift her head. "Give it to me. Hurry."

Within moments, Cat's restless head-tossing and moaning had slowed. Although she didn't sleep, she remained quiet for the next hour. Emmaline fried some bacon and made tea for herself and Tommy. When she tried to give her mother a cup of tea, Cat shook her head. "More," she croaked. "More Godfrey's."

Emmaline supported her mother's head as the woman swallowed the laudanum with urgent gulps. "That's all for now, Mother," Emmaline told her, pulling away the bottle. "We must save some for later." As she let her mother's head ease back onto the pallet, she felt a slight pressure on her arm.

Tommy's eyes were clouded with tears and distress as he held Emmaline's arm. He pressed his hand over his heart, the sign Emmaline had taught him for Mama, and then raised his palms in a question. Emmaline knew what he was asking.

She nodded. "Mama will sleep now, Tommy. We'll look after her together, and she'll get better." *Better soon*, she signed.

Thanks be for this magic, Emmaline thought. *And that we have money enough to buy more, enough to get Mother through the worst of the pain.* And she ran her thumb, still stained with her mother's blood, over the front of the bottle.

"I'm sorry, Mother," Emmaline said sharply.

"But I need it, Emmy. I need my medicine. Get it for me."

It had been two weeks since the accident. Every night Emmaline unwrapped the bandages from her mother's hand, sniffing for the odor of rot and looking for telltale streaks traveling up her mother's arm. Either sign would mean the black stinking disease was creeping in, and for that there was only one cure. She could also die from the cure itself, which would be to cut off the whole hand.

And every evening Emmaline breathed a sigh of relief, for Cat's hand, although terrible to look at, was losing its swollen puffiness, and there was no blackening, no warning smell of decay. Emmaline had been able to remove the tiny stitches, and although the seams she had sewn together were raised and purple-scarlet, they remained clean.

It appeared that Cat would live, and keep her hand, although Emmaline saw that her fingers were twisted oddly into unnatural, stiff positions. The hand would never work properly again, and without her right hand, her mother would never be able to get another factory job.

It was barely five in the morning. Tommy was still asleep on his pallet. Emmaline looked longingly at the chunk of hard, watered-down cheese and thick slice of onion and gritty white bread wrapped in a cloth on the table. She took a full mug of water from the pail and drank it down, hoping it would help to take away the gnawing pain in her empty stomach. She hadn't eaten anything in Milk Court for the last week, leaving what they had for Cat and Tommy. She relied now on her one staff meal a day in the Slater kitchen.

"There's enough food for you and Tommy for today," she said to her mother. "Make sure you get him up soon, so he'll get down to Bethany's on time, to start work."

"I'm not hungry. And I said I need my Godfrey's!" Cat's voice was raised, petulant. Her lips were chewed, the skin ragged. "You're not my keeper. Now go and get me some more before you go to work." She grabbed at Emmaline's arm with her good hand. "The chemist on Newton Street will be open."

Emmaline smelled the staleness of her mother's breath, saw the dull tangle of her once gleaming dark hair. "No," she said again. "You mustn't, Mother. You're taking too much, and all you do is sleep."

Cat struggled out of bed to stand before Emmaline. With no warning, she slapped her hard. Emmaline reeled back, stunned, pressing her own hand against her stinging cheek.

"I'm still your mother, and you'll not tell me what I can and cannot do," Cat said, and then collapsed back onto her pallet.

"There's no more money for medicine, Mother," Emmaline said, her voice low and cold. "I told you that yesterday when you finished off the last bottle. I expected it would last you another few days at least, maybe even to the end of the week. With only my wage now, and Tommy's few pence, we need everything for food." She didn't add what had been worrying her: without her mother working at the mill, how long would they be allowed to stay in the millhouse? "And surely the pain is lessening," she added.

"It's not. It's not, Em. It hurts something dreadful."

"I have to go to work," Emmaline said, trying to ignore the heat in her cheek. "Don't forget to wake Tommy, and make sure he eats before he goes off," she said, but her mother didn't appear to be listening. "And you eat something, too. I'll be home as quickly as I can after work."

Emmaline pulled the door behind her, but before it closed entirely she heard her mother murmur, "Don't forget to get me more medicine. I need my medicine."

Distressed, Emmaline hurried to the Slater house. The way Cat was drinking the laudanum was using up their savings – savings that had to last them until the next quarter pay – in a frightening hurry. And she was troubled about what her mother might do to get more of it.

"What are you doing here?" she had asked Justy Dilton, when she'd come across him loitering outside their door a few evenings before, as she arrived home from work.

The boy had rubbed his nose across his sleeve. "Yer muvver sent Tommy to get me," he said. "She's givin' me tuppence to go on an errand for her."

Emmaline had slipped in their door to find her mother on her knees in front of the hearth, prying up the stone that hid their money.

"What are you doing, Mother?" she asked, and Cat had sat back on her heels.

"I was almost out of Godfrey's, and I'm sending Justy to get some," she said, no expression on her face.

Emmaline had pushed her mother aside and gathered the coins into her own hand. "Go to bed," she told her.

Cat stayed on her knees, in front of the fire, while Emmaline went to the door. "We don't need your help after all, Justy," she said. "And please don't do any errands for my mother, no matter what she promises. Is that clear?"

The boy had shrugged and left. Later, after Cat was asleep, Emmaline had cut a small opening in the hem of her apron, put in the last of their coins, and stitched the hem together again.

When Emmaline came home that evening, she found Cat on her pallet in the cold dark room, her head nodding and eyelids heavy as she slumped against the wall. Tommy lay across from her, on the pallet he shared with Emmaline, looking dully at his mother.

Emmaline immediately recognized the blissful look on her mother's face. She touched the small ridge of coins at the bottom of her apron. "Mother?" she said, shaking the woman until her eyes focused. "Mother? Where did you get the money to buy laudanum?"

"It's just for a while, Emmaline," her mother said, smiling tenderly at her. "We'll get them back in a while."

"Get what back?" Emmaline demanded, but Cat didn't answer. Watching her, Emmaline knew, with a sudden painful jolt, what her mother was talking about. She hurried over to the straw-filled mattress, which she saw now was pulled to one side. Ignoring Tommy, who jumped up, she found what she had hoped she wouldn't: the tin boxes, empty, their tops lying carelessly beside them. Her books and Jasper's writing box and the beautiful shepherdess were gone. She whirled around to face her mother.

"No! You can't have sold the only things I care about. You can't."

Her mother smiled and shook her head. "I wouldn't sell them, Emmy. I only pawned 'em, is what I did. Only pawned. They're at the shop over on Pilchard Lane. We can get 'em back."

Emmaline knelt in front of her mother. "How, Mother? We barely have enough to buy a loaf of bread every few days. Where will we get the money to get our things back?"

"They're at the pawnbrokers over on Pilchard Lane," Cat repeated. "We have lots of time to get them back, Emmy. Don't worry." She smiled again, closing her eyes. "I'm going to rest, now." She turned over on her bed, and there was a faint clinking.

Emmaline saw, half hidden beside her mother in the mess of her bed, four bottles of Godfrey's. Large, dark bottles. She sat at the table and wept, letting the tears run down her face freely. Even when Tommy put his arms around her and patted her cheeks, murmuring, "Em, Em," she couldn't stop crying.

A NECESSARY PLAN

ess than a week later, Emmaline came home from work to find Tommy sitting in front of a dying fire. The steady winter rain leeched through the walls. Patches of damp rose on them in an intricate pattern of black mold. They were down to their last chunks of coal, and had only enough food for another day or two. There were no coins left in her hem.

She wouldn't be paid until quarter day, another month away. The overlooker at the mill wouldn't hand over the wages Cat had earned before she'd hurt her hand until then, either. She realized that soon she and Tommy would be reduced to scrabbling in the streets for bits of old paper and wood shavings to burn for heat. What they'd eat, she didn't know. As it was, Tommy had begun whimpering from hunger in his sleep, and shivering, no matter how tightly Emmaline hugged him.

She knew that her mother had drunk the final drop of her Godfrey's the day before. Although she had heard Cat through the night – moving restlessly on her bed, scratching at herself, sometimes crying softly – Emmaline had left for work that morning with a tiny feeling of hope. As there was no way her mother could get any more of the drug, she would start to return to normal. Maybe she could even find some small job, something that she could do with one hand. All day Emmaline had held this hope close.

But now, thirteen hours since she'd left, her mother was sleeping the unnatural, deep sleep of too much laudanum, her face slack, her mouth open.

"Mother?" she said, shaking her shoulder. "Mother?"

But Cat only sighed, languidly turning onto her side. Emmaline pulled aside her tangled blankets, looking for a bottle. She wrinkled her nose at the faint but distinct odor of urine wafting up from her mother's dirty bedding.

Emmaline left her and crouched beside Tommy. He wouldn't lift his eyes to meet hers.

"Tommy," she said, pointing and moving her fingers in the secret language only the two of them knew. *Where did Mama get the medicine?* She put her hand under his chin and tilted his head back sharply. "You know perfectly well what I'm asking, Tommy. How did Mother get more medicine?" *Show me.* She put her hands on his shoulders and gave him a shake. He finally looked into her face.

Taking a quick, nervous peek at his sleeping mother, Tommy went to the side of her mattress, and reaching under it, pulled out something. He came back to Emmaline, and on his open palm she saw a small glass vial. She knew it was a dram, a more highly concentrated – and more expensive – form of laudanum. The vial contained straight opium suspended in wine.

Where did you get this? she signed.

Tommy shrugged.

Emmaline knew there was only one way that Tommy would have acquired this dram, as well as however many her mother had already consumed that day.

"Oh, Tommy," she said, shaking her head sadly. "We're not thieves." She wondered what her mother had said – or done – to Tommy to get him to resort to stealing the vials from the chemist. Tommy was clever, and he was so small, with such a pleasing open face, that he probably slipped into the crowded chemist shop, perhaps unnoticed, or at least ignored, and then slipped out again with the tiny vials hidden in his hand.

She took the vial from Tommy, shaking her head and making her lips form a firm line. "You know this is wrong," she said, shaking the vial in her hand for emphasis. "Wrong and evil. You must *never* do this again." She waited for him to nod. He did, his face solemn, a shimmer of tears in his eyes. He gave a stifled sob.

At the sight of his tears, Emmaline pulled him close and hugged him, feeling his painfully frail body shake as he cried. "I know you didn't want to do this. We'll get through, we will. Just promise me," she pulled away from him and looked into his tear-streaked face, "promise me you'll never do this again, no matter how Mother begs." *No more*, she signed. *Medicine is bad now. Makes Mama sick. No more.*

Tommy ran his sleeve across his nose.

Although it was difficult, Emmaline smiled at him. He smiled back with a sweet shaky grin.

Emmaline thought, *I can't count on Mother to find a job at this rate. And surely we'll be turned out of Milk Court any day now, with Mother not working at the mill. We'll have no roof over our heads. What will we do? Where will we go?*

And with that thought, she knew there was only one thing to do, only one person to turn to, as there had been only one thing for her mother to do five years ago when they were forced out of their home in the village.

Emmaline woke Tommy before she left for work the next morning, and he sat up sleepily, rubbing his eyes and shivering in the morning cold. She instructed him to eat all that was left of their food – the cup of cold barley gruel and one small herring she'd set on the table – and then go on to Bethany's. As she left, she glanced over her shoulder at her mother. Cat hadn't come out of her deep, drug-induced sleep all night.

The streets were wet, the air gray and heavy with rain. *Coming near the end of February*, Emmaline thought, *and still a chill in the air that goes right into the bones*. She pulled her shawl tight around her and kept her head down, making her plans.

Emmaline hated what she knew she had to do. There was no way open but to go to Aunt Phoebe, swallow her pride at having to ask – no, beg – for help.

Emmaline knew she would have to move into her house, leaving her mother and Tommy. She would become the daughter Phoebe had always wanted, as long as Phoebe would let Cat and Tommy stay on in the millhouse. And one other thing. She would tell her aunt that she would have to see them – at least once a week – and that she would be allowed to give them money so they had enough to eat. *It wasn't so much to ask, was it?* Emmaline was no longer a girl of ten. She was grown now, coming sixteen, and if her aunt wanted her to be a part of her life, she would have to accept Emmaline's terms. Surely the woman would show some pity, for it would mean that she would finally have Emmaline.

All that day, as she worked on Aunt Phoebe's new spring sets, she thought about how she would present her plan to her aunt. She would give herself just this one last day, she promised, to get everything straight in her head, and tomorrow she would ask Mrs. Brill to arrange an appointment with her aunt.

She walked home that evening, the sky still heavy and wet, her neck and shoulders aching with the tension of her work and the worry of meeting with her aunt. Her feet were soaked and cold, and she was light-headed with fatigue and hunger. She tried to push away a tiny voice deep inside, the one saying that after today she would never again be this tired, or this cold and wet, or this hungry. Living in the Slater house would mean she would always be warm and cared for.

But then the small voice disappeared. *Tommy.* She hurried the last few streets, splashing through puddles, needing to feel her arms around him and see his trusting face.

CAT'S BARGAIN

he was cheered by the sight of her mother out of bed, sitting on the stool near the table. Her hands were hidden in her lap. She was alone.

"Mother? Isn't Tommy home yet?" When Cat didn't answer, she peered at her, and her heart sank when she saw the unfocused, dreamy state of her eyes. "Mother," she said, louder. "It's too late for Tommy to be at work. Where is he?"

Cat started, and looked up at Emmaline as if she hadn't been aware of her coming into the room. "Emmaline," she said, and then her brow furrowed. "Tommy. I had to. It was for the money. We need money, Emmy, and I got us some." She lifted her right hand, using it without thinking. She had taken off all of the bandages. Crumpled in the bent claws that had been her fingers were pound notes, three – no, Emmaline saw, touching them with her own shaking fingers, five – as much as her mother would have been paid for working in the mill for half a year.

In the safe drugged haze, Cat smiled a small sad smile. "He gave me the money, Emmaline. He brought me more of my medicine, and he gave it all to me. Medicine and the money. He said it was important I keep taking my medicine."

"Who? Who gave you the money?"

"He was such a gentleman, Emmaline, in a fine black suit," Cat said slowly, her tongue sounding too big for her mouth. It tripped on every second word. "He brought Tommy home from the chemist's. Tommy got caught, Emmaline. The chemist caught him with my dram and was beating him, and the gentleman rescued him. He might have been hurt bad, or even killed – our Tom – him being so small and all. The gentleman saved his life. He brought him back home, and gave me my dram. My dram and two more. He'd paid for them himself."

"But why did he do this for you? Why did he give you the money?" Emmaline tried to think of who the "fine gentleman" might be, and why he would have given her money. Of course there had always been the men from the factory who were kind to her mother, but none of them were gentlemen, and none had extra pounds to give away, she was sure.

Cat's pupils were huge, leaving only a rim of iris. Emmaline saw this, and also the black flatness in them, reminding her of the small horse she'd seen, fallen in the street only the week before. A drayman's horse, overworked, dying from exhaustion on the cold wet street. There had been nothing in its eyes anymore. No light, no fear, no hope.

"It's only for a short while," Cat said, as she'd said about the books, and the writing box, and the shepherdess. "Only a short while, he promised. And then he'll bring Tommy back. And he didn't even mind that our Tom can't hear, nor speak more'n your name."

A dark quiet grew inside Emmaline.

"It's not for so long, Em. And he'll treat him fine."

You sold Tommy, she thought, afraid to say the words out loud. But when Cat's head nodded in sleep, she blurted it, her voice loud in the low-ceilinged room. "You sold him? Into what trade?" she demanded, thinking, *No, I'll take the money and go to the spinner's, or the weaver's, or whichever mill Mother has sold Tommy into. I'll give back the money, and say it was a mistake, that my mother is not in her right mind, and that Tommy cannot work the mills – he's too young – not until he's nine. I'll go to wherever it is and get him back tonight.*

"Weren't none of 'em here, Em," her mother said. "Weren't none of 'em here in Tibbing. I don't rightly know what the gentleman did, but he said Tommy would be well treated, and get a hot meal every night. He'll be apprenticed into a trade. I thought it was the best thing for our Tom. Don't you think so too? There's nothing for the lad here."

Emmaline sat down, hard, in front of her mother. "It wasn't to a mine, was it?" No one would want Tommy for mine work. He was small enough, but didn't have the strength to be a hurrier, one of the children who crawled through the narrow passages, pushing and pulling wagons of coal. "You couldn't have sold Tommy into the mines. Anyone looking at him would see he doesn't have the strength."

Her mother shook her head. "Nay. Weren't a mine. Weren't a mine," she repeated, dully. She got up, and, carefully, as if walking on a swaying bridge, crossed the few steps to her mattress. Her clothes were filthy, her hair matted as a rat's nest at the back.

The dark quiet reached out a cold finger and stroked Emmaline's spine. "If it wasn't to one of the mills, and not a mine . . . Mother. Where is Tommy?"

"The man was from London, Emmaline." Cat lay on her back and feebly plucked at the blankets piled beside her. "Imagine that. Our Tom apprenticed down in London. I remember him saying that it was a fine opportunity for any young lad. And he gave Tommy fresh cakes. He had a whole sack of them, and he gave two to Tommy, and oh, Emmaline, you should have seen the lad's eyes light up as he ate those lovely cakes. Gave one to me, too, I think. It were for the best. And 'tis only for a wee while, I'm sure. A few months, I think the gentleman said. He wrote it down here." She fumbled through the blanket, finding her uneaten cake and dropping it onto the floor, then pulling out a folded square of cheap paper. "I told him I don't read, but my lass does, and if he'd wait for you . . . but he said t'weren't possible, he had to get on back, but it was all right and proper, and here's the proof." She lay the paper on her stomach, smoothing it with her good hand, over and over. "He showed me where to put my mark."

Emmaline looked at the paper for a long time before she went and took it. Outside the door was the clatter of something being kicked along the cobbles, the coarse shout of a man's voice, the wail of a child.

"There's no factory work for Tommy," she said, as if convincing herself. "He's too young." She was stalling. She could see what was on the paper as if it were reflected in a wavy mirror – the darkness of the ink, the scrawl of the letters, and, on one corner, a large black thumb print. Soot. It looked like soot. The sight of that sooty print moved the darkness forward from her spine to the pit of her stomach. It felt like an uncooked lump of dough.

There wasn't enough light for her to read the words. She went to the fireplace, where a few chunks of coal glowed red. She read what was written in the one misspelled sentence, looked at the meaningless name and address, and at her mother's shaky cross at the bottom. Then she simply stared at the embers.

Finally she turned to her mother. Cat was asleep, the drug having put her into the deep numbness that she so desperately craved now. Her head was thrown back, her mouth open. A silvery line of drool – like the track of a snail – glistened from one corner of her mouth down to her jaw. She cradled her right hand in the crook of her other arm, as if it were a priceless treasure. Short, huffing snores filled the room.

Emmaline fought to push down the cold churning mass in her stomach that was cramming its way up her chest into her throat. She put her hand over her mouth, partly to try and hold in the meager contents of her stomach, and partly in horror.

Her mother had sold Tommy to a master sweep – not, as she tried to tell Emmaline, for the boy's sake. It had been a way to have money for the drug, for the drams of opiate that took her away from everything – the pain in her hand, the noise of the mill, the smell of the street. The poverty of her own spirit.

And because of this need, Tommy would be a climbing boy, condemned to spending the next five years of his life forced into narrow flues in the high houses of London, sweeping and dusting the soot from the chimneys.

Five years. If he lived that long.

EARLY MORNING DARKNESS

ven though Emmaline's body was exhausted, her mind raced from thought to thought, not letting her sleep. Shivering in a sudden cool whisper of air that snuck in through the rag in the window, she pulled Tommy's blanket over hers.

Where is Tommy now? Is he safe and warm, his belly full, or is he cold and hungry and frightened? Emmaline wondered. The images in her head were terrible. "Tommy," she whispered, over and over.

Across the room Cat uttered a sudden garbled sentence, followed by a whimper. Emmaline didn't know whether her mother's distress was caused by her need for another dram, or the terrible realization of what she had done in order to have it.

Cat's eyelids were red-rimmed in the glare of the lit rush Emmaline held over her. "I must sleep, Em. I'm tired," she said, her voice lifeless. She scrabbled in the bedding, holding up first one, and then a second empty dram, tipping each to her chapped lips even though the tiny bottles had already been drained.

Watching her, something cruel clutched at Emmaline's heart, holding it with a pinching painful grip, surrounding it so that it felt dead, and hard, to match her mother's eyes. Emmaline wondered, for just a moment, if the life she had lived back in the village, the life she imagined she'd one day escape back to, was all just a dream.

Is this where Mother goes when she takes her dram? Back to those times when Father was alive, before Tommy's illness, before life in the mill and this wretched place?

She took the pound notes off the table, where her mother had left them, and tucked them down the bodice of her dress. She put the folded note into her apron pocket.

"My money," Cat whispered. "My five quid. I must have 'em, love."

Emmaline knelt in front of her mother. "I'm taking them, Mother, for I'm off to find Tommy. I'm going to find him, and when I do, I'll give the master sweep back his money, and he'll have to let Tommy go."

"But –" Her mother's face dissolved in bewilderment. She clutched Emmaline's hand. "But I *need* that money," she said. "For my pain."

"The laudanum is harming you, Mother. It muddies your thoughts. And you're not eating, or even cleaning yourself. You mustn't have any more. Now come with me."

Cat's grip on Emmaline's hand grew fierce, her knuckles white and waxy. The confused look changed to fury. "I'm only sick because I don't have it, Emmaline. I'll be better if I have some more." Her voice was harsh. "And I'll not go anywhere with you," she said, her good hand almost crushing Emmaline's.

Emmaline was surprised at how much angry strength her mother still had, and winced at the pain, but she didn't look away. "You can fight me if you wish. But if you act this way, I'll take the money and leave you here – in the cold, with no medicine, and no way to get more. Is that what you want?"

Her mother let go of Emmaline's hand.

"Where's your shawl?" Emmaline asked, then finding it crumpled in Cat's coverlet, picked it up and gave it a brisk shake.

"Where are we going?" Cat asked. "Is it the chemist? Are you taking me to the chemist?"

Emmaline didn't answer. She tried to smooth her mother's tangled hair back with her fingers, and took a clean rag, wet it, and wiped her mother's face. Then she knotted the plaid shawl firmly over the woman's chest. "Come on. Get to your feet," she said, and her mother, obedient, stumbled along after her, holding tight to the back of Emmaline's shawl.

As they passed Slater's mill, someone called Emmaline's name.

"Fanny!" Emmaline said, turning to see the slight figure slipping around the corner of the sooty brick building.

"Where are you off to with yer ma then, Emmaline?" Fanny asked.

"I don't have time to talk, Fanny," Emmaline said, stopping. Her mother bumped into her. A strong, bitter wind gusted through the narrow streets, swirling rubbish around their legs.

"Nor do I," Fanny said. "I've overslept by a good quarter hour, and now I'll be in trouble. I thought I'd just close my eyes for another minute, but when I opened them the others had left. And now I've missed my breakfast, as well. I'm hoping I can slip in without the overlooker spotting me. I'm not up for the bite of his cane across me back. She's not coming back to work, is she?" she asked then, raising her chin in Cat's direction. "She don't look up to it, not one bit."

Emmaline shook her head, seeing Fanny's small front teeth chatter slightly in the cold wind.

"No, she's not coming back to the mill right now. Look, Fanny, I won't see you for a while."

Fanny's low forehead furrowed. "Why's that, then?"

Emmaline shook her head. "There's no time to tell you what's happened. But look after yourself," she added, and then instinctively gave the girl a quick hug. She felt the strange slope of her friend's spine – the spinner's slouch – and as she stepped back, unconsciously straightened her own shoulders.

Fanny had been at the mill since she was five years old. She was pitifully thin and so pale, the dark circles around her eyes and the dullness of her lank hair making her look years older.

"Aye. I will. An' you and all. Look after yourself, Emmaline." She wrapped her arms around herself and then ran through the front doors.

Watching her, Emmaline thought that no matter how awful a job in the mill might be, it would still be a sight better than the life of a climbing boy.

She knew they took only the smallest boys – those between four and seven years of age. After that, they were too big for the tiny flues they were forced up with their brushes and rags. A nightmarish image of Tommy, trapped and terrified in a dark, airless, and confining space, having to use his bare knees and elbows to climb the brick flues, made Emmaline break into a trot, grabbing her mother's hand.

But Cat pulled back, panting and clutching her chest, so that Emmaline was forced to slow down. Cat appeared stunned, as she lurched behind Emmaline through Tibbing in the early morning darkness, her head down against the wind.

"What are we doing here?" Cat asked. They had walked through the gates of the Slater house and were at the side, on the curved walk banked by trimmed bushes of cotoneaster and ornamental cherry taller than Emmaline's head. It was the first time Cat had spoken since they'd left Milk Court. She let go of Emmaline's hand. "I know this place. Why are we here?"

Emmaline turned away from her mother, facing one of the leafy bushes. She saw that it had been stripped of its winter berries by hungry birds. After a long few moments she said, "I'm going off to find our Tommy."

She wouldn't look at her mother, although she could feel Cat's twitchy hand plucking at the back of her dress. One large raindrop hit the leaf in front of her, and the leaf bowed with the weight. Then another drop hit, and another, the pattering on the leaves sounding like the feet of tiny, scurrying creatures. The rain was icy on Emmaline's hands and face.

"Do you hate me, Emmy?" her mother finally said, her voice low.

Emmaline made a sound of disgust. "Yes. I do hate you, Mother. I'll *never* forgive you for what you've done," she said, swallowing and swallowing around the hard knot at the back of her throat. She pressed her hands over her eyes, trying to stop the tears that burned there. She didn't want to cry, afraid that if she started she wouldn't be able to stop. But with a choking sob, the tears came. She cried for Tommy and she cried for her mother, for she didn't hate her. She loved her, for all her weakness and neediness, but she also wanted to hurt her the way Cat had hurt Tommy.

Finally she took a deep breath, wiped her face with the damp edge of her shawl, turned back to her mother, and pulled the woman along the path and opened the back door. Mrs. Brill was there in the kitchen, giving instructions to Cook for breakfast, while two girls who assisted Cook scurried about, setting out dishes and rolling pastry.

"You're earlier than usual," Mrs. Brill commented, seeing Emmaline in the doorway. A frown creased her forehead. "Well, don't expect to leave any earlier this evening. Why are you standing there, gawking? Get on to the sewing room."

"I must see my aunt. Now," Emmaline said.

"That's impossible. She's still asleep. And don't use that tone with me." She looked around Emmaline. "Heavens above," she said, eyeing Cat. "Who is *that*?"

Emmaline turned, and saw her mother as Mrs. Brill must see her. Little more than a scarecrow, emaciated and dried out, her hair uncombed and clothes, a filthy wrinkled mess. How had the beautiful Catherine Roke become this hollow-eyed, bony, stinking creature? "It's my mother," she said.

"Your mother? Well!" Mrs. Brill shook her head and took a step back. "Well! There's no place for such a one as *her* on these premises. Take her away. Away now, I say, Emmaline."

But Emmaline dragged her mother into the kitchen. "I won't. Now take me to Mrs. Slater. Please."

"I'll do no such thing," the woman said.

"Fine. Then I'll go to her myself," Emmaline said, marching toward the door that led to the rest of the house, tugging her mother behind her. Cat felt weightless.

The housekeeper grabbed her arm. "Stop. Stop, girl. What is all this nonsense about?"

Emmaline bit down hard to stop her lips from trembling. "It's very, very important, Mrs. Brill. Please. Tell Mrs. Slater . . . tell her it's *imperative* that I speak to her."

The housekeeper's eyes widened, then she reluctantly nodded. "Well, all right. But it will take awhile. Come back with your – with her," she raised her nose in Cat's direction, "in a few hours' time. Mrs. Slater doesn't rise for at least two hours, and then she'll bathe and have her breakfast, and –"

"NO!" Emmaline exploded. "I must see her now. I can't wait hours. Take me to her, or I swear, Mrs. Brill, you'll not stop me."

Throwing down the page of notes she was holding, the housekeeper shook her head. "Wait here. I'll go and see what I can do. And mind you, don't let your mother touch anything."

Emmaline directed Cat to a chair at the long kitchen table, and sat beside her.

The fire roared as Cook and the two girls worked, their red faces gleaming with sweat. They occasionally glanced at Emmaline and Cat, but said nothing. The steamy kitchen was an island of silence.

LEAVING TIBBING

ithin fifteen minutes Mrs. Brill was back. "She'll receive you, in her bedchamber," she said, with a slightly injured tone. "Now come along."

Emmaline and Cat followed the woman's quivering false chignon, pinned low on her scalp. The creaking of her whalebone stays accompanied by the harsh melody of her jangling keys sounded too loud in the wide, silent hallways and staircases. Finally Mrs. Brill stopped in front of a green baize door and rapped softly.

Phoebe yanked open the door. She was wearing a dressing gown, her hair pinned up under a nightcap, although blonde tendrils escaped around her face. Her eyes were slightly puffy with sleep.

Phoebe's mouth opened in an oval of surprise as she spotted Cat, cowering behind Emmaline. "Catherine? No," she breathed, in a hushed, shocked whisper. "Hurry. Come in," she said, and Emmaline stepped forward, still pulling her mother.

Her voice normal once more, Phoebe spoke to Mrs. Brill. "That will be all, Mrs. Brill," she said, shutting the door in the housekeeper's face.

Emmaline didn't wait for even a second after the door closed. "It's Tommy, Aunt Phoebe. He – my mother . . ." Emmaline could not admit to her aunt that her own mother had done such a dreadful thing. "Tommy's gone. He was taken by a master sweep, Master Sweep Hillis – taken to London – and I need your help."

"Taken? Stolen, you mean?"

"No," she said, quietly. "It's Mother. She's in a bad way. Look at her, Aunt Phoebe!" she demanded, although Phoebe was already staring at Cat, her hand over her nose and mouth, as she was close enough to smell the woman.

"This is the worst she's ever been. It's her hand, you see," Emmaline said. "Surely you know she was injured, and she can't work, and she needed medicine, and there wasn't enough money for it, and she didn't know what she was doing, Aunt Phoebe. Really, she didn't."

Her aunt moved her own hand from her face to her throat. "Do you mean . . . has your mother . . . has she *sold* the boy into service?"

Emmaline could only look at the floor. When she raised her eyes, she saw revulsion on her aunt's face. At that look, any dread she had about approaching Phoebe for help was replaced, suddenly, by a surge of rage. And the rage made her strong. "So I'm asking for your help, Aunt Phoebe. I can't do all of this by myself anymore. Could you speak to Uncle Nathan? See if he would allow someone to take me down to London, and help find this Master

Sweep Hillis who took Tommy? I have the address – Steeplemount Way. I'm sure that if we go straight to this area, and find him, it would be a simple matter to –"

"We? Who, exactly, are we?" her aunt asked.

"Well, like I said, if you could ask Uncle Nathan to send someone with me, in a carriage, and then once we've found Tommy, I'll come right back, and –"

"Your Uncle Nathan is on business in Scotland. He won't return for a week."

"Couldn't you, then? Couldn't you arrange it?"

Phoebe blinked. "Mr. Slater is a complicated man. He runs his business and our lives in an orderly fashion. I – I'm not permitted to make these kinds of decisions."

Emmaline wanted to shout at her aunt, to run at her, tear the woman's soft cheeks with her own fingernails. Instead, she concentrated on keeping her voice even. "I realize that, Aunt Phoebe. Of course. Then I'll go to London on my own. But I beg you to keep Mother safe while I'm gone. I wanted you to see for yourself that she can't be left on her own."

One of Phoebe's feathery eyebrows raised, just the slightest, as she watched Cat.

Her sister-in-law was looking at an oil painting that hung on the wall at eye level in front of her. It was a pastoral scene, two small children – a girl and a younger boy – frolicking with lambs in a meadow. As Emmaline and Phoebe watched, Cat reached out her right hand, and, with her stiff useless knuckles, gently touched the smaller of the two painted figures.

"Please don't touch, Catherine," Phoebe said. Her tongue clucked once against the roof of her mouth. One loud *quack*.

"It's like Tommy. Tommy and Emmaline, how they might have been, back home," her mother said, so softly that Phoebe leaned closer.

"What's she saying?" Phoebe said.

"Tommy," Cat said, in a soft singsong, as if she were calling him, calling him in from play, calling him from the picture. Then she gave a sudden shiver, and scratched violently at her scalp with her good hand.

"Please, Catherine. That's a very expensive piece I had commissioned."

Cat's scratching moved from her head down to her shoulder. She scratched as if there was something alive under her skin. "It's my children," she said.

"It's not Tommy and Emmaline," Phoebe snapped. "It's Jasper. Jasper and me." Then she rubbed her forehead with her long, white-skinned fingers, the nails perfect ovals, buffed to a sheen. When she spoke, her voice had lost its harshness. "I don't know. I'll have to think about what's to be done."

Emmaline took a deep breath. "Aunt Phoebe, we can't go on the way we have been." She took another breath. "If you'll help us now, I'll come and live with you, as you've always wished." The room was quiet except for the muted ticking of an ormolu clock on the mantel.

Finally Phoebe spoke. "You'll live here?" she said.

Emmaline nodded.

Phoebe looked beyond Emmaline, at the gilt-framed mirror over the mantel that reflected Emmaline from the back. Her eyes were fixed on the spill of the girl's dark blonde hair. She put her hand to her own hair, then lowered it. "As a daughter?"

"Yes," Emmaline said.

Phoebe smiled, a small cautious smile, as if she were afraid showing too much joy would change Emmaline's decision. "You will be happy here, Emmaline. You'll see."

"But you must promise me two things," Emmaline said. "You must promise me that you'll look after Mother – not just while I'm gone to London, but afterwards, too, once I've brought Tommy back. That they can stay on in the millhouse, and won't want for anything. And that I'll still be able to see them."

Phoebe nodded. "I'll not see my brother's wife and her child be turned out in the streets to starve. That I'll agree to. But the rest must be under my terms. You'll cut all ties with them, Emmaline. You won't see them. Is that clear?"

Emmaline watched Cat as she stood in front of the picture, staring.

"Do you understand, Emmaline? You can go and look for your brother, although I can't imagine you'll actually find him, and I'll make sure Cat is cared for until you get back. Afterwards I will provide for her – and for the boy, if he returns – but you cannot see them again. Those are my requirements for this . . . proposition."

Emmaline lowered her head. "They won't want for anything?"

"No."

Emmaline hesitated. "I'll agree to your terms," she said quietly. She watched her aunt moving about the room, and heard the clink of coins.

"Take this," Phoebe said, putting a small knit bag into Emmaline's hand. "It's all I have right now. As I've said, Nathan keeps a careful watch over his accounts, and I've nothing but pocket money."

Emmaline nodded, then went to her mother. "Good-bye, Mama," she said. "I'll be back in a fortnight, surely, if not sooner."

Her mother looked at her. "I'm sick, Emmy," she whispered. A muscle under her left eye twitched, a tiny frantic dance.

"I know, Mama," Emmaline said, then gave her one swift hug, and left the bedchamber with its scent of lilacs.

As she stepped through the green baize door into the hall, she knocked into Mrs. Brill. Clustered around her were two parlor maids. Mrs. Stanley was standing behind Mrs. Brill, her fingers pressed over her mouth.

As Emmaline passed Mrs. Stanley, the woman reached out to touch the girl's arm. Emmaline looked into her face, and saw pity and something else – *horror*?

"He's never been taken as a climbing boy, your Tommy, has he?" she whispered. "I'm sorry, Emmaline. You'll find him. Surely you will. Good luck," she said, and put her arm around Emmaline's shoulder.

"Aye, good luck, Emmaline," the parlor maids chorused. For once, Mrs. Brill said nothing.

"Mrs. Brill, could I collect what's owing to me for this quarter year, before I go?" She squeezed the small bag of coins in her hand. "I'll need money, once I'm in London."

Mrs. Brill unexpectedly looked flustered. "Well, no now, pay isn't due until Lady Day, March 25, a full month off. You know that. And besides, that's Master Slater's business, not mine."

Mrs. Stanley squeezed Emmaline's arm. "Never mind, dearie. Come along with me, to the sewing room."

Emmaline turned her back on Mrs. Brill and followed Mrs. Stanley, and in the little room under the stairs the woman handed her two small worn books. "One by Fanny Burney and the other a very macabre one, my daughter says, by Mary Shelley," she told Emmaline. "I was going to give these to you this morning; my daughter passed them on to me only last night. How I wish I had a few bob for you as well, but I've not a penny with me."

Emmaline looked around the cluttered room where she had spent the last five years of her life. "My aunt gave me this," she said dully, lifting the small bag.

"How much money do you have?" Mrs. Stanley asked. Emmaline emptied the coins into her hand.

"Not enough for a coach, not near enough," the woman said. "I expect you'll have to take a wagon, then. They come by on the main road, regular-like, and many go all the way to London."

Mrs. Stanley sighed, but gave Emmaline a lopsided smile. "You'll find him," she said. "A smart lass like yourself, aye, you'll find that brother of yours in no time. People will pay attention to you, Emmaline, for you carry yourself like a lady, and your words are fine, yes, quite fine, from all your reading. If only . . ." She paused, studying Emmaline's patched dress and apron and scuffed boots. Then she rifled through a wardrobe that held the staff's cast-off clothes that were to be sold to the rag-and-bone man.

The woman pulled out a poplin day dress of deep purple, and a lilac shawl. She thrust them, along with a tiny housewife – a case containing needles and thread – at Emmaline. "Take these clothes. They won't fit you, and they're a bit the worse for wear – Mrs. Slater's lady's maid has worn them as well as the Lady herself. But you'll be able to stitch them up in no time. If you could only brush and polish your boots, why, you could easily be taken for a lady's maid, or even a governess. Go on, now," she said, when Emmaline opened her mouth and shook her head, as if to protest.

"She owes it to you, the nasty glut," Mrs. Stanley said. "So go on now." She gave Emmaline a gentle push.

"But what about the fancywork?" Emmaline asked, suddenly realizing her leaving the sewing room would affect Mrs. Stanley.

"Never you mind about that," Mrs. Stanley assured her. "That's not your problem. Your worry now is to find that boy of yours, and get him away from the chimneys before it's too late. I had a nephew once . . ." She stopped. "No. There's no use going on over what's in the past. So you get yourself off, now, and be quick about it."

Emmaline put the bag of coins into her bodice and wrapped the books inside the dress and shawl. She thanked Mrs. Stanley, and then did as the woman told her. She was off.

THE ROAD TO LONDON

ercifully, the freezing rain had stopped, although now there was a heavy mist in the air. Hidden by the high hedge at the side of the house, Emmaline took the five greasy pound notes from her bodice. She pulled open her hem, slipping them into the opening, and, using a needle and thread from the housewife, stitched the hem closed. She knew she couldn't touch the money until she found the master sweep, and she didn't want to take a chance on losing it or having it stolen.

She tramped to the main road, and within a quarter of a mile came upon a knot of people, all of them hunched against the cold haze. Emmaline approached a haggard woman carrying a large straw basket.

"Will there be a wagon soon?" she asked.

The woman nodded.

"Will it go to London?"

"Roundabout, aye. Not straight through, like a coach. The wagons stop at towns along the way."

"How long does it take?" Emmaline asked.

"I'd say four days, given these roads. Less in summer, when the roads are better. But you can count on four, surely, this time of year," the woman told her, one eye squinting as she looked at the marbled sky.

"How much does it cost?"

The woman shrugged. "Depends," she answered, looking at Emmaline's bundle. She picked at a sharp eyetooth with broken, dirty fingernails. "The journey itself ain't too dear. But you'll have to buy food, if you have none with you, and pay for lodging at night. And then there's the road tariffs, as well. How much do you have?" Her eyes suddenly brightened. Something in her expression made Emmaline shrug cautiously.

"I'm sure I have enough," she said, and moved away, her fingers clamped over her bundle.

She stood with her back to the woman, watching the gloomy mist as it rolled up from the wide verges and over the road, watching for the wagon that would take her to London.

Eventually a long Berkshire wagon rumbled into sight. It was pulled by two teams of horses; passengers sat on the three rows of wooden benches that ran the width of the wagon. Two of the people got out, and the six people waiting with Emmaline climbed on.

"I'm going to London," Emmaline told the driver. "How much will it cost?"

"You pays by the day," he said. "Tuppence for all of today's ride, with a ha'penny more for the turnpike at Fellis."

Emmaline fished the coins out of her bag and handed them to him, then found a space at the end of the one of the benches.

That first day on the wagon passed in a daze.

The road was long and winding, pocked with half-frozen puddles. They passed an occasional wagon or cart as they dipped into shallow valleys, where the mist turned to thick fog. Cattle and sheep stood mute – humped shadows beside the road. The horses' breath emerged in long, quavering white bursts. Their hooves squelched through the mud as the iron wheels churned with agonizing slowness, sometimes grinding over wet stones, making Emmaline's jaw ache. The road was lost in fog on either end. On the backless wooden bench, Emmaline was jostled back and forth, back and forth, her shoulder constantly bumping the grizzled old man on one side of her, and her hip banging against the hard wood of the cart on her other. Her back ached, her feet grew icy.

By midday the last wisps of fog had faded away as the wagon pulled up outside a nameless inn, and the driver and some of the passengers went inside. Emmaline followed others to a privy at the back of the inn, then walked back and forth in front of the wagon, swinging her arms and stamping her feet, trying to drive away the numbness. The passengers who stayed outside pulled out food they'd brought: chunks of sausage, withered apples, boiled eggs. Emmaline tried not to watch them eat, her own stomach contracting as the sky darkened in shifting patterns.

Eventually the driver came out, the smell of beer and warm meat and smoke clinging to his clothes. They set off again as rain began to fall.

That first night they stopped at an inn called The Pheasant. Emmaline bought a mug of tea and a pickled egg, and paid the innkeeper to sleep over the stables. Travelers from other wagons were already there – some talking quietly, some sleeping. The room was old and creaky, the roof low-pitched, but at least the heat of other bodies, all forced into closeness with each other, kept it warm. She spread her own shawl over straw gray with age, and lay down beside a young woman with a smiling baby girl. She covered herself with her Aunt Phoebe's lilac shawl, using the purple dress as a pillow.

She was so weary, her clothes damp and her body aching from the wagon ride, that she fell quickly asleep. She was awakened a number of times by harsh coughing and the shrill cries of the baby, but each time fell immediately back to sleep.

In the morning she went into the inn, trying not to watch those feasting on pigeon pie, ham and cold boiled beef and buttered toast, trying not to breathe in the tantalizing smells. She used one of her precious coins to buy herself a small currant bun, and drank handfuls of icy water from the pump in the yard.

The day was warmer than the one before, the sky clearer, the road busier, and Emmaline felt her spirits rise. Although still terribly hungry, she was less uncomfortable than she had been the day before, and sat next to the woman with the baby, holding the infant for her from time to time.

They passed through hamlets and villages, dingy with coal dust. After a few hours the road turned to macadam, the packed broken stone keeping down the mud. Dogs ran alongside the wagon, barking, and there were animals being driven to markets. Men and women worked in fields, and the road was busy with carriages and spring carts, ponies and traps and dogcarts. The young woman beside Emmaline shared a half-loaf of dark bread and heel of hard cheese with her. Tears sprang to Emmaline's eyes at this kindness.

"I'll be home by tonight, thank the Lord. You're going all the way to London, then?" the woman asked, chewing a piece of bread to mush and putting it into the baby's mouth. The baby gummed it.

Emmaline nodded. "My little brother," she said. "He's been taken as a climbing boy, and I'm going to find him and bring him home." She surprised herself by telling the woman her story, but there was something about traveling with strangers that created an intimacy. She gnawed a chunk of cheese.

"Oh, yes," the woman said. "You mustn't let him be a climber, if you can stop it. Terrible, terrible for those poor boys. Some of them get trapped and die in those tiny black flues, you know. No light but what might come in from above. Can't pull them up or push them back down."

The cheese turned to chalk in Emmaline's mouth, and she spit it into her hand, her throat suddenly closed and unable to swallow.

"They don't last long," the woman went on, unperturbed by Emmaline's expression. "If it's not one way, it's another. Even if they get stuck but survive, they're turned out on the street because they're too big. Nasty business. I hear they're trying to make some special brushes what cleans the chimneys, instead. My husband's brother, he was once apprenticed to a master sweep, but he was only a chummy – one of the bigger boys, paid to keep an eye on the littleuns, make sure they does their job. Prodders, some calls 'em, as they give the climbers a good jab with a pin, in the feet or legs, if they don't go up quick enough." She chattered away cheerfully, thoughtlessly, while Emmaline squeezed the wet cheese tighter and tighter in her fist, until it was a soggy, inedible lump.

That night she had a terrible sensation of being pinned, of being unable to move. She gasped for air and sat upright in the pitch blackness. She couldn't catch her breath, and couldn't see her hand in front of her face.

"Help," she croaked, although she didn't know who she was asking, or what help she needed. "Help me, please."

"Shut yer bloody gob," a male voice snarled, and Emmaline remembered where she was. She lay down again in the crowded, windowless loft with its stench of unwashed bodies, but was afraid to fall asleep – afraid of the desperate, trapped, dark feeling.

By the end of the third day Emmaline was out of money. She'd put her last coins into the dirt-lined palm of the driver that morning, and sat in swaying silence on the wagon the whole day. When they stopped at a hamlet that night, she asked him how much farther it was to London.

"We've made good time, with these last two dry days," the driver told her, helping the hostler unhitch his horses outside the stable. "Only a few hours' drive tomorrow."

With one longing glance at the warm light spilling from the glazed windows of the inn, Emmaline slipped around behind it. She found a narrow lane tunneled through trees, and walked down the soft wintered grass and weeds as darkness fell. At the edge of a strip of dusky meadow, she made a nest in the soft bracken and settled in. There was the sound of a nightingale from deep in the woods, and, far in the distance, something that might have been the comforting, rhythmic sound of an ax. And there was a crescent moon. Emmaline watched the slice of white in the sky until her eyes closed.

She slept in the fresh night air, slept deeper than she had for a long time, awakened at daybreak by the piercing, inquisitive cries of chickadees and jays and the rustling of small animals in the underbrush. She stood and stretched, stiff and chilled in the thin morning air, seeing, in the distance, a cottage that she hadn't noticed the night before. It had a friendly low brow of thatch, and a curling white ribbon of smoke from the chimney. She had a sudden rush of aching pain that might have been caused by the sight of the cottage, so like her old home, or that might have been caused by hunger. The hunger sat like a constant stone in her belly.

As she started her walk through the woods back to the road, she found a handful of whortleberries and ate them. Although it was too early in the season, and the small blue berries were hard and bitter, the act of chewing was comforting. A few steps further, she discovered the slender drooping stems and delicate white flowers of snowdrops. She hadn't seen snowdrops – or any flower – since she'd last walked under the trees near Maidenfern with her father. He had told her that these were the winter flower of hope, and that they were edible. She pulled a number out now, devouring the bulbs and leaves.

"Today," she said, swallowing the last of the leaves, the taste strange but not unpalatable, "today I will be in London. Today I will find Tommy."

IV

London

1836

When my mother died I was very young,
And my father sold me while yet my tongue
Could scarcely cry, "'weep! 'weep! 'weep! 'weep!"
So your chimneys I sweep, and in soot I sleep.

– William Blake
from "The Chimney Sweeper"

ALL UP!

ondon, huge and gray, rose on the horizon. The sheer immenseness of it shocked Emmaline. Even though she had heard about London all her life, and read about it, nothing could have prepared her. On the outskirts of the city she was jostled and pushed along with the growing crowd, and was soon enveloped in a surging mass of frightful noise and activity.

Grit stung her eyes, and the endless shouting of people, the barking of dogs and high squeals of horses, all topped with the maddening clanging of nearby church bells, made Emmaline put her hands over her ears. But then she was shoved roughly from behind by a large woman carrying a honking goose under one arm. An elderly man stepped down hard on her foot as he attempted to pass. She hurried to make her way out of the middle of the street, and draw closer to the open market stalls and carts.

There were stalls heaped with fabrics, others hung with large bunches of rags. Peddlers opened their coats to show her ribbons and jewelry pinned on the lining, and one, grinning lewdly, made kissing noises at her. And the smells – in the air mingled the odor of the hot blood and offal from the butchers' stalls and the unmistakable smells from the fishmongers'. Emmaline saw wrinkled dull-eyed cod and neat rows of sole, while half-dead eels feebly writhed in open baskets. There was the cloying smell of rotting fruit hidden below the fresh, all crawling with flies, while underfoot, gutters ran with an endless, stinking trickle of human and animal waste.

Emmaline tried to ask for directions to Steeplemount Way, but people ignored her or pushed her aside as if she were begging. She wondered if it would help if she put on Aunt Phoebe's dress, but she had nowhere to change, and she knew it would hang like a sack on her unless she was able to alter it.

As she walked, she stared up at the tall narrow chimneys on every building. *Is Tommy in one of these?*

She passed a street corner where a man wearing an apron smeared with filth stirred at something in a barrel, slopping water over the sides. Glancing into the barrel, Emmaline saw that there were live trout, snouting at each other, and then, as she smelled a piece of the fish frying over an open brazier beside the man, her stomach cramped in on itself.

"Only a ha'penny apiece, ha'penny apiece," cried the hawker, and Emmaline thought of the pound notes in her apron hem. *No*, she told herself firmly. If she had even a shilling less than what Master Sweep Hillis had given for Tommy, she couldn't bargain to get him back. In the next instant, the scent of the frying fish in her nostrils and down her throat, she was overtaken by lightheadedness. She thought she saw something – a dark shape – out of the corner of her eye, and heard harsh whisperings behind her. She shook her head, but the same thing happened again. She turned her head to bring whatever was just beyond her vision into sight, or see who it was murmuring behind her, but there was nothing, no one. Finally she passed through the busiest streets, and saw that she was away from the shops and market stalls and peddlers, and into an area of finer houses. Many of them were like her aunt's, although smaller and less grand.

"Excuse me, Miss," she asked a young woman, walking with her lady's maid on one of the streets. The woman ignored her. She reached forward, only intending to ask directions: "Excuse me, can you please tell –" But the woman looked down at her, horrified at Emmaline's dirty hand on her sleeve, and stepped back, shaking off the hand as if it burned the fine wool of her dress.

"Away with you," her maid said, pushing her face close to Emmaline. "This isn't a street for the likes of you. Get away back to Covent Gardens or St. Giles or wherever you ply your trade. Go on, now," she said, menacingly, while her mistress stayed to one side, shaking her head in annoyance. Emmaline smelled something fruity on the maid's breath.

"I'm not plying any trade," Emmaline said. "I'm not begging. I simply –"

The two women swept past her, their heads high. Emmaline suddenly realized they thought she was a girl of the streets, selling herself like the girls in the market at Tibbing. She looked down at her mud-streaked dress and filthy boots. She drew a deep breath and unsteadily touched her forehead, trying to smooth back her hair. The light-headedness was becoming almost constant.

She set out again, putting one foot in front of the other with dull, heavy steps. As she neared the end of a street that felt miles long, for the first time since she'd left her Aunt Phoebe's the utter hopelessness of what she was trying to do overwhelmed her. She had no idea any place could be this immense and confusing.

She turned toward a high iron fence, leaning her arm against the cold railings, and put her head against her arm, giving way to tears. She was hungry and exhausted and lost. Lost, with no directions except for the name Steeplemount Way, written on the note in her apron pocket. A light rain was falling. The tears that collected under her lids were hot, scorching her eyes, and she turned her face up, into the drizzle, to cool them.

"Oy!" she heard. "Oy – you there. Watcha think you're playing at?"

Turning in the direction of the voice, Emmaline saw a young woman on the steps of the house inside the iron fence. A dripping rag hung from the young woman's hand, and a pail sat near her feet. She looked to be about the same age as Emmaline. The girl's eyes were red-rimmed and swollen, as if she'd been weeping. Emmaline wondered, suddenly, if her own eyes looked the same.

"Get off," the girl said, waving the rag in Emmaline's direction.

Emmaline rubbed her arm against her face. "I'm sorry," she said. "It's just that I'm . . . I'm not sure where I am, and I can't seem to find anyone to give me directions. And I'm looking for someone."

The girl pursed her mouth and narrowed her eyes. "Well, ain't you a surprise, with that silky talk come out of one who looks as rough as you. Wot's yer story, then, eh?"

Emmaline opened her mouth to speak, but nothing came out. There was an odd buzzing in her ears, and the street beneath her feet tilted. Emmaline held fast to the railings. As she slumped against them, closing her eyes, she heard the girl's voice, as if from a great distance, softened around the edges by the buzzing. "Are you sickening for something? You don't have the plague, do you?"

With great effort, Emmaline lifted her eyelids, and the noise in her ears diminished. "No. I'm not sick."

"Why's your mouth green then, eh?"

Emmaline touched her bottom lip. "I . . . I've been eating . . . plants. In the countryside. I've just arrived in London."

The other girl threw her rag into the pail. To Emmaline the splash was faint, deadened, as if heard through a thick wall of cloud. "Is it that much of a hunger you have, then?"

Emmaline nodded, trying to clear her vision. Something in the other girl's voice had changed.

"Aye," the girl said now. "I know what that's like. Well," she sighed, "there's not much sense washing the steps in the rain. Come round back, then, but be quiet about it. Cook's out just now, at the costermonger getting fruit and veg. If we hurry I can slip you a veal pie afore she's back." She picked up her pail. "Hurry, now."

The idea of savory meat encased in a flaky pastry made the saliva rush into Emmaline's mouth, and she had to swallow before she answered. "Thank you," she said, following the girl around to the side of the house and then across a courtyard and down a steep set of steps, supporting herself with the wall of the house the whole time. She kept her eyes on the cross of the girl's apron straps. She wore a uniform: a blue striped cotton dress with a white apron with broad straps edged with lace. Her dark brown hair was pulled up in a knob under a white frilled cap.

"Sit yerself," the girl said, as they entered the dim basement kitchen of the house. "What's yer name?"

"Emmaline."

"Mine's Sukey," the girl said, dumping the pail of dirty water into a massive stone sink in the scullery, and then setting the empty pail in the corner with a clatter. "And this here is Thorn House."

The quietness of the room revived Emmaline. She sat at the scrubbed table and looked around the kitchen. One wall was covered with shiny copper pans, hanging in neat rows. There was a large open fireplace with an iron spit, and beside it a round oven.

"Hope Cook won't miss one pie," Sukey said, taking a large tin container down from an open shelf in the larder. "Sometimes she counts, but today she had in a tradesman she's sweet on, and she was being right generous. He et a number of 'em, so likely she's lost track of how many she made." She started to pry the lid off the tin.

"I don't want to get you into any trouble."

"Long's as you're out of here before she gets back —" Sukey was interrupted by the harsh clang of a small bell. She snicked her tongue and looked at the row of bells on a board on the wall at one end of the kitchen. "There's the old master in his bedchamber, wanting something. Likely it's nothing. You wait here, now, and I'll go see. I'll be right back." She jammed the lid back on the tin, then hurried up the wooden staircase that Emmaline knew would lead to the main floor of the house, closing the door behind her.

It felt so good to sit, feeling safe and calm, for even a few moments. Emmaline tried not to think of the tin of pies, so close. When a few minutes passed and Sukey didn't come back, she put her arms on the table and rested her head on them, thinking of how it would feel to sink her teeth into the pie. *Is Tommy as hungry as I am at this moment?* she wondered.

A loud male voice on the other side of the stairway door startled her out of her daze. She jumped up, her head spinning from the quickness of her movement. She stared at the stairway. *Please come back, Sukey*, she willed the girl. But the voice only got louder and closer. Emmaline knew if anyone walked in and found her in the kitchen, they could accuse her of thieving, and she didn't like to think what trouble it might bring.

She whirled and raced out the side door, up the steep stone steps, and as she turned into the little walkway that would lead her back to the street, collided with someone. She would have fallen but was grabbed around her upper arms. She was aware of someone tall – a boy with a shock of wavy black hair – but she broke free and ran down the street, away from Thorn House.

She hurried along, her heart fluttering. After half a block she pressed her hand to a stitch in her side and slowed to a walk, asking herself why she was running. She hadn't done anything wrong. But the voice she heard behind the stairway door was loud and harsh, full of authority. And something about it sent a shiver through her. Her face and neck were wet with perspiration, and even though she now stood still, her heart wouldn't stop its painful thudding. Emmaline tried not to think of the pie, willing her mouth to stop imagining the taste, willing her stomach to stop its bitter gnawing as if it were angrily trying to devour itself. A strange new pain bloomed behind her eyes.

She leaned against a building, the bricks hard and cool, trying to get her bearings. She hadn't come this way before. Now she was on a busy street corner, a crossroads of some sort.

As she stood in the midst of the rumble of carriage wheels, the clanking of horses' hooves on the rough paving, the tapping of the pattens strapped onto ladies' shoes to keep them dry on the wet streets, the cackling laugh of a gull overhead, she heard another sound. A voice, from high above her.

"All up!" the voice cried. Emmaline tilted her head, seeing the small sooty face of a child poking out of the narrow flue of a chimney on the house across the street.

"All up!" it called, a second time, shouting back down through the flue, and Emmaline watched as the child climbed up on the edge of the chimney and tottered on the sloped roof of the house, his bare toes curling over the rough wet slate.

"Tommy," she said, although she knew it wasn't Tommy. There was no way of recognizing the boy, for he wore only a short torn pair of filthy trousers. His legs and chest and arms and face were blackened with oily soot, and he clutched his brushes tightly. His head was shaved. It could have been Tommy, but for the voice, for of course Tommy would never be able to call out.

The ache inside her grew. Seeing the state of the little boy – painfully thin, the small round rib cage barely covered with flesh, the ragged pants flapping about the knees, which were too large and knobby for the matchstick shins – was heartbreaking. There was a liquidy roaring in her ears, coming from far behind at first, and then growing closer and louder. At the same time, church bells began to ring, first one set, and then another and another. The chiming blended with the rushing sound in her own head until Emmaline couldn't tell which was the true sound and which was the echo. And then all the sounds faded, and she was cocooned in a blessed shroud of white silence.

"Tommy," she said, her voice coming from somewhere in the back of her throat. "Tommy . . ."

She knew she was falling. And as she fell, she sensed a shadow pass over her. The side of her face hit the hard cobblestone, jarring her temple and cheek and jaw with shocking force. And then there was a breath near her ear, and she heard quiet words, although she wasn't sure whether she actually heard them, or just imagined them.

I'm here.

"Tommy?" Emmaline wanted to say more, but she had no strength, not even in her tongue and lips. She wasn't sure whether she just thought, or actually said, the words. *Is it you, Tommy? Are you really here?* As the darkness came over her – a thick, suffocating blackness – she was answered.

"Yes, it's me. I'm here."

And then she heard no more.

THORN HOUSE

n and out, light and shadow, the edges of an unfamiliar room came into focus. Emmaline squeezed her eyes tightly, trying to remember, to sort out what had happened, why she was lying on – she touched the softness beneath her – a mattress of some kind.

As she twitched the material between her fingers, she opened her eyes and stared at the low sloping ceiling above her, covered with water-stain shapes that reminded her of places she had seen on an old map in the back of a book. The whitewashed walls were cracked and bulging. She turned her head, slowly, and saw a low chest. Jammed beside it was a rough table. On it was a candle stub and a book, and pulled up to it a ladder-back chair with the middle slat on the back missing. There was only a tiny window, its glass cracked, high on one wall – too high to see out of.

Fragments of images came back to her: running down the street, the hard press of a building against her back, the chimney sweep who wasn't her brother, the pounding in her head, the shock of stone rising up to meet her face, her own voice calling out, and then another voice. *Yes. It's me.*

Emmaline sat up, and saw her bundled shawl on the floor beside the bed. The door of the dark room was half open, light spilling onto the floor in a yellow wedge. She became aware of weeping – quiet, muffled weeping – from somewhere beyond the door.

She swung her legs to the floor, but the sudden movement brought a quick fist of pain to her cheekbone. She put her fingers to the spot and gingerly explored the hot throbbing lump.

Walking unsteadily toward the open door, she softly called out. "Hello?"

The weeping stopped in midsob, then she heard the sound of nose-blowing and the long low stutter of tears held in the throat.

"Yer finally awake, then, are you?"

Emmaline recognized the voice before she saw the face. "Sukey," she breathed.

"Aye." Sukey poked her head around the door frame. "You're lucky I sent Paddy out after you."

Paddy? Who is Paddy? "I don't understand," Emmaline said.

"When I came back to the kitchen, I realized you'd have been scared off by Master Eugene; I run into him when I made my way back. I'm only glad he didn't catch you; there'd have been no end of trouble." She folded her handkerchief and tucked it into the waistband of her apron. "And I saw the pie tin, still closed tight, and knew you'd gone off without one, so I sent Paddy after you with it. And here he comes back, with the pie in one hand and you like a sack of oats over his shoulder." She shook her head, her eyes studying Emmaline's cheek. "Paddy said you'd fallen like a lead weight on Goddard Street. Good thing he found you; if you'd lain there too long you'd have been picked up and took to the poorhouse or the prison, each as bad as the other. He brung yer bundle, too, grabbed it up afore someone snatched it."

Emmaline gently touched the lump on her cheekbone again. "I don't remember being carried, or . . ." *All I remember is calling Tommy's name, and a soft voice answering. Yes, it's me.*

"And you're in luck now. You've been like dead a few hours. Master Eugene has gone out for the evening, as usual, and Cook is off to check on her sister, what's been taken with fever, and she won't be home until late. The old master is poorly and will sleep all night. There's only me and Paddy. You're in his room," she added. "We thought it best to put you in a place no one ever looks. So come on into the kitchen and we'll get you that pie, and some soup as well." She sniffed, took out her handkerchief again, and mopped her nose.

"Are you all right?" Emmaline asked. The young woman's face was blotchy and streaked.

Sukey shrugged, balling the handkerchief in her hand. "Bring yer bundle, and come on, then."

The room Emmaline had been in was just off the kitchen, and, judging by its size, had probably been a store cupboard at some time. As they stepped into the kitchen, Emmaline saw a large copper kettle over the fire, steam rising from its spout. "Could I wash my hands and face?"

"Suit yerself," Sukey said, and poured boiling water into a bowl on the counter, adding a cup of cold water from an enormous jug. "There's washing soda there," she said, nodding toward the back of the counter.

Emmaline slowly lowered her hands into the hot water, sighing with pleasure. After scrubbing them, she did the same to her face, then used the clean drying rag Sukey handed her.

"Now. Sit down."

Emmaline did as she was told, and in a moment Sukey set the meat pie and a bowl of steaming soup in front of her. Emmaline could see that the soup was full of barley and vegetables and generous chunks of meat. As the warm meaty aroma drifted into her nostrils, she fought for composure, wanting to grab the bowl by its sides and put her face right into it, slurp it up as if she were an animal. Instead she picked up the spoon Sukey had left beside the bowl. "Why are you being so kind to me?" she asked, feeling the start of tears behind her eyes again.

Sukey shrugged again, going into the scullery. "T'weren't too long ago I were in much the same position as you," she called back. "Alone and hungry." Her voice was heavy, as if her own tears were threatening to come on again. She wiped at the inside of a pot with a rag.

Emmaline took one spoonful of soup, and then another and another, making small involuntary sounds of satisfaction. "But it looks like you've landed on your feet here, with this job," she said, stopping to catch her breath.

Sukey was still turned away. "For now," she said. "But . . ."

Emmaline waited. But when Sukey went on with her cleaning, saying nothing more, she returned to the soup, finishing it and then eating the pie more slowly. She savored each bite, licking her fingers to catch the last buttery, flaky crumbs of the crust.

She took her soup bowl and spoon and set them in the sink in the scullery. "Thank you, Sukey," she said. "I don't know what I would have done if –"

"Never mind," Sukey interrupted.

"I'll be off, then," Emmaline said.

"Let me wrap up some bread and cheese to take with you," Sukey told her, grabbing a round of bread and a long knife.

There were footsteps from the kitchen stairway, and Emmaline made a start toward the back door.

"No, no, don't run off. 'Tis only Paddy," Sukey said. "I told you; there's nothing to fear for now."

In a moment a boy came through the doorway. He was tall, and had to duck his head to avoid hitting it on the low lintel. He clattered down the stairs, his thick black hair wafting back from his face in the breeze he created. He carried a load of rumpled linens. Without saying anything, he stared at Emmaline.

"This here is Paddy, the lad what brought you here," Sukey said.

Emmaline flushed. "Thank you. For finding me. And . . . carrying me here." It was shameful to think of her body pressed against this stranger's.

"'Tis fine," Paddy said. "I'm glad you're all right."

It was this voice – the quiet, gentle voice – that she had heard as she slipped under the surface of the darkness. *Yes, it's me. I'm here*, he had answered, when she'd said her brother's name.

She recognized the Irish in it. The Meehans in Milk Court had been from Ireland.

Sukey had said his name was Paddy. "I'm Emmaline," she said. "You're . . . Paddy?" A question in her voice. "But –"

"It's only my house name," he interrupted. "Because I'm Irish. Master Eugene has always called any of the Irish help Paddy."

"But your real name," Emmaline said. "What is it?"

The boy's eyes stared into Emmaline's. "It gave me quite a start, hearing you call out my name, there, on the street, just as I came upon you."

"So you *are* Tommy?"

He nodded. "Although no one's called me Tommy for many a year. I'm Thomas. Thomas McLinn. There's been no one call me Tommy except –" He stopped. "Well, no one for a long time. How did you come to know my name? You don't possess the special powers, do you, now?" He gave Emmaline a half-smile.

Emmaline was almost sorry that she had to disappoint Thomas. "I was calling my brother; he's Tommy. I thought I saw him, but it wasn't him, after all."

Thomas then set down the mound of linen with a thump. A newspaper lay folded on top of it. If Emmaline's story meant anything to him, his face didn't show it. "I've brought down the bed linens and soiled clothes from Master Eugene's room." He picked up the newspaper and opened it on the table, leaning on his elbows and studying the page.

Sukey sighed. "Lord have mercy. I don't know how we'll get this done, what with Mary not here." She started sorting through the dirty laundry. "Girl who does the extra around here was hit by a carriage last week. She'll heal eventually, will Mary, but one of her legs is broke, as well as something inside of her, and she can't work for some time. Master Thorn doesn't want to hear about our domestic worries. I told him, but he just waved his hand and told me to look after it. Cook and I have to find someone for the scrubbing and kitchen dirty work right smart; there's plenty to choose from at the workhouse, but we've been that pushed for time that Cook hasn't had a chance to get down there." She talked quickly, hardly pausing for breath. It was almost as if she were just thinking out loud.

"Maggie is day help in the laundry out back a few days a week; she does the rinsing and mangling, and we've old Peg coming in one day a week to iron, but it were Mary what did the scrubbing out in the laundry, and all the peeling and chopping and washing up in here, as well as carrying up the coal and cleaning out the ash." She shook her head. "The Lord just doesn't provide enough hours in the day for me to do it all. This house has gone downhill badly, since Lady Lucy died. Gone to rack and ruin, if you ask me."

"There's no mistress?" Emmaline asked.

Sukey shook her head, leaving a shirt on the table and piling the rest of the dirty clothes into the basket she pulled from under the table. "Look at that," she said, still more to herself than Emmaline. "Torn right around the shoulder. How does he spoil his clothes so?" She gently fingered the ripped seam. "Oh, yes, up and died did the Lady Thorn," she said. "Was her heart. She were always poorly. Since then – oh, it were about a year ago now – things have gone badly. Master Thorn has let most of the staff go. Says we don't need so much help with no entertaining and much of the house not used and only he and the young master to provide for." She set the basket by the back door and picked up the shirt again, running her hands over the smooth cotton.

"So now there's just a few of us, rattling around like pebbles in a jar. And a house with no mistress is like a horse with no rider. No real order, no direction. Cook told me that, and she's proved right."

Emmaline glanced at Thomas, but he seemed engrossed in the newspaper.

"Ain't even a proper housekeeper or butler or footman no longer, no extra housemaid, neither," Sukey prattled on, "so it's fallen on Cook to look after things, plan all the meals and do all the cooking, without even a kitchen maid, and just Mary for the scullery. She has to organize what Thomas and me are to do an' all. And I've been reduced to not much more than a mere maid-of-all-work, 'stead of my old job as upstairs parlor maid. Thomas here has to look after all the fetching and hauling, and trimming the lamps, and keeping Master Eugene's clothes and boots in order. Old Master Thorn takes little care; he rarely dresses and eats no more'n a bird. All he cares about is his books. The house feels right strange, and we're all overworked. Ain't that so, Thomas?"

Thomas nodded, his eyes still on the paper. "It feels like the skeleton of a house."

Emmaline looked down at the newspaper, *The Penny Magazine* written in bold type across the top. Underneath, in smaller type, was an article entitled *The Catacombs of Kief.*

"Where is Kief?" she wondered aloud.

"You read, then?" Thomas asked.

"Of course," Emmaline said, although she didn't know why she chose those words, or why she heard her own voice use a slightly contemptuous tone.

Thomas turned away, quickly, and busied himself with ladling soup into his bowl. "Kief is the capital of a Russian province. Situated on the banks of the Dnieper River."

"Oh," Emmaline said, ashamed of the way she'd spoken.

In the silence that followed, with Sukey pulling out a needle and thread to repair the torn shirt, and Thomas eating his soup, Emmaline licked her lips. "I need work, and a place to stay. Just for a short while. I've been apprenticed," she said, folding one edge of the newspaper into a neat triangle, "as a seamstress. In Tibbing. I worked for a fine house in Tibbing. Do you know of any seamstress positions going? Just as an assistant." She saw that Sukey's seam was loose; the sleeve would tear again the next time the shirt was worn.

Sukey gave a grim chuckle. "London is gagging with trained seamstresses out of work. It's the cheap slopwork what's put them out of their jobs. People willing to pay much less for carelessly done piecework, long as it's done quick. Nay, I doubt you'll find any jobs going for a real seamstress these days. Not around here." She tied the thread and broke it between her calloused fingers, shook out the shirt and threw it onto the pile in the basket. "Do you have a letter, from your last job?" she went on.

Emmaline shook her head.

"No chance, then," Sukey said. "You'll never be hired on anywhere without a recommendation." She slapped her hands on her aproned thighs as if the matter was closed.

Emmaline hardly waited a heartbeat. "If that's the case, perhaps I could help out here. Surely a laundry scrubber or scullery maid won't need a letter of recommendation. And I could do any sewing that's needed." She glanced at the shirt in the basket.

Sukey snorted. "You're not short on boldness, are you? Why'd you not have a letter from your last mistress? You get the shove?"

"I wasn't let go. I . . . left," Emmaline told her.

Sukey studied Emmaline. "Not usual to leave a place once you've settled. Never heard of it. You get a good position, and you stay on, for as long as they'll keep you. Nobody up and leaves of their own accord."

Emmaline took a deep breath. "I had to leave, to find my little brother, Tommy," she said, hesitating then. "He's been sold, into the sweeps." Saying the words out loud created a fresh wave of pain that made her injured cheek throb more deeply. She covered it with her palm.

Sukey and Thomas exchanged a glance. Thomas set his spoon on the table with a tiny *clink*.

"Lots o' climbin' boys here, Emmaline," Sukey said. "Lots and lots. You really think you'll find him?"

"Yes," Emmaline said, her voice louder than she intended. "I *will* find him. I'll search until I do."

There was silence in the kitchen.

"Is there a chance?" Emmaline finally asked. "Of me being hired on here?"

"But you're not trained for laundry work, or for the scullery," Sukey said. "You can't change your job. If you've been trained as a sewer, you'll never manage laundry and heavy kitchen work."

"Why not?" Thomas asked, quietly. "Surely some of us are capable of more than one thing, and can make a change in what we're handed."

Emmaline saw how blue his eyes were, so light in comparison to his dark eyelashes. But it was his words that made something slide through her ribs – a knife, but soft, pleasurable. Hadn't she thought this very thing herself, over and over?

"I know that laundry and kitchen work are harder than sewing, but I'm sure I'd take to it in no time. I've always done both in my own family." She tried not to sound too anxious or pleading. Or too bold. If she acted too pushy, she might scare off Sukey.

Sukey's expression grew thoughtful, and Emmaline realized the girl was older than she'd first believed, quite a bit older than her, and older than Thomas. "How'd you come to reading? Seamstresses, and those fainting in the streets from hunger, they're not usually the ones to know their letters. Let's see your hands."

Emmaline obediently held out her hands, palms up. Sukey studied them, then turned them over and looked at the backs.

"My father taught me to read," Emmaline said.

Sukey sniffed, still bending over Emmaline's hands. She touched the faint rinds of scars – memories of the slip of sewing shears – the callouses from the needle. "Well, there's no doubt these hands have seen work." She looked at Thomas, then back to Emmaline. "But Cook won't like that you've no letter from the last place," she said.

"But surely no one from the workhouse has a letter."

"And even if she says yes, mind, 'tis only for a short while. Until we find a real maid-of-all-work. And your pay as scullery and scrubber will be the lowest."

Emmaline tried to control her breathing. "I'm a hard worker. You'll see, Sukey. Thomas."

"We're not the ones with the final say, I'm afraid," Thomas said. "As Sukey said, you must meet Cook's approval first."

Emmaline picked up her bundle and started toward the back door. "I'll come back tomorrow, then. Before dawn."

"Where will you sleep?" Thomas asked.

"I'll find someplace nearby."

"Sukey?" Thomas said, and the girl sighed, giving a slight dip of her chin.

"You might as well take Mary's side of the bed for this one night at least," Sukey told her. "My room's up in the attic, beside Cook's. Only we can't let Cook or either of the masters know you're here. You can creep down with me real early, when I get up to light the fires, and wait outside until I tell Cook about you."

Emmaline raised her eyebrows and smiled. "Thank you. Thank you ever so much, both of you."

Thomas and Sukey nodded back at her, but neither smiled.

They look as if they've the weight of the world on them, Emmaline thought. *Here's the pair of them, living in such a fine house, with plenty to eat and warm beds. What could possibly make them appear so downcast?*

The tiny room at the top of the silent house was cramped and stuffy, but the mattress was an improvement over the hay in the stables, or the ground at the edge of the field outside London. It was even more comfortable than the pallet she'd shared with Tommy in the room on Milk Court. As she lay rigidly on her back in her chemise beside Sukey, waiting for sleep to come, Emmaline tried not to think of her mother, or of Tommy. She knew that if she let the pictures start in her head – pictures of what might be happening to Tommy, of how Aunt Phoebe was treating her mother – she would never get to sleep. And she needed to sleep; she needed to be able to stand up and speak properly to Cook and

this Master Eugene. She wanted this position, no – needed it.
Even if she had to work fourteen hours a day to keep up, it would
be no more than she'd have to put in at a factory, and the food and
lodging would be better. And she would still find time to search
for Tommy, and she'd find him quickly, so she'd be here only a few
days, a week at most . . .

Sukey let out a low moan. "Jesus, help me," she murmured.

Startled, Emmaline sat up. "Are you all right?" she whispered.

But Sukey had her back to Emmaline, and didn't answer.

LAUNDRY SCRUBBER

ong before daylight Sukey had shaken Emmaline awake, and the girls tiptoed down the three flights of stairs into the dark kitchen. Emmaline sat stiffly on the outside step leading to the kitchen door. As she waited, she studied the courtyard. It was enclosed by old brick with crumbling masonry, partially covered with thick ivy. There was a small wooden shed with a slanted roof. To one side of it was a garden surrounded by a knee-high border of trimmed boxwood. Down from the shed was a low stone building. There was a horse chestnut tree and leggy rosebushes.

A cat, its coat a mixture of tawny and brown and white, emerged from behind the shed. It sat and stared at Emmaline as it daintily washed first one white paw and then the next, the morning light shivering across its brindled fur. Sukey opened the door and beckoned to her. "Cook's down," she said. "I give her a while to get settled, and to get breakfast over, afore I told her 'bout you. And she says she'll see you now. She's not in the best of moods, but don't worry. She acts hard, but underneath her heart's a big lump of butter."

Emmaline went into the kitchen, clutching her belongings. Cook was an elderly woman, very heavy, her plump florid cheeks trembling as she pounded her solid fist into a mound of dough in a huge crockery bowl.

"This here's the girl I told you about, Cook," Sukey said. "To fill in for Mary."

Cook stopped punching the dough, and turned it out on a floury board before she looked at Emmaline. "You say you know this girl, Sukey?" she asked, her small dark eyes looking Emmaline up and down.

Sukey nodded. "Aye. I've known her a while, ain't that right, Emmaline? And she's hardworking, and honest. She'll do fine, Cook."

"Doesn't look like anyone from the workhouse to me. Meatless as she is, and with that patched dress, I can tell that. Looks like she's got her head about her."

"Oh, she does, Cook. She does. And I didn't say she were from the workhouse. I just said I knowed her. From . . . from around."

Cook kneaded the elastic dough, pushing and stretching it, picking it up and slapping it back down on the floured surface. "Where'd you work last, girl?" she asked.

"I was apprenticed to a seamstress, up north, in Tibbing. I worked for one Mrs. Slater for five years," Emmaline answered.

Cook's eyes made her think of currants. "And why'd you leave? Thievery, or insolence?" Cook concentrated on her dough.

"Oh, no, Missus. I left on my own. I came here to –" She stopped herself. "I thought I might find something different here." She twisted the tied ends of her bundle.

"So you've given up a good clean job as a seamstress to work as a runabout – a laundry scrubber and scullery maid?" Cook looked up from the dough, her shrewd eyes boring into Emmaline's. Then, as if she'd discovered what it was she was searching for, she shrugged her plump shoulders. "Well, since Master Eugene doesn't give a monkey's about what goes on below stairs, and there'd be no use in bothering the old man about such matters, I may as well take you on. Something tells me I may be making a mistake, but it'll save us a trip to the workhouse. I'll hold you responsible, Sukey, should anything go missing. It'll come out of your wages if this girl proves to have light fingers." Cook wagged her own thick floury finger at Sukey.

"I'm not a thief, Missus," Emmaline said.

Cook didn't acknowledge Emmaline's words. She plopped the round of dough back in the bowl and covered it with a clean square of bleached cotton. "Now you, Sukey, get upstairs and get them grates cleaned. And you," Cook said, raising her chin at Emmaline, "you'll call me Cook. None of this Missus business. Leave your pack and come out to the laundry with me. Maggie and Peg should already be at work. If you can sew, as you claim, you can fix up Mary's uniform to fit. You'll have to take in the waist, and let down the hem, from the looks of you."

Emmaline followed Cook across the courtyard to the stone building tight against the back fence. Thomas was in the garden, bent over and hacking at the ground with a hoe. As they passed, Emmaline saw mounds of green rising from the earth.

"That there's Paddy," Cook said. "Paddy, here's Emmaline, to take up Mary's work," she called.

Thomas and Emmaline silently dipped their heads at each other, but Emmaline detected the beginning of a smile around Thomas's finely curved lips.

"He's got a right good hand at growing," Cook went on. "We get a nice bit of produce from that patch."

As Cook opened the door, the strong smell of disinfectant made Emmaline's nose burn. Inside the steamy heat of the small room, she saw that there were two other women in the laundry. One bent over what looked to be a pair of trousers, rinsing and wringing them in a shallow tub of dirty suds. The other, whom Emmaline knew must be Peg, was thumping a heavy flat iron with expert strokes over a frilly shirt. Both women's faces were slick with steam and sweat, and their hands red and rough.

"This is the new girl," Cook called. The women looked up at the same time. "She'll fill in for Mary for now."

Cook led Emmaline to a shallow wooden trough, in which stained aprons were soaking.

"Maggie will show you what to do out here, and you'll answer to her. If I hear a word from Maggie that you're not working hard, you'll be out."

Emmaline nodded.

"You'll get a tanner a week," Cook said, "paid monthly."

"Sixpence?" Emmaline asked, calculating in her head. Even if she worked an entire year, she'd make only two pounds fifty-two pence. But that didn't matter. She didn't intend to be here at month's end anyway. And she already had the money to buy Tommy back. All she needed was food and a place to sleep for the next few days.

"You heard me. All you can expect, being at the bottom. You have your breakfast in the kitchen, start work at seven sharp every morning, and finish at seven in the evening. At two o'clock you'll receive a hot dinner, and after seven, a glass of ale and cold food from dinner. I preside over morning and evening prayers. Don't be late for either. You'll sleep up top with Sukey, as did Mary. Now, get your sleeves rolled up and get to it," Cook said, and was gone, slamming the door behind her.

"Well, then," said Maggie. She looked to be in her late twenties, and had a cruel twist to the left side of her mouth. Her left eye drooped in a peculiar manner as well, but the right one was piercing and restless. "You bin scrubber afore, then?" she asked, and Emmaline saw that the left side of her face didn't move at all, so that her words came out pinched and slightly slurred.

"No. I . . . I worked as a seamstress."

"Sewer, was you? Well, we'll have no fancy airs here, I warn you. Young Mary was a right hard worker, and if you don't match up to her, I'll have you out on your ear before you can say yer name. What is yer name, anyway?"

"Emmaline."

"Emma*leen*, is it?" Maggie mimicked. "Emma or even plain old Em ain't fancy enough for you, is that it? Seems to me, Peg, what we have got ourselves here is a fancy name to match a fancy sewing girl with a fancy voice." Her speech held a sneer. "Grab that brush and get to scrubbing those aprons. Pour boiling water and more soap into the trough, and be quick about it. We've got extra work today, what with Mary not here the last wash days."

Emmaline set to work. By dinnertime her hands and arms felt scalded by the hot water and the harsh washing soda, all the tiny fissures and nicks on her fingers stinging, but she said nothing, just filed into the kitchen with Peg and Maggie.

She sat down at the table and saw her plate, brimming with mutton stew and boiled potatoes and batter pudding. It was more than her mother and Tommy and she would have eaten between them in two days. Bile rose in her throat. *What is Tommy eating today?* She couldn't swallow.

"You going to eat that, or just stare at it?" Maggie asked. "Or maybe it's not to your liking, is that it? Who do you think you are, Miss?" she muttered, then turned to Sukey. "Who does she think she is?" she repeated.

"That's enough, now, Maggie," Cook said.

Emmaline lowered her head and forced herself to eat every bite that was on her plate, even though her stomach had shrunken. The food began to rise back up, and she fought against choking on it. *I am the Moon King's daughter*, she repeated to herself, chewing and swallowing, chewing and swallowing. *That's who I am. I am the Moon King's daughter. I must be strong.*

She followed Maggie and Peg back to the laundry, her stomach bloated, and worked until she thought her legs would fold under her. Maggie and Peg left her alone, heaping more clothes and sheets in front of her just when she thought she was coming to the bottom of the pile. But by the end of the day, as she dried her hands and arms on a piece of coarse sacking and straightened her shoulders, she thought she saw a glimmer of something that might have been grudging admiration, or at least acceptance, on Maggie's unsmiling, lopsided face.

That evening Emmaline was so weary that she could hardly chew her cold mutton and bread. The thought of heading out into the street to start searching for Tommy was overwhelming.

"First thing tomorrow we'll get you helping out Sukey with the housework," Cook said, and Emmaline nodded, rubbing her eyes.

I'll leave it for this one day, this first day of work, she thought, dragging herself up to the top floor and collapsing, still fully dressed, facedown on the bed. She touched the reassuring thickness of the money sewn into her hem. *Come tomorrow evening I'll set out in earnest. I won't let another day go by without looking for Tommy.*

And she had barely finished the thought before she was asleep.

THE OLD MASTER

arly the next morning, Emmaline altered Mary's uniform to fit her. The feel of the needle, coursing in and out of the fabric, was familiar, comforting. For a few moments it diminished the ache over missing Tommy.

After breakfast, Cook proudly showed her the astounding array of cleaning powders and solutions kept in a cupboard near the stairs. "There's fuller's earth, blacklead, borax, sweet oil, ox-gall, camphor, and sifted wood-ash on this top shelf," she said. "Here." She took a wide-necked jar from the next shelf, and handed it to Emmaline. "I've already mixed up a linseed oil, turpentine, and beeswax polish. You'll do all the furniture in the sitting room. The polishing has been left this last while. Be careful, there can be nothing broken. Clean out the fireplace as well. Then go on upstairs and try to make some order out of young Master Eugene's room; he didn't come home last night. Sukey went up with his breakfast, but he weren't there. You'll recognize it by the state it's in. Sukey," she continued, "you keep an eye on her. And you brush all the hallway carpets."

"Yes, Cook," Sukey and Emmaline said together.

"And when you're done, Emmaline, I'll need help down here," Cook added.

Loaded down with the polish and rags, an ash pail and slop bucket, she followed Sukey through the door off the back stairs and into the spacious foyer of the main floor.

"You'll find your way around," Sukey said. "Just don't disturb old Master Thorn upstairs, in the last room. He can be as prickly as his name."

"All right," Emmaline answered, and Sukey, lugging a pail and a wide brush, left her standing at the foot of a wide elegant staircase with curved railings and gracious bannisters.

She entered the large sitting room, which had a dark and shut-up feeling about it: all the curtains were closed, and the air stale. Through a doorway she could see a smaller smoking room. Even though the rooms were neat and well decorated, they felt airless, unused.

She polished all the wooden furniture – most of it rosewood or mahogany – to a high luster. There was a Gothic breakfront bookcase with glass, tables of all sizes, a kneehole desk, and a number of delicate curved chairs. There was even a wooden case holding a fierce-looking stuffed bird, its sharp beak curved, its once far-seeing eyes replaced by hard shiny glass. Once she'd swept out the ashes from the fireplace and deposited them in her pail, she started up the stairs with the pail and slop bucket. She realized she was tiptoeing, but didn't know why.

The first bedroom she came to was obviously a guest room, as was the second, the beds neat and fireplaces clean. The third bedroom was, she could tell, the late Mistress Thorn's. A silky dressing gown was draped over a rose-patterned sedan chair, and a pot of rouge and perfume flasks, arranged tidily, still sat on the small dressing table. Gilt figurines decorated the mantel. A thick blanket lay on the end of the bed, while on the table beside the bed was a silver salver holding what looked to be invitations.

The room across from it was Master Eugene's. In contrast to the other orderly bedrooms, this one was a terrible mess. The bed was a jumble of linens, drawers were pulled out, the wardrobe doors stood open, and shirts and pants were strewn about. A pair of tasseled Hessian boots, spattered with mud, were tossed carelessly in one corner. The room smelled of cigar smoke and stale food. On a small table Emmaline saw a plate with a half-eaten slab of beef sitting in gravy that had congealed into a greasy crust with lacy white edges. There were also a number of glasses around the room – delicate wine glasses and short heavy tumblers, stinking of whiskey. There was an empty wine bottle on its side on the floor beside the bed.

She cleaned and tidied the room, emptying the chamber pot and wash water into her slop bucket, sweeping out the fireplace ashes, gathering all the clothes and bedding to take to the laundry house, making up the bed with fresh linens from the linen press she found in the hallway, closing all the dresser drawers and the wardrobe doors, and then leaving the window open a few inches at the bottom, to try and dispel the stench. She left the wine bottle and dirty plate and glasses sitting outside the door, beside the items for the laundry, to be picked up on her way downstairs.

There were only two doors left, and Emmaline knew the last one – which was closed – should be avoided, for it was Master Thorn's. But the second last door was open, and she glanced in and stood blinking in the semidarkness. "Oh, yes," she breathed, setting down her pail and bucket. The four walls were covered from floor to ceiling with shelves of books. She had never imagined so many books in one place.

The room smelled musty, of ink and old paper, but it was a warm comforting smell to Emmaline. She crossed the thickly carpeted floor and pushed back the heavy velvet curtains that covered the large arched window. Dust motes danced out of the curtains in the sudden light. Emmaline ran her fingers over the spines of the books, stopping to pick one out here and there, glance through it, and then put it back. There were so many wonderful books – some covered in morocco or moleskin, others gilt-spined. She'd never seen such a collection.

As she wandered along the shelves, she heard a sudden gasping, as if someone was struggling for breath. She looked toward the sound, and realized, then, that there was a second door, slightly ajar, in the room. It was in one corner, and almost hidden by the jut of a bookshelf.

She pushed the door open the tiniest bit; the ragged breathing grew heavier and she saw an old man hunched in a disheveled bed that was placed at an odd angle in front of the window. A thick cord, to ring downstairs, hung to one side of the bed. The old man had a woman's deep blue shawl over his shoulders, and on his long white hair was a black skullcap. He wore small, dark-lensed spectacles, and held a slender book almost against his nose. Emmaline saw his lips moving as he read, and the sounds that came from his chest were labored and painful. *This is Master Thorn, then*, she thought.

Without any warning, the old man hurled the book across the room. It knocked over a tall empty vase, sending it rolling to the carpet with a dull thud. The book landed only inches from Emmaline's foot. She let out a quick shriek.

"Who's that? Who's in here?" the old man said, his head swiveling in Emmaline's direction.

Emmaline put her hand over her mouth, aware of what she'd done, then lowered it. "'Tis only me, Sir," she said.

"Only Me? Come in, come in, Only Me. Don't stand there like a fool."

Emmaline stepped into the room, over the book, *Lyrical Ballads* by William Wordsworth.

"Who is it?" he called again, his voice lifting with hope, as if he was expecting someone.

"It's Emmaline. Emmaline Roke, Sir."

"And who might this Emmaline Roke be?" he asked. His face was curtained by his uncombed hair, and from where she stood Emmaline couldn't make out his features.

"I work below stairs, Sir. I've only just started. Or rather, I work in the laundry and kitchen, but I'm helping out upstairs today. I didn't mean to disturb you, Sir, but I was next door, and I heard –"

"Come closer. I don't recognize your name, or your voice. Strange voice. From up north, are you? Where, exactly?" His tone was demanding, but not unkind.

As Emmaline came to the side of the bed, she saw the thickness of his dark spectacles.

"Born in Lancashire, Sir. Late of Tibbing, near Manchester."

The old man nodded. "Although you most certainly are a Lancashire lass, it's not entirely pure. Your voice is . . . well, perplexing is the only way I can describe it. Although charmingly so. Now come closer." He reached out his hand. It was spotted with age and crippled with arthritis. But the trembling fingers were long and had once been slender and well shaped, she could see. His hand reminded her, without warning, of her father's.

Emmaline didn't move. She was already touching the side of the bed. "Sir?" she asked.

"Don't be a damn fool, girl," he said. "I only want to get a better look." He pulled on her sleeve, and she was forced forward. Master Thorn's face was only inches from hers, now, his cheeks a cobwebby map of broken capillaries. She smelled the odor of rusty nails. He let her go as suddenly as he'd pulled her forward. She took a step back, far enough that he couldn't touch her if he reached out again.

"Where's that other girl? Susie, is it? She usually does for me," he said.

"It's Sukey. I'm helping her today," Emmaline told him, wanting to get away from this room, with its smell of decay and age. "Your Wordsworth, Sir. The *Lyrical Ballads*. Shall I bring it to you?"

Master Thorn shook his head. "What's the use? Can't read anymore; all I can make out is the bloody title, if it's in big enough letters. Damn these eyes. As if I didn't have enough taken from me." Suddenly he stuck his chin forward, as if he had just realized what Emmaline had said a moment earlier. "Don't tell me you read, as well?"

Emmaline bit her lip, afraid she might be getting herself into some kind of trouble. Sukey had warned her to stay away from Master Thorn. "Oh. Well, only a little, Master Thorn. Really, not much at all."

The old man suddenly slumped back against his pillows, waving his hand in the air in a distracted manner. "Pity. I could use someone to read to me." He cleared his throat. "Now you, you sound like someone who could do that."

Emmaline saw that the bones of his wrist and hand resembled brittle sticks. She suddenly felt sorry for him. "Is there anything I can bring you, Sir?" she asked. "Perhaps you'd like a cup of tea? Or something to eat? Cook is making a chestnut and orange custard."

Master Thorn shook his head. "Don't enjoy my food any longer," he said. "There's not much point anymore, not much point at all." He sighed heavily, and took off his glasses and set them on the windowsill beside him, but his eyes were closed. "Will you send my boy in? I haven't seen him for days."

"Master Eugene, Sir? I don't believe he's –"

"Not Eugene," he said, almost petulantly. "He never has time for me. No. It's Wallace I want. Get Wallace up here to read for me." His voice grew weaker.

Emmaline stood still.

"I want Wallace to read to me." The last words wavered and finally became a helpless whisper.

Emmaline didn't want to say that she'd never heard of Wallace. She waited until the old man's breathing quieted, with a rattly, even rhythm, and then left, closing the door behind her with a quiet click.

AS IF HE WERE HER BROTHER

or the rest of the day Emmaline worked below stairs, willing the hours to pass so she could go out to look for Tommy. Following Cook's terse orders, she scoured dishes and pots, scrubbed the stone kitchen floor and all the way up the wooden back stairs, swept out the courtyard, peeled vegetables and rolled pastry dough. As soon as she had finished her supper, she told Cook she was going out for a walk.

"A walk? Oh, no, we'll have no young women from this house out wandering the streets of an evening. There's only trouble beyond the gates at night. If you're here, inside, there's no harm can befall you."

Emmaline heard a small strange sound from Sukey at the scullery sink.

"There'll be no wandering about after hours," Cook said. "You get up them stairs and to bed. You get Sunday afternoons off. That'll have to do for any walking."

Panic closed around Emmaline's throat like a tight harness. How could she look for Tommy if Cook wouldn't allow her out?

From his spot at the table, Thomas clanked his knife against his plate as if by accident, raised his eyebrows at Emmaline, and shook his head.

"It's just . . . it's the smell, Cook, from all the cleaning powders," Emmaline went on. "It does get into my nose, and down my throat, and I need some air to clear away the burning. Could I not slip out for even a few minutes?"

Cook curled her fleshy hands into fists and set them on her hips. She was so solid, her short shape so square, that for that moment she reminded Emmaline of a handled jug, her head a small round stopper. "One day, and you're arguing with me? That'll get you nowhere, my girl. You may have been able to speak your mind at your last position, but I'll not accept that in my kitchen. Now get away upstairs with you. Take a drink of weak ale to clear your nose and throat. And if there's any more nonsense from you, hard worker or no, you'll be on your way. Do I make myself clear?"

"Yes, Cook," Emmaline said, but she knew she'd have to get outside somehow. She headed up the back stairs. As she was passing the second floor, she heard the same loud voice that had frightened her out of the kitchen the first day Sukey had brought her into the Thorn house: "And I tell you, Father, that I don't agree!"

There was a loud slam. Emmaline had stopped on the back stairs, her hand on the splintered railing. The thumping of footsteps passed by the door, but just as Emmaline started up the stairs again, she felt a pull on the back of her skirt.

Startled, she whirled around. It was Thomas. "What is it?" she whispered, aware of the voice she had just heard on the other side of the door.

"I was trying to let you know that it's not wise to go against Cook." He stepped up one riser, closer to Emmaline. "Is it to go out looking for your brother? Is that what the business about a walk was?"

"Yes, but how can I find him if I'm not to leave the house but for Sunday afternoons? I have to find him right away! It's been a whole week now since he was taken. Anything could happen to him, could be happening to him right now . . ." She picked at the skin of her bottom lip. "Perhaps I was wrong in taking work here."

"You'll have no more freedom in any house or factory, Emmaline," he said.

Emmaline liked the way her name sounded with the Irish in it. "I'm going to look for him, Thomas."

Thomas glanced behind him. "Cook will be up for bed any minute. Once she's in her room, and you hear her start to snore – Sukey says she snores dreadfully – come back down to the kitchen, and maybe we can sort out something. Just be careful crossing this second floor doorway, for this floor is the Thorn bedrooms, and if Master Eugene is home, and hears you, there might be trouble. You don't want to get in his way, especially not after he's been out on the town."

"All right. Thank you, Thomas," she said, but he had already turned down the narrow stairs.

Emmaline did as he had said, sitting on the edge of her bed and waiting until she heard the sounds of Cook in the next room: the splashing of water being poured from the jug into the washbasin, off-key humming along with the rustling of layers of clothing being removed, Cook saying her prayers, and finally a heavy sigh as the woman settled herself in her bed. Within five minutes the snuffling fits and starts of her breathing began, just as Thomas had predicted. Emmaline realized she must have been deep in sleep before Cook came upstairs the last two nights, or she would have heard the woman.

Once the snoring was regular, Emmaline tiptoed out of the bedroom, past Cook's door, and down to the kitchen. She found Sukey and Thomas sitting there at the table. Thomas had spread newspaper on the tabletop, and on it was a pair of gleaming boots and a pair of equally shiny shoes. He was in the middle of blacking a second set of boots.

"Weren't a good idea to get up Cook's nose," Sukey said. She had a mug of steaming cocoa in front of her, and she wore white cotton gloves. She was polishing a silver gravy boat that was tarnished around the lip. A pile of gleaming platters and salvers she had already finished were at her elbow.

"Thomas told me," Emmaline answered.

"Sit with us. I'll make you some cocoa, if you like," she said. "Cook's usually first to bed. Me and Thomas, we sit up a spell. Sometimes Thomas reads to me – ain't that right, Thomas?"

Before Thomas could answer, Emmaline moved toward the side door. "No, I can't stay. I've got to go out, and look for Tommy," she said.

"You're not serious!" Sukey said, her voice rising. "It's gone dark. It's true, what Cook says. There's all sorts of dangers out there." She held the polishing rag motionless over the gravy boat. "A girl on her own. . . . No, you mustn't go out."

"But that's why I'm in London, Sukey. My brother is here and –"

Thomas interrupted. "There'll be no sweeps about after dark, Emmaline. They start work early in the morning, before the fires are lit in the stoves and chimneys for preparing breakfast."

"Then I'll go out in the morning, before I start my work."

Sukey took a sip of her cocoa. "Aye, that's a better way; what Thomas says about the sweeps is right. And the streets will be busy with working folk, instead of the wicked sort you might find after dark."

Emmaline sat down across from Sukey.

"Where will you start?" Thomas asked. "This is a big city. It could take you forev –"

"His name is Hillis," Emmaline said, "Master Sweep Hillis of Steeplemount Way."

"Steeplemount Way? That's about a mile and a half from here, going west."

"West?" Emmaline repeated.

"Yes. I'll get up and unlock the door for you in the mornings," Thomas added. "Just make sure you return before Cook is down."

"Thank you, both of you. Shall I help you with the silver, Sukey?" she asked, covering her mouth as she yawned.

"No. I just aim to finish up this last piece. Thomas, you're done, too, aren't you?"

Thomas put the shoe brush into a small wooden box holding the assortment of polishes and brushes. "Yes."

"Off to bed, then," Sukey said to him, as if he were a child, although he was only a few years younger than her. Emmaline thought Thomas must be in between her and Sukey in age, maybe seventeen.

He half grinned at Emmaline, embarrassed. "She thinks she's my big sister," he said. "She's right bossy."

Sukey slapped at him with the white gloves she had taken off. "You need someone to tell you what to do," she said. Emmaline recognized something in Sukey's face that she had often felt herself when she looked at Tommy. *She really cares about him, loves him as if he were her brother*, she thought.

"Both of you!" Sukey said. "Away you go. I'll be up shortly, Emmaline."

Heading toward the stairs, Emmaline turned back to say good night to Sukey, but the girl wasn't looking in her direction. Instead, she stared at the dark square of the kitchen window with a distracted look on her face, chewing at her thumbnail, while the other hand ran over the toe of Master Eugene's polished boot, in front of her on the table. She ran her hand over and over it, gently, as if she were stroking a kitten or some other small beloved creature.

STEEPLEMOUNT WAY

mmaline wasn't asleep, even though she was bone weary. She had left the bedroom door open, partly for Sukey, and partly to try and get more air into the small room under the eaves. There was only one tall narrow window that opened up onto the courtyard. It was a surprisingly warm evening for early March. Emmaline knew the room would be stifling in the summer months, and, with no fireplace, freezing in the winter.

Not that I'll be here for the winter, she thought. *Or even for the summer. Surely I'll find Tommy in the next few days, and be back in Tibbing with him.* Then she thought of Cat and Phoebe. *What if Aunt Phoebe has thrown Cat out, after all? What if Mother has resorted to thieving, or worse, to get her medicine, and has been caught and sent to prison?*

What if Tommy has somehow escaped from the master sweep and made his way back to Tibbing, but found Mother and me gone, and has no one to turn to? What if he thinks I've abandoned him? The black thoughts whirled faster and faster in Emmaline's head, until she put her hands on her ears and whispered, "No, no," into the dark room.

"I can't think this way," she said. "I must think about good things. I must think about finding Tommy. That's the main thing. I can't worry about anything else right now."

She lay still and closed her eyes, hearing the muted chiming of a clock from somewhere below. She had heard clocks chiming and bonging and dinging at other times while she worked that day, realizing there were a number of them throughout the house. She willed herself to listen for the four o'clock chimes, willed herself to awaken at that time, in order to get dressed and downstairs and be out on the street before anyone in the house stirred, so she could have a few good hours to search. As she tried to keep her dismal thoughts at bay, she became aware of voices. Muffled, faint, but unmistakable. There was a low rumbling one, and a high soft one. A man and a woman. The voices were drifting up to the attic window from the courtyard.

Emmaline got out of bed and looked down. The figures were partly hidden by the horse chestnut tree, but as she watched, Emmaline saw the woman reach out and clutch the sleeve of the man. He shook her off, then walked away. Or stumbled. He was tall, and well built. At first Emmaline thought, because of his uneven, lurching walk, that he had a crippled leg, but then realized it was simply the effects of alcohol. He left the courtyard, going through the side gate, clanging it behind him.

Then the woman stepped out of the shadows. Even in the darkness, Emmaline recognized Sukey by her uniform.

Sukey stood for a moment, one hand reaching after the man. Then she covered her face with her hands and sank to her knees, her body shaking with silent sobs.

Emmaline opened her eyes in the darkness. Something had wakened her. A distant church bell rang. *One*, Emmaline counted. *Two. Three. Four.*

A house full of clocks, and a city full of bells. It wouldn't be difficult to keep track of the time.

Sukey was sound asleep on her back, one arm thrown over her face. Emmaline thought of her crying in the courtyard the evening before.

Emmaline quickly put on her uniform and rinsed her eyes with water from the jug on the washstand. She grabbed her shawl and slowly tiptoed down the back stairs. The fourth stair from the top gave a warning creak, and she stepped to one side, making a mental note to remember that stair.

In the kitchen, she saw a line of light under Thomas's door, and, going to the side door, found the padlock undone. As she looked at the hanging lock, thinking, *Thank you, Thomas*, there was a light touch on her shoulder.

Emmaline gasped, turning. "Will you not creep up on me, Thomas? That's the second time you've frightened me," she whispered harshly, thinking of his hand on her skirt the evening before.

"I'm sorry," he whispered back. "I'm coming with you."

"That's not necessary," Emmaline said, straightening her shoulders. "I'm perfectly capable of going on my own."

"Just to show you the quickest way to get to Steeplemount. There's a fast way through the back streets."

"All right," Emmaline said. "But just this once."

"Just this once," Thomas agreed. "Come on, then."

Emmaline wrapped the shawl over her head, and hurried after him. The streets were already filling with men and women on their way to work, heads down as they passed. Children were hawking everything from oranges to violets to watercress. They called out their goods in the predawn, with voices husky from years of shouting the streets. As Thomas and Emmaline waited for a carriage to pass, she watched a girl no larger than Tommy carry a basket on her head, her cotton-velvet bonnet crushed, her neck cricked by the weight.

Within fifteen minutes they were on a street of tall shabby houses.

"This is it. Steeplemount Way," Thomas said. "It's a large area – goes on for about two miles each way. See, it's bounded by stone arches on this side and the Thames on the other."

Emmaline looked around her. "I'll make a plan," she said, "I'll take each street in turn. I'm bound to see sweeps, if you say they start work before dawn."

Thomas agreed. "And you'll be able to find your way back to Thorn House in time?"

"There are enough church bells to tell me the time," she said.

A middle-aged man in a stained jacket murmured something to Emmaline as he passed by her.

"Pardon me, Sir?" she asked. Before she knew what was happening, Thomas had sprung at the man, grabbing him by the arm and pulling back his fist. The man cowered, putting his hands up over his face. Thomas let him go with a shove and a curse.

Emmaline was shocked at Thomas's transformation. His face had filled with blood, and the muscle of his jaw formed a tight knot.

"Who was that?" she asked.

"Just a rude-mouthed lout," he answered, straightening his coat. "With no right to speak to you like that."

"But – I didn't even hear what he said."

"Just as well," Thomas said. "Look," he added, glancing around the street. It seemed as if he was about to say something, but then he turned, and before Emmaline had a chance to thank him, he was off down the street.

Thank you, Thomas, she thought, for the second time that morning, then she started up the street, her head turning from right to left and up to the chimney tops, looking for any sign of a climbing boy.

She spotted three sets of sweeps, always a small climber and his larger chummy. The boys were slipping around alleyways and in and out of shadows. They were little more than shadows themselves – so small and dark – staying close to buildings and seeming invisible to those on the streets. The first pair disappeared almost the same minute that she realized she was seeing them, scampering down a set of cellar steps. She called out to the next set of boys, saying, "You! Climbing boys. Wait!" but the boys ignored her. By the time she turned the corner after them, they'd disappeared. She ran silently after another pair, and caught up with them. But when she touched the older one on the shoulder, he turned around with a snarl, showing broken, browning teeth. Before she could speak he broke into a run, and the smaller boy ran too, sacks of soot bouncing against their backs.

hat evening after Cook had gone up to bed, Emmaline sat with Sukey and Thomas in the kitchen. As they drank their cocoa, she told them how she'd met Master Thorn the day before. "Who is Wallace?" she asked.

"Oh, Wallace is his boy what died," Sukey told her.

"I didn't know he had another son."

"Master Wallace were quite a bit older than Master Eugene, and the apple of his father's eye. It were him what hired on Thomas and me to Thorn House."

Thomas laughed, a warm sound that filled the room. Emmaline realized she had never heard him laugh.

Sukey grinned. "Aye. We tricked Master Wallace that day, me and Thomas."

"Tricked him?"

"When Master Wallace come to the workhouse, and picked me out, I pulled Thomas alongside me, and – for I were still disrespectful then, new off the streets and hadn't learned my place –

I opened me gob and asked, 'What about him? Do you have a position for him 'n all?' Before Master Wallace had a chance to answer, Thomas ups and steps forward, shaking the gentleman's hand with his own small one as if he were being introduced at a fancy ball. And he gave Master Wallace one of his bright smiles." Sukey winked at Thomas, and he grinned at her. Emmaline liked the tiny space between his front teeth.

"I could see Master Wallace givin' in," Sukey continued. She took a sip from her mug. "'Well, all right, bring him along,' he says to me, 'for I likes the look of him, darkly handsome.' Remember, Thomas, how he called you that – darkly handsome?"

Thomas made a *tsking* sound. "Go on with you," he said.

"And it weren't until we were here, at the house," Sukey continued, "that he asks Thomas if he knows how to clean and trim lamps and black boots, and Thomas speaks up right smart to him. Well, you coulda knocked Master Wallace over with a feather. I'll never forget the look on his face. 'What's this?' he cries, lookin' at me. 'How is it you speak like a London street urchin and your little brother like an Irish?'

"'I never said he was me brother,' I tells him. An' don't Thomas pipe up, 'I's Thomas McLinn, come from County Clare,' and Master Wallace gives a right hearty chuckle. 'So it appears I've been hoodwinked,' he says. 'But as it's too late to take him back, he may as well stay on. I've nothing against the Irish myself,' he says. 'I believe everyone should be given a chance,' he says. Ain't that right, Thomas?"

Thomas nodded, smiling at Sukey in an indulgent way, as if she'd told the story many times before.

Sukey sighed. "He were a right gentleman, he were," she said. "We all miss him sorely."

"What happened to him?"

"Knocked out of his phaeton, square onto the cobbles, by another carriage with a horse gone raging. He lived for a few days, but never opened his eyes again." She sighed. "It were a sad day for all Thorn House. Master Thorn bought the phaeton – beautiful and rakish as it was – and chopped it to bits with an ax. And after that things were never right again. It seemed that without him the spirit went out of the house. It were shortly after that Lady Lucy started to sicken, and within a year she were gone, too, and him upstairs taken to his bed."

"But there's still Eugene," Emmaline said.

"Cook says the old man couldn't get over his disappointment that Eugene could never be the son Wallace was," Thomas added.

"And Master Thorn is nearly blind, isn't he?" Emmaline asked.

"Lady Lucy used to tease him about having the time to read as much as he wanted, once he was finished with his law practise. But then he began to lose his sight. It's ironic. That now he has the time, but can't read," Thomas said.

Emmaline ran her finger along the lip of her mug. "What about his son?" she asked Thomas. "Doesn't Eugene worry about him?"

"Master Eugene? No. They've had too many falling-outs. There's little that passes between them anymore. Anytime they do speak, it ends in an argument."

"He was confused as he was falling asleep, calling for Wallace to read to him," Emmaline added. "He seems such a sad old soul."

"It's no wonder, shut up there by himself, with no one to talk to," Sukey said. "He just lies abed all day now. And it's a right job to even try and get him washed, or change his clothes. He grows weaker by the day; it's the cough and wasting disease, that much is clear, although he rarely lets the physician near."

Thomas murmured in agreement, then they all silently drank their cocoa.

The next afternoon Sukey came into the kitchen, where Emmaline was peeling vegetables under Cook's supervision.

"You'll never believe it," Sukey said, her eyes round. "I've just been cleaning Master Thorn's room, and he's asked me to fetch Emmaline."

Cook frowned. "How does he know about Emmaline?"

"I – I met him, the other day. When I was cleaning upstairs," Emmaline said.

Before Cook had a chance to pry any further, Sukey grabbed Emmaline's arm. "Hurry. Leave the potatoes. She must go, mustn't she, Cook?"

"I suppose," Cook grumbled, as Emmaline scrubbed her hands in the sink.

Drying her hands on her apron and rolling down her sleeves, Emmaline hurried along with Sukey to the last room in the long hallway upstairs. Sukey gave a quiet knock on Master Thorn's bedroom door, and then opened it.

"Master Thorn? Here she is. I've brought up Emmaline Roke, as you asked." Then she left.

The old man struggled to sit up in bed. He didn't have his glasses on, and his eyes were tiny red slits. He blinked rapidly, peering in her direction, and then doubled over in a coughing fit.

Emmaline approached and patted his back, tentatively at first, then harder and harder. Coughing with an alarming choking sound, he motioned to a pipkin on the floor beside the bed. Emmaline picked up the little clay dish and held it in front of Master Thorn's mouth, and he coughed watery strings, laced with pink, into the bowl. Finally he stopped, wiping his mouth with his sleeve, and collapsed against the pillows.

"Give me a portion of Madeira. It's on the table near the door. Good for medicinal purposes. Damn spectacles. Where have they got to? They don't help my sight much, but they keep the light out. Light hurts my eyes something fierce."

Emmaline searched in the bedclothes and found the spectacles, then fitted them on the old man's face. "There you go, Sir," she said. She poured Master Thorn a drink of the ruby liquid.

"I've a desire to hear some of my Wordsworth, read in a soothing voice. Emmaline? Are you still here?"

"Yes, Sir," Emmaline said, bringing him the glass.

"*Lyrical Ballads*, pronounced without a stumble on the tongue. You're not fooling me for one minute. I know you can read, and I'd like to hear you today." He took a short sip, sighing. "That does go down fine. Now, my book is just there, on the windowsill."

Emmaline reached across him for the book, and then pulled a gout stool up beside the bed.

"Is there something special you'd like to hear, Sir?" she asked.

"Read the *Lucy* poems, will you? Both Wordsworth and I mourn a Lucy."

Emmaline found the set of poems, and began reading. She had to stop, after she finished the pair of stanzas that read:

In one of those sweet dreams I slept,
Kind Nature's gentlest boon!
And all the while my eyes I kept
On the descending moon.

My horse moved on: hoof after hoof
He raised, and never stopped:
When down behind the cottage roof,
At once the bright moon dropped.

Her lip quivered at the images the poem was creating in her mind: of the night Tommy was born, of her father, and their cottage garden in the moonlight.

"Emmaline? Why have you stopped?" Master Thorn quietly asked.

"I'm sorry, Sir," she said, but before she could begin again, Master Thorn spoke.

"I've decided I'd like you to read to me every day. Tell Cook I'll expect you up for an hour every afternoon, and that you're to be given the time off from your other duties."

"I'm sure she won't like that, Sir," Emmaline said, running her palm over the page.

"Don't give a damn whether she does or not. If she has an argument about it, tell her to come and see me."

"Yes, Master Thorn," Emmaline said, and began the next stanza.

And as she sat on the low stool beside the old man's bed, with the calming act of reading aloud in the quiet warm room, something around her heart loosened its grip just the tiniest bit, the grip that had been there since she'd first come home to Milk Court to find Tommy gone. The easing of that hard tightness – for even one hour – was such a relief that she had to stop, midline, on the pretense of clearing her throat, and take a deep breath to steady herself.

ALL SAINTS

mmaline kept up her routine for the rest of the week, rising early to head out to Steeplemount Way, full of hope. Each morning, when she came down the stairs, she found the side door unlocked. And after near two hours combing the streets, she would rush into the kitchen, breathless, her cheeks pink and hair windblown. Sukey would be there, lighting the fire and starting the breakfast chores before Cook got down.

"No sign of 'im, then?" Sukey would say, and Emmaline would shake her head, more distressed each day. Why hadn't she found him? She had seen climbers every day. They would always be darting down back alleys or coming out of side doors in pairs, carrying sacks of soot and cleaning brushes. All of them and none of them looked like Tommy. When she'd approach and ask them about Tommy or Master Sweep Hillis, she'd be met with either blank frightened stares, or a rude gesture.

"None of them will talk to me," she said, trying to keep the hopelessness out of her voice. "They ignore me, or run off."

"Likely think you're bringing trouble on their heads," Sukey told her. "Climbing boys see someone wantin' to talk to 'em, their first guess is they done something wrong, or will be accused of something. Maybe a parlor maid thinks they made too much of a mess in her clean morning room, or Cook's noticed an egg or slice of bread gone missing, and remember they had the climbers in. Nobody's got a good word for those little lads; they learn fast to keep their mouths shut and their heads down."

Emmaline did the same in her own work. She kept her mouth shut and her head down as she scrubbed until her knuckles were raw and burned by the boiling water and lye washing soda. The calluses on the fingers of her right hand, raised and hard from years of the needle, softened and dwindled. Sometimes when she was caught up with the scrubbing, she helped Peg with the ironing or worked the tablelike contraption of a mangle for Maggie, flattening the clothes between two rollers turned by a handle. She learned that the bedclothes and table linens and undergarments needed the hottest water, and that Master Eugene's white shirts had to be blued and starched, and that his merino wool trousers and silk cravats and bright waistcoats had to be washed in cold water. The Belgian lace ruffles on the cuffs of his best shirts couldn't stand water, but had to be dusted with bran to take out the grease.

When Maggie saw how handy Emmaline was with a needle, she had her stitch split seams, sew on loosened buttons, and repair torn lace. With no mistress in the house, there was little fancy sewing to be done, mainly maintenance. Maggie and Peg weren't friendly, but they tolerated her, for they quickly saw that Emmaline would carry out her duties with no supervision, as well as silently do the extra work they gave her.

And every afternoon at two o'clock, when the midday meal was done, Emmaline was allowed to hurry up the staircase for her hour with Master Thorn. That one daily hour made the rest of her life bearable.

The worst times were the nights, while she lay in bed both dreading and longing for the morning.

"I did love the look on Maggie's face this afternoon when Cook told her you're to be excused from work for the hour after dinner," Sukey said, with a giggle, as she and Emmaline did the supper dishes in the scullery that evening.

"And she won't ask me why, for she likes to pretend she doesn't care one bit about me or my business," Emmaline said.

Sukey looked behind her. Cook was vigorously grinding meat in the kitchen. She put her wet hand on Emmaline's sleeve. "Listen, Emmaline, I know the old master has got you doin' this reading business for him, but –"

"But what?"

"It's best if not everyone knows about it, so you be right quiet when you're above stairs."

"But everybody already knows. You, and Cook and Thomas. Who do you mean?"

Sukey licked her lips. "It's the young master, Eugene. He don't like it one bit if the help knows their letters. Thomas found that out the hard way."

"I haven't even see him."

"Nor have I, at least not much these past weeks." Sukey's face was suddenly stiff.

"What's he like?"

Sukey merely shrugged, and then made a great splashing and clanking with the last of the dirty pots in the sink.

Emmaline was always exhausted by the time she finished her supper, and sometimes would get into bed even before Cook came up from the kitchen. She thought, more than once, about Sukey and the man in the courtyard, but there was never the right opportunity to ask her about him. Once Sukey's muffled weeping woke her, and she murmured, "Can you not tell me why you weep, Sukey?"

Sukey said, her voice choked with tears, "It's nothing you can help me with. Nothing anyone can help me with." And she'd say no more.

The first Saturday night that Emmaline was at Thorn House, Cook said, "You'll attend church with us, in the morning, Emmaline. Sukey and I go over to All Saints." She lowered her voice. "Thomas goes off somewhere to worship on his own. The less said about that the better." She tightened her lips and bustled about the kitchen, wiping the table as she passed by. "And then you can go out for your afternoon walk, if the weather is fair. You've worked well this first week."

Emmaline went upstairs and took in her Aunt Phoebe's dress so that it fit her snugly, realizing the sweeps wouldn't be working on this day of rest, so there was no point in going to Steeplemount early. But surely they would be out, playing on the streets in the afternoon, for they were just little boys, after all. She would be able to take her time, and wander freely through the afternoon hours.

The next morning, when she came down to the kitchen in the deep purple dress, made fuller with the petticoat Sukey had given her, a thin shaft of early morning sun was coming through the window. Thomas was sitting at the table, reading, and he looked up as she walked down the stairs. She saw him through the golden haze. For a moment she thought she saw a look of surprise on his face, and then some emotion, deep within his eyes, although, she told herself, it might just be the sun playing tricks. A piece of her hair had slipped loose, and she busied herself tucking it behind her ear.

By the third full week Emmaline was in Thorn House, a desperation started to grow inside her. She had left Tibbing nearly a month ago, thinking she would be back within ten days or a fortnight, and she was no closer to finding Tommy than she had been her first day in London. The hope that had been so strong was waning, and Emmaline felt that a piece of herself was now missing, along with her little brother.

She tried to find comfort in church that morning. She loved All Saints, for it reminded her of St. Martin's. She hadn't attended church for the five years in Tibbing, for the closest one was miles away from the workers' quarters, and she and her mother had simply got out of the habit.

That morning the yellow spring sunlight fell through the stained glass windows, flickering over the gleaming wooden pews and white walls and decorated altar, creating beautiful moving shapes of color and warming the stone floor underfoot. Emmaline sat between Cook and Sukey on the servants' benches at the back of the church. Up front, the finely dressed had cushioned pews. The street noises were muffled as the congregation stood and sang. Emmaline lost herself in "When I Survey the Wondrous Cross." The words came back to her, and she didn't even have to glance at the hymnal. But she had more trouble concentrating during the sermon. The minister's voice was sonorous, and she was distracted, thinking of the afternoon. *Might this be the day I find Tommy?* Beside her, Cook's stomach growled, and there was the soft *thump* of a Bible accidentally dropped, the rustle of a cloak being removed, the scrape of a shoe on the stone floor, the knock of a knee into the back of a pew. Emmaline glanced over at Sukey, and saw that she had her eyes squeezed shut. Her hands were in her lap, clasped so tightly over her Bible that her fingertips were purplish. She was praying, but her prayers were obviously not giving her any pleasure or relief. Instead, it looked to Emmaline as if Sukey was in some kind of pious agony, her plain features twisted as she swayed slightly, her lips moving rapidly.

After the final benediction, the people in the back rows waited for those in the front to file down the aisle: the ladies in their sweeping dresses and decorated bonnets, the men in their fine redingotes with the cutaway fronts, the young girls in silk dresses, accompanied by their governesses carrying their prayer books in red morocco cases. Emmaline noticed that Sukey continued to pray with the same intense fervor, and she had to tug on her arm when it was their turn to leave.

When they got home, Cook and Emmaline finished preparing the dinner – leg of lamb – that had been cooking while they were at church. Sukey served Master Eugene and took a tray to

Master Thorn. Cook and Emmaline and Sukey and Thomas then had their own dinner, with a jam roly-poly for dessert. Cook went upstairs for a lie-down before she left for her weekly visit to her sister. Thomas went out to work in his garden, and just when Emmaline was about to leave for Steeplemount, Sukey asked her to go for a walk to a nearby park.

"But I was – Sundays are my best days to search for Tommy," she said. She counted on these afternoons, the precious daylight hours, all week. But Sukey hooked her arm through hers and begged, "Please."

Emmaline, remembering the misery on Sukey's face in church, and thankful for all Sukey had done for her, said, "All right, Sukey. It is a beautiful day."

The park was a small treed green, surrounded by an iron fence. Sukey and Emmaline strolled slowly along the gravel paths, looking at the spring flower beds: narcissus leaning on their stalks, hyacinths with their proud stems, daffodils and tulips preparing to bloom. But after only one turn around the park, Sukey stopped and put her hand to her face, wiping at her upper lip with her glove.

Emmaline saw that her skin glowed damply, with a waxy pallor. "You look ill, Sukey," she said. "Come, sit down." She led the girl to a bench.

"I'll be all right in a moment," Sukey said, closing her eyes. "I just come over sick. Too much dinner, I expect. And it's awful hot, for so early in spring."

Emmaline didn't say anything, but watched Sukey take deep quavering breaths, untying her bonnet ribbons.

"That's better," Sukey eventually said.

"Can you tell me?" Emmaline asked, her voice soft.

Sukey picked up one of the loose bonnet ribbons, rolling it up into a coil and then letting it unroll. "Tell you what?"

"What's wrong with you. Why you're always crying. And . . . and I saw you, Sukey. One of the first nights after I came. In the courtyard, with a man."

Sukey turned her face away from Emmaline. "Weren't me. You didn't see me with nobody," she said, still rolling and unrolling her bonnet ribbon.

"But I did, Sukey. I saw you. You can tell me, really. Maybe I can help."

"Leave it, Emmaline," Sukey said, letting go of the ribbon and studying the green square where a group of small boys were kicking a ball.

"But —"

Sukey got up and shook out her skirt. "I told you you was mistaken. You didn't see me with no man. Is that clear?" she said sharply. "Is that clear?" she repeated. "You'll say nothing about what you might see or hear around Thorn House, things you don't understand. Otherwise, I'll see that I did wrong in helping you."

"If you say so," Emmaline said. "I'm sorry, Sukey. Please. Sit back down." She patted the bench.

"No. The day is ruined for me now." Sukey tied her bonnet with quick angry movements. "I'm going home. Stay here, for all I care. Do as you please." She walked off, her head held high, although Emmaline saw that her steps were a little unsteady.

LOST IN SEVEN DIALS

mmaline wandered through the streets of Steeplemount Way, still distressed about Sukey and what she was hiding. She didn't keep to her usual morning pattern, feeling freer, as she did on Sundays, with no strict time limit, no listening to the bells.

Hours passed and she hadn't seen a single child who looked like a sweep. Deeply disappointed, she started back in what she thought was the direction of Thorn House. But nothing looked familiar. She realized she must have strayed farther than she ever had, and was well out of Steeplemount.

She found herself in much narrower streets, with decaying buildings and houses attached to each other higgledy-piggledy. The smell of offal and rotting food was strong, and she had to sidestep piles of filth, emptied from slop pails outside of doors. Many of the windows in the buildings had no glass, but were filled with crumpled brown paper. She tried to retrace her route, but before long she realized she was deep into a maze of dark lanes. The crumbling brick structures leaned on each other, sometimes separated at the

bottom by narrow, zigzag passes that led to eerie secluded court-
yards. Emaciated dogs snapped and growled at each other over
reeking bits of garbage. People were loitering in the doorways:
sometimes women with small children clustered against them,
silent and pale, their faces empty; sometimes a man and woman,
pressed back into the deepest recesses, creating moving shadows,
and Emmaline turned her face away. And there were girls on the
street corners, always two or three standing together, their faces
bleached with white powder, their mouths stained crimson. Their
dresses were low cut, light cotton or merino; some wore bonnets
with waving feathers, and others slouched straw hats. They stood
with one hip thrust forward, laughing with each other, too loudly,
and beckoning boldly to men who passed by. Some sang out, in
practised, weary voices, "Would you like some company, Sir?"

Emmaline hurried by them, her head down, realizing, help-
lessly, that she was spiraling deeper into the labyrinth of narrow
court upon court. Desperate, and not wanting to attract attention
to herself by talking to anyone on the streets, she called up to a
woman sitting in a second-floor window. "Please, Ma'am, could
you direct me to Steeplemount? I've lost my way."

The woman threw back her head and laughed. Her mouth
was an empty black hole. "You'll find naught what you want up at
Steeplemount, dear heart," the woman hollered down, her voice
coarse. "Anything a lass needs can be found right here, in the
Seven Dials. Aye, anything a lass needs can be found in St. Giles,
anything and then some," she said, with a rude cackle. "Why don't
you stop there, my sweet? For a few pence I can take you to a gent
that I'm sure would be more than willing to help you find what
you're looking for."

She disappeared from the window, and Emmaline raced away, ducking into the next alley and running all the way to the end before she slowed to a walk, her heart thudding against her ribs. She remembered the lady's maid, that first day in London, who had told her to go back to St. Giles to ply her trade. She understood where she was now.

She looked neither left nor right, not wanting to encourage anyone to approach her. When she reached the end of yet another alley, she heard singing. Off-key, one loud adult voice and a jumble of children's voices. Emmaline tilted her head toward the sound. She couldn't make out the words, but she recognized the familiar strains of "Guide Me, O Thou Great Jehovah." If there was a hymn, there must be a church, and no harm could befall her in a church.

She walked toward the voices until she came to a deteriorated three-storey building that looked as if it had once been a small factory. Beside the open doorway was tacked a hand-painted sign that read CROW ALLEY SUNDAY SCHOOL. She stepped inside.

At the front of the wide dusty room stood an enormously tall man, skinny and straight as a rake, his eyes closed and his mouth stretched wide as he sang. His voice was so flat that it made Emmaline wince. To one side of him was a woman, thinner still, but not as tall. She sang just as badly. She held a small pitch pipe in one hand, and waved the other hand in the air, up and down and then through the middle, up and down and through the middle, as if she were painting a cross in the air.

The woman watched Emmaline step forward hesitantly, and smiled and nodded, all the while conducting and bleating the hymn.

Emmaline wondered at the strange gathering. Ragged and dirty children sat cross-legged on the floor in front of the man and woman. Some had their heads tilted back as they stared up at the couple, trying to mouth along with the words they obviously didn't know. The result was a kind of tuneless babble. Others stared off to the side of the room, not even pretending to sing. Emmaline followed their intent gaze, and saw a small table with plates piled with squares of cake. There was also a mound of what Emmaline realized were combs.

"Bread of Heaven, Bread of Heaven, Feed me till I want no more," the man bellowed, one last time, and the song ended – *mercifully*, Emmaline thought.

The man put his hands together. "We will pray," he said, and the children dutifully folded their hands, imitating him. Many bowed their heads, but some could not tear their eyes from the food.

"Oh, Lord," the man began, "we beseech thee to take these lost lambs to your heart. Listen to their pure young voices as they do their humble best in your name. Our Father," he said, opening one eye and nodding at the children, encouraging them to repeat after him. "Our Father, who art in Heaven," he said, beckoning with both hands now, and smiling with long square horse teeth when the chorus of high voices echoed his own.

The woman approached Emmaline. "Welcome, child," she whispered. "We are all welcome in the house of God, even a miss of the streets. Sit with the others." Her face was sallow, her eyes small and set close together, but her smile was warm.

"I'm not one of the . . . the misses," Emmaline said. "And I'm not able to stay. I just . . . I heard the singing, and followed it."

"You can open your heart here, my child, and lay down your mantle of guilt. Have you chosen to give yourself to Jesus, and lose your wicked ways?"

"No," Emmaline said, shaking her head. "No. I've told you. I'm not one of them."

The woman ran her eyes over Emmaline. "It's true that you don't wear the costume, nor does your face hold any trace of powder or paint. And there's your voice. Certainly not common." She sounded disappointed.

"Who are these children?" Emmaline asked.

"They are the lost lambs of Jesus," the woman said. "Our own dear wee lost lambs. Suffer the little children of Crow Alley."

"Amen," boomed the man, after his flock had droned the last line of The Lord's Prayer. His *amen* was followed by a chorus of shouted *amens* from the children. Emmaline stepped out of the way of the wild scramble as the children pushed and knocked each other to line up in front of the table that held the cake and the combs.

"During the week they are profane, riotous, miniature criminals-to-be, I'm afraid," the woman said, shouting over the sound of the children. She rubbed her hands along her arms as if she were chilled. "They spend their lives in the mills or chimneys or on the streets. Brother Newglove and I try to provide a bit of charity, to keep them away from evil on the Lord's Day. Charity means love in action, Brother and I say —"

"Sister Newglove? Can you not spare a hand?" the tall man hollered, swamped with the crowd of ragged children. "We've a larger than usual number."

The woman waved at him. "I must assist Brother. Are you hungry, child? You do have a hungry look." She blinked rapidly, her sparse eyelashes fluttering involuntarily. "We can always find enough for one more. We have seedcake today, and combs. Some weeks there is more, others less, but we always make sure no one leaves empty-handed."

Emmaline shook her head. "Sweeps?" she shouted, over the din. "There are climbing boys here?"

The woman called Sister hurried away from Emmaline. "Oh, yes, many. They come and go, poor little savages," she called over her shoulder. "We get new ones every week."

"I'm looking for one, for a sweep by the name of Tommy. Do you know him?" Emmaline yelled after the woman, her eyes swinging back to the children and noticing, suddenly, a few telltale shaved, soot-ingrained skulls. "Do you know a sweep named Tommy?" she shouted, louder this time, but the woman didn't hear. She was surrounded by the waving arms of the clamoring, noisy crowd of hungry, dirty children.

Emmaline pushed after her. For an instant they blended together: boys and girls in filthy torn clothing, all with cheekbones and collarbones protruding. *Is Tommy among them?*

CROW ALLEY SUNDAY SCHOOL

mmaline planted herself beside the table as each child reached for cake and a comb, waiting, watching, until she knew for certain that Tommy wasn't there. Near the end of the line was a climbing boy with one eye swollen shut. She took hold of his wrist as he reached for his cake.

The boy ducked, putting up his forearm to protect his head.

"I'm not going to hurt you," Emmaline said. She also assured Sister Newglove, who, holding a square of cake, had stepped forward at the sight of Emmaline's hand on the boy. "I just want to ask him if he's seen my brother. Tommy," she said, loudly, into the climbing boy's face. His eyes wouldn't meet hers, and he bit his chapped bottom lip. "Do you know a climbing boy named Tommy who can't hear or speak?"

He shook his head, trying to pull his wrist out of Emmaline's grasp. He concentrated on the cake in Sister's hand.

"Do you understand what I'm saying?" Emmaline asked. "The boy I'm looking for can't speak," she repeated. "His name is Tommy."

But the boy just continued to shake his head.

"Leave the poor mite be, my dear," Sister said. "It's clear that he doesn't know your brother."

Emmaline dropped the boy's wrist. He grabbed the cake from Sister Newglove and bolted out the door.

"Wait!" Brother Newglove called. "He didn't take a comb," he said, as if to himself.

"You're forgetting that the climbing boys don't need them, Brother," Sister said. "They've not a hair on their heads to bother with."

The children had shoved their squares of sweet seedcake into their mouths in a few huge bites, wolfing them down, hardly seeming to chew through the thick texture, dotted with caraway, before they were back at the table, prowling, reminding Emmaline of small anxious foxes.

Brother and Sister Newglove divided what was left of the cake among the children who had stayed, then encouraged them to use their combs on their dirty matted hair. "Clean hands, clean face, and tidy hair are better than fine clothes," Sister Newglove chanted rhythmically. "Come, see if you can pull through the tangles. You'll feel better with combed hair, you'll see."

To Emmaline, given the neglected state of the children, worrying about them combing their hair seemed laughable. But she saw how Brother Newglove kindly patted the shoulder of one boy, and absently straightened the child's half-torn shirt collar. She watched a small girl press against Sister Newglove, smearing her nose, running with thick mucous, against the woman's skirt. Sister Newglove merely put her ungloved hand on the child's matted head.

"Have you been doing this for a long time?" Emmaline asked.

"Ah, yes," Brother Newglove sighed. His eyes were bloodshot.

"Would you remember seeing my brother? His name is Tommy. The thing that would set him apart is that he's deaf, and unable to speak."

"I wish I could tell you that we've seen him, dear," Sister Newglove answered, "but to be honest, I wouldn't know if any of the boys were deaf or mute. Many of these working children — slaves, I call them — who come here of a Sunday don't speak much anyway, and many have a faraway look in their eyes, as if they're confused. It's the lack of proper food and sleep and care, you see. Gives them a blank look. What brought you to search in this particular area? Do you suspect him of being here, in St. Giles? It's highly unlikely. Nobody does much cleaning of any sort in this area. The climbing boys you saw here today would just be making the rounds, in search of Sunday schools and their free food, all over the city."

"No. Actually, I've been looking in Steeplemount. I have a note that says he's there, from the master sweep," Emmaline said, pulling the worn slip of paper from her pocket. "You see?" she asked, handing it to Sister Newglove. "Master Sweep Hillis, of Steeplemount Way. If I can just find him, I'll find Tommy. You might know of him, this Hillis fellow," she continued, her voice lifting.

Sister Newglove's face softened. "Ah, my poor girl. There's nobody named Hillis. Leastways not a Master Sweep Hillis."

"But it says so. There," Emmaline said, pointing to the scribbled name.

"It's part of the ruse," Brother told her. "Many of the filthy beggars who travel about the countryside and towns, looking to employ – to use the word loosely – the poor boys, all call themselves Hillis. It's a bit of a code name, in these parts. The men who buy boys from desperate parents try to make their shady dealing appear proper with a so-called contract. As if using a name could take away from the illicit nature of their deeds."

Sister put the paper back in Emmaline's hand. "So that if someone has a mind to come looking, as you have, it will be impossible to trace the child. I'm sorry."

Emmaline closed her eyes. "Is it even slightly possible, then, that he is employed in Steeplemount?"

"Oh, it's possible," Brother Newglove said. "Oh, yes, quite possible. Could most definitely be in Steeplemount."

Emmaline opened her eyes.

"There are so many sweeps about those parts," Brother Newglove went on, taking a large handkerchief out of his pocket and blowing his nose with a loud honk, "because of the height of the houses, and the tiny flues. Oh, yes, the sweeps are numerous there, although of course they're used all over the city. But there is a big proportion of the more slippery master sweeps in the Steeplemount area. Isn't that right, Sister?" He swabbed the end of his nose, refolded his handkerchief and stuffed it back in the pocket of his frock coat.

His sister agreed with him. "Houses aren't so fine, and the home owners not as picky. In the better areas of London there are higher class sweeping outfits, with more respectable treatment of their sweeps. In the more genteel neighborhoods the residents insist on the boys being cleaner, and hire a familiar sweep team on a regular basis. But in Steeplemount the sweeps generally just call the streets, walking up and down and shouting out for business. Master sweeps and their boys come and go. The boys are the most poorly treated of the lot, and often the smallest."

Emmaline swallowed. "I'll keep searching there, then."

Brother and Sister Newglove both looked down at their hands. Emmaline thought she saw an almost imperceptible shake to Brother's head, but she ignored it. "I will find him," she said. "It doesn't matter how long it takes," she added, firmly. "I'll find him."

She tried to picture Tommy in her head at that moment, but found, to her horror, that she couldn't remember exactly what he looked like.

She just couldn't remember.

MEETING THE YOUNG MASTER

hen the last child had left, Sister Newglove remained behind to clean the room, while Brother Newglove led Emmaline out past the Seven Dials. It was growing dark along the seven streets leading out from the main area of St. Giles, like spokes of a wheel, and the street lamps were being lit. The area hadn't yet been switched to gas lamps, and the smell of singed oil made her eyes smart. Nobody bothered Emmaline as she walked beside the tall man in his black frock coat, and she was grateful for his kindness. Eventually he led her onto a High Street, and gave her easy directions to get back to the area of Thorn House.

It shocked her to see how far she had wandered, and it took so long to get back. She hoped Cook wouldn't be furious with her at staying out past dark.

She undid the latch of the tall iron gate and slipped through, shutting it soundlessly behind her. She hurried into the courtyard, then stopped, bending down to peer in the kitchen window to see if Cook was waiting up for her.

She was suddenly pulled roughly by the shoulder, turned, and her forearm was grabbed tightly. "What do you think you're doing, my fine lass?"

Emmaline looked up. It was a well-built young man with shining dark red hair and a gingery mustache. His skin was ruddy, his teeth even and white. He was, Emmaline realized, quite attractive, although there was a downward slope to his chin that stopped him from being handsome.

Had she been out on the street when the man grabbed her, she might have been afraid, but here, in the courtyard of Thorn House, she knew that if she screamed, Cook or Sukey or Thomas would hear her.

"Excuse me, Sir," she said, using the same confident tone as the man, and looking him directly in the face, "I would appreciate you letting go of my arm. You had no right to follow me in here. This is my place of employment, and should you insist on detaining me, you will answer to the house."

The man's mouth dropped open, and then he smiled. In a moment the smile widened, and he threw back his head and laughed, a loud long laugh. Emmaline smelled the stale reek of cigar smoke and the harshness of strong whiskey. "Well," he said, his grip on Emmaline's forearm never lessening, "Whoever trained you has done a remarkable job. There aren't too many common thieves who are able to pretend that they are as wellborn as you." He pulled her closer to the house and studied her in the light from the kitchen window. "Let me give you a hint, though. Although your skin is quite fine, and your hair a marvelous color, the clothing will have to go. Have your accomplice provide you with a finer dress – perhaps a green silk, which would do wonders with those eyes. Although I must admit," he stopped, and let his eyes travel down the length of Emmaline, "that even without enough petticoats to give it shape, this deep purple is quite fetching on you. With gloves and a stylish bonnet, and perhaps carrying a parasol, you might pass as a proper lady. Who knows? Had I been introduced to you in a drawing room, in a seemly costume, I might have been quite taken with you. You might have even worked your way into my home through the front door, instead of sneaking in a window to do your dirty work."

"Your home?" Emmaline said. *Of course. That voice.*

"Don't play me for a fool," the man said, losing his smile. He squeezed Emmaline's forearm even harder, and she bit down so she wouldn't cry out. "I think that perhaps I should drag you down to the constabulary. We've nobody the likes of you working in Thorn House. Do you think I wouldn't know? I'm the master here. You've picked the wrong man to try and deceive."

"I'm not deceiving you, Sir. You would be Master Eugene. It was Cook herself who hired me. I sleep in the attic, with Sukey."

The man loosened his hold a bit. "Cook hired you?"

"Yes. I'm just here to fill in for a girl who was injured. Please, Sir, if you don't believe me, come into the kitchen and ask Cook."

There was something about Master Eugene's smile that made his face appear wolfish. "Well, well. I must apologize." He dropped her arm and took a step back. "What is your name?"

"Emmaline. Emmaline Roke."

"Emmaline," he repeated, rolling the name off his tongue, reaching out to touch her hair. "A beautiful name for a beautiful young woman, even when you look so angry. I can imagine how glorious it would be to see you smile."

Emmaline kept her mouth shut. Eugene's fingers played with the curl at the side of her cheek, gently, letting the hair slide between his thumb and forefinger.

"So you won't smile for me?" He moved his hand down from her hair to rest on the side of her neck. His fingers were smooth, uncallused, the nails trimmed.

Emmaline felt the beat of her pulse under his fingertips. "I must get inside, Sir. I may have upset Cook."

"Have you been out with a gentleman friend, then?" The smile grew secretive. "I'm sure you must have a number of them. Or at least one special one." His fingers were warmer now, caressing her neck, straying lower. His ring finger touched her collar bone. He left it there.

"No, Sir. I . . . I had business to attend to."

Eugene leaned closer. Under the tobacco and alcohol, Emmaline smelled the fragrance of apples from his hair pomade and the spicy scent of cologne. "Business?" he said. "I can't imagine what kind of business –"

The kitchen door swung open. "Emmaline? You're to come inside now. Cook has kept your supper for you," Thomas called loudly.

Eugene lowered his hand, but didn't move away from Emmaline.

"Good evening, Master Eugene," Thomas said.

Eugene nodded. "You should have let me know we had new staff, Paddy," he said.

"Cook said you weren't to be bothered with any below stairs bits and pieces," Thomas answered. "Come now, Emmaline," he said, moving toward her. "You must excuse her, Master Eugene. She's late coming home from an errand."

Eugene ignored him, reaching out to trace his finger down Emmaline's cheek. "I'm sure I'll be seeing her around, now that I know she's here," he said.

Emmaline turned her face from Eugene's touch, and followed Thomas through the door. Once inside, she shut it and leaned against it, letting out a sigh of relief. "I'm ever so glad Cook sent you out when she did," she said. "What an awful man. Is Cook huffed off with me for being so late?"

Thomas reached behind her head to lock the door. "Cook's gone to sleep," he said.

Emmaline breathed deeply. There was no unpleasant odor of bad habits about Thomas, no artificial scent of hair pomade or cologne. He smelled of washing powder and fresh air. She stayed where she was, her back against the door.

"When Cook came in from her sister's a while ago," Thomas said, his arm still over Emmaline's shoulder, hand on the door, even though it was locked now, "I said you and Sukey were already in your beds. I was speaking the truth about Sukey. She felt poorly and went straight to her room from supper."

Emmaline had to stop herself from leaning forward. She wanted to lay her cheek against Thomas's chest, to close her eyes and not think about anything – not about the hope that was slowly diminishing, not about her next day in the laundry, not about where Tommy was that minute. Not about the sly searching look on Eugene's face as he studied her body.

She saw, over his shoulder, the deserted, brightly lit kitchen. A book lay facedown on the table beside a covered plate.

"So it wasn't Cook that sent for me?"

Thomas shook his head. "I . . . I was waiting for you." His face colored slightly. "To lock up after you, of course." He pulled his arm away, but didn't move. "Watch out for Master Eugene, Emmaline. You must keep your wits about you where he's concerned. Usually he doesn't bother much with coming to the kitchen, but now that he knows there's a new lass . . ." He didn't finish his sentence, fussing with the button on the cuff of his shirt. "I just wouldn't want any harm to come your way," he said, his voice hardening. "Your supper's just there," he added, glancing at the covered plate.

"Thank you, Thomas," Emmaline said.

Thomas hesitated, but then abruptly said good night, and went into his room, shutting the door.

Emmaline took the cloth off the plate, and quickly ate the cold slice of lamb pie. As she finished the last crumb, she saw the rim of light under Thomas's door go out.

She blew out the lamp and went up the dark back stairway, tiptoeing with great care past the second-floor landing that she knew opened into the Thorn House bedrooms.

WE ALL HAVE OUR STORIES

ukey was a dark lump under the covers, but as Emmaline undressed silently in the inky blackness of the moonless night, the other girl turned over, and Emmaline heard her voice, husky with sleep.

"You're finally back, then?"

"Yes," Emmaline whispered, mindful of Cook in the next room. "I got lost." She didn't want to tell Sukey what she had discovered about Master Sweep Hillis.

Sukey sat up. "You had no luck, then?"

Emmaline was relieved that Sukey was her old self. It was as if the incident in the park hadn't happened. "No," she answered, trying to keep the despair out of her voice. "And I won't give up, Sukey. Not ever. But it's taking so long." A moment of silence followed while Emmaline tried to still the dark panic that wouldn't leave. "I did see a lot of children in a Sunday school, though."

"Oh, I remember them Sunday afternoon times well," Sukey said. "Me and me brothers and sister would make the rounds, going to as many of the Sunday schools as we could, to fill our bellies for at least once in the week."

Emmaline got into bed and sat beside Sukey. "Where are your brothers and sister now?"

"We all worked, my three brothers on the streets as crossing boys or holding horses. My sister and me helped me pa as mudlarks, dredging the Thames for whatever we could find to sell for scrap." Sukey's voice was low, faraway. "We worked down on the shore of King James Stairs, in Wrapping Wall. That were our spot. Me ma did what she could, wherever she could, collecting pure – the dog dirt from the streets, to sell to the tanner – or selling stay laces to the working girls, when she had a few pence to buy a supply. Between us all we earned enough to share a room with ten others, and buy a pinch of tea and slices of bread most days. And then one winter we were all taken ill with the fever. Me pa and ma and youngest brother went first. After that we were put out on the street, my brothers and sister and me; we couldn't pay, so couldn't stay in the room any longer."

Emmaline waited in the darkness, remembering the poor huddled wretches she'd seen in doorways and alleys just hours before.

"The last I remember is my head hurtin' something awful, and the sound of my sister crying. That's all. And next thing I woke up in a workhouse, my hair all cut off. I never seen them again, my sister and two brothers. I don't know whether they's alive or dead." Her voice was steady and smooth, without a hint of distress. "Weren't nothing nobody could do about it."

"You met Thomas there, at the workhouse?" Emmaline asked.

"Aye. He reminded me a lot of my second youngest brother. Thomas were all alone, too, and we drifted together. It were six years since we come here. Thomas were eleven; I were somewheres around my fourteenth year. I'm not overly sure what my birth date is; me ma couldn't quite remember." She stopped.

Emmaline waited, wanting Sukey to go on.

Finally she did. "Thomas and me did get on, and I often worried about what would happen to him when it came my time to quit the workhouse, and leave him on his own. There were something – I don't know the word – that made me fret about him, in a way I never fretted about me own brothers. They were a tough, scrappy little lot, ready to fight for anything. Now Thomas had the temper, 'tis true. Terrible, it were at times. But there was something different, as well. I think it were that he trusted people, and could fall to harm if he weren't careful."

"Vulnerable?" Emmaline said. "It means he would be easy prey."

"That sounds about right. Aye, that word you said – when he were a younger lad. Seems he's grown out of that, but not the temper. He works sore hard to not let it get the better of him, and he's just as quick to be sorry for letting it out, as well. What were that word, again?"

"Vulnerable."

"Cor. Don't you use big words, though. Mind, you're a lot like Thomas, with his big words. It'll be the book readin', for both of you. Seems that them wot reads books forgets the common man's speech."

"I could teach you, if you like," Emmaline said. "To read."

"Wot, me? Learn to read? Not half likely. I haven't got the brains."

"Who says that?"

"Well, nobody said it. But I always figgered only real smart people could read. Thomas offered to teach me, more'n once, too, but I said no to him an' all. I knew I'd be no good at it."

"Nonsense. I'm sure you could learn easily. We could start with you learning to write your name, at least."

"Maybe. It would be right handy, knowing the letters of my own name."

Emmaline wrapped her arms around her knees. "So shall we start tomorrow?

"Aye." Sukey muffled a yawn.

"Maybe I could find something in Master Thorn's library that would be easy to start with. If he wouldn't mind."

"He wouldn't. I've been sneakin' Thomas up there to borry books for years now. Longs as we puts 'em back, Thomas and I don't reckon it causes any harm. He even seed us once, old Master Thorn, lookin' at some books, but he said naught. No, he's all right, is the old boy. Him and Master Wallace were one of a kind. The young master is a different sort."

"I can see that."

"What do you mean?"

"I met him. Master Eugene. This very evening."

Sukey turned to Emmaline. "Where?" The question came out in a rush of breath, all trace of sleepiness gone now.

Emmaline studied the pale oval of Sukey's face. "Outside the house. I was coming in, and he caught hold of me and stopped me, not knowing I worked here. He seemed like he could turn nasty if he had a mind to."

"Oh, well, he would be acting queer if he'd been out to the fancy clubs on Pall Mall. Takin' a drop. But he's not always so. There are times when he's . . ."

When she didn't continue, Emmaline prompted her. "When he's what?"

Sukey shrugged. "Nothing. It's nothing. He just takes too much to drink now and again. He's not at his best with the drink in him."

Emmaline thought of Cat, reeling with ale, angry and lashing out. "Tell me some more about Thomas," she said.

"What about him?"

Emmaline was glad that Sukey couldn't see the warm flush that she knew was on her cheeks. "Well, how did he come here from Ireland? Does he have any family?"

"Thomas don't like to talk much about where he come from. We all of us has our stories, and some find it easier to forget as much as possible. Some likes to tell the story over and over, to anyone who'll listen. And others push the past away. Seems like that's how it is for Thomas."

Sukey and Emmaline lay down, side by side, in the warm darkness. Emmaline thought of Eugene's fingers touching her hair, caressing her cheek and neck. "Is he – Master Eugene – ever unpleasant to you?"

"Cook ain't too bad-tempered, as you can see, and that's one thing to be grateful for," Sukey said, ignoring Emmaline's question. "It's a fair house. Cook and Thomas make it feel almost like a family. And the old man don't ask for much but cups of weak tea and a tray of food now and then. Yes, it's not a bad house," she repeated.

"But Master Eugene. What do you think of him?" Suddenly Emmaline remembered Sukey stroking Eugene's polished boot; saw the image of her pulling at the arm of the drunken man in the courtyard. Thought about all the tears she tried to hide.

There was a moment of silence. "No more talking tonight," Sukey said. "All of this chatter has me right wore out."

The coverlet rustled as she pulled it over her shoulder and turned on her side, away from Emmaline.

In the darkness, Emmaline thought about Master Eugene and Sukey. *Of course.*

SUKEY'S SECRET

he next morning when Emmaline came in from her rounds of Steeplemount, she found Sukey sitting at the kitchen table. Just sitting, her hands not busy, for once. She was more pale than usual. There was no fire, no breakfast started.

"Where is Thomas?" Emmaline asked, seeing his door open, and his bed made.

"He's upstairs, packing for Master Eugene. The young master is off to the country for a fortnight." Her voice was dull and expressionless.

"Well," Emmaline said, "that'll mean less cooking, and less laundry then, won't it? No towels and bed linens from his rooms. And how it will lighten the amount of his clothing to wash and iron! He must change three or four times a day. How can he wear so many clothes?" She kept her voice light, trying to cheer Sukey.

"He loves to dress well," Sukey answered, not meeting Emmaline's eyes. "He has his morning dress, for breakfast and walking to fetch the post and newspaper; his dinner dress, for dining with friends; another set o' clothes for the afternoon and more visiting; and then his finest evening wear, for the clubs. The dance and gambling halls in the West End."

Emmaline started the fire and got out eggs and bread and oatmeal. She hoped that Cook would be slow coming down. "It must be quite a life, doing nothing at all but indulging oneself in pleasures."

Sukey leaned her chin on her palm. "We'll never know, will we?" she said, more to herself than Emmaline.

Emmaline sat down across from Sukey, noticing dark smudges under her eyes. "Are you still not feeling well?" she asked. "Yesterday, in the park, you —"

"I'm fine," Sukey said sharply, studying her fingers. "There's not a thing wrong with me. I just get tired these days, that's all."

"Are you sure? Is it something to do with . . . with Master Eugene?" Emmaline asked, hesitantly.

Sukey's head snapped up. "Who's bin talking about me? Were it Maggie? She's got a mean tongue. Whatever she said is a lie. There ain't nothing between Master Eugene and me, so you just shut up and leave me be." She jumped up, knocking over her chair, and ran out into the courtyard, slamming the door behind her.

With Eugene gone, there was much less work to do, as Emmaline had predicted. In the evenings she and Thomas and Sukey sat longer in the warm glow of the lamp in the center of the table. She and Thomas talked about the books they had read, and Sukey practised writing her name, and sounding out simple words. And in the day, there was sometimes an hour or two that she could spend with Thomas, helping him in the small garden.

One afternoon they weeded around the feathery green tops of the carrots and cress and radishes, and under the emerging cabbage leaves. "Have you ever grown herbs?" Emmaline asked. The brindle cat had come out from behind the shed and sat on a flat stone that was warmed by the sun. It watched them with its long topaz eyes.

Thomas picked tiny insects off the beet tops. "No. I don't know much about them."

"My father had wonderful herbs, back in Maidenfern, when I was a child. He won a prize once. For his basil."

Thomas smiled, and Emmaline suddenly remembered something that he'd said the first night she'd come to Thorn House. *Surely some of us are capable of more than one thing, and can make a change in what we're handed.*

"Do you think you'll stay here, at Thorn House, always?" she asked.

Thomas straightened, looking at the cat. "I think about a lot of things. I think about County Clare, and that perhaps my grandfather's still alive there. He had a stone cottage, not far from the sea. When the wind blew in off the water, the air . . ." He stopped. "No. I know I can never go back. Not to that place, and that time. But I think about a lot of other things. That might be, someday."

"I do, too," Emmaline said, watching the cat with him.

It sat, still and tense, its eyes following a small white moth that fluttered over its head and in front of its nose. With no warning, the cat leapt into the air, snapping its jaws at the moth. But the tiny winged creature was too fast, and the cat fell, twisting awkwardly on the soft ground. In the next moment it was back on its feet, giving itself an indignant shake and looking accusingly at Thomas and Emmaline, as if they were to blame.

Emmaline laughed, the burst of sound surprising her. She realized she hadn't laughed for a long time. "Did you see that?" she asked, pointing at the cat, still laughing.

Thomas nodded, and then he joined her, and the two of them laughed, long after the cat had settled itself back on the warm stone, and was gazing at them with a disdainful tilt to its broad head. But suddenly Emmaline clapped her hand over her mouth. How could she laugh, with Tommy gone? How could she allow herself, for even a moment, to feel happiness? *Oh, Tommy. Don't give up on me. I'll find you.*

On the fifth day that Eugene was away, the spring weather turned nasty and cool toward evening. Emmaline couldn't fall into a deep slumber that night; she tossed and shivered, always just over the thin edge of sleep. The wind had come up, gabbling like a lunatic in the flimsy window frame. It created a high, keening wail that went on the length of a scream, and then faded to a moan, a squall of rain ticking sharply against the pane. The sound of it jerked Emmaline from her restless half-sleep. She sat up and looked at Sukey's side of the bed.

The bedclothes were thrown back, and Sukey wasn't there. *Where would she have gone?* Emmaline got out of bed, the floor cold under her bare feet, and looked out the window, pressing her forehead to the chilled glass. The courtyard was empty and desolate.

Perhaps Sukey was in the kitchen, having a warm drink. Emmaline wrapped her shawl around her shift and tiptoed downstairs. But there was no one in the kitchen, and Thomas's door was firmly shut. As her eyes adjusted and made out the familiar shapes in the darkness, she realized that the side door wasn't padlocked. She opened it all the way and looked out.

There was a faint candle glow from the window of the laundry house.

The ground was wet and cold, patches of lichen yielding and unpleasantly spongy under Emmaline's bare feet as she made her way across the courtyard. The wind tugged at the end of her shawl, and she had to hold it firmly to keep it from being swept away. She peered through the window, but it was steamed over.

As she pulled open the door, she heard a splash and the clink of glass. Before she could call out, the wind rushed through the open doorway, and in the next instant she saw the flame of the candle lean, flutter like a rag, and then go out.

A small, frightened cry came from inside the dark laundry.

"Sukey?" Emmaline called, shivering. "Is that you, Sukey?"

"Go away!" Although the voice was hoarse with crying, and strange, raspier than she had ever heard it, she knew it was Sukey's. She dropped her shoulders and sighed with relief, stepping inside the laundry house. It would have been dark as pitch, but for the glow of embers in the stove they used for heating the wash water.

"Where are you?" she said, shutting the door behind her.

"I told you to go away. Can't you just leave me be?" Sukey's voice was low with anger and something else.

Emmaline made her way to the stove and lit a piece of rush from the embers. Then she found the candle and lit it, holding it up. "Where are you?" she repeated. Then she saw her.

Sukey was sitting in her thin shift in one of the washing tubs, up to her waist in water that Emmaline could see was very hot. Steam was rising around Sukey. She wrapped her arms around herself and wouldn't look up at Emmaline. Beside her, on the stone floor, was a long-necked bottle.

"Why are you taking a bath at this time of night?" Emmaline asked. "And why here, in the laundry?" The usual place for bathing was standing in a small copper tub in the kitchen, with a curtained stand pulled around it.

Sukey reached for the bottle, put it to her mouth, and filled her cheeks. She squeezed her eyes shut and grimaced as she swallowed. "Go 'way," she said. "None o' yer business."

"I'm not going until you tell me what you're doing. What's that you're drinking?"

"Med'cine," Sukey said. "It's med'cine. I bought it with me own wages, from an old woman on Threadneedle Street. It'll do the trick, she told me. Sit in water hot as you can stand, and drink it all down. That'll bring it on, and it'll be over by morning." She unsteadily set the bottle down beside the tub again.

Emmaline stood very still.

"She took one look and told me it were too late for coffee berries to do any good, and I've already tried brews of tamarisk. Didn't work. So you go on back to bed, like a good little girl, Emmy," Sukey slurred. "I need to finish my med'cine."

Emmaline set down the candle and picked up the bottle. She put it to her nose. "'Tisn't medicine of any sort, Sukey," she said. "It's just rum. Cheap rum."

Sukey looked up at her, her mouth loose, her eyes desperate. "Not med'cine? It won't make the baby go away?"

"Oh, Sukey," Emmaline said, softly.

"I used all my savings on it," Sukey said. "She told me it were dear, but worth it, because it would take away my problem. Now what will I do?"

Emmaline took a piece of toweling from the drying rack, and put it around Sukey. "Come out of there, Sukey," she said, helping the other girl up.

"What will I do?" Sukey repeated. Her face was flat and blurred, like a coin handled over too many years.

"I don't know," Emmaline told her. "But we'll think of something," she reassured her, although at that moment there wasn't a single thing that came to mind.

Emmaline got Sukey back up the stairs, into a dry shift, and into bed, thankful that Master Eugene was away, and that Cook was such a sound sleeper. For the rest of the night, the rain continued to lash the window. Sukey's sharp elbows and knees jabbed into Emmaline as she thrashed and mumbled in her drunken sleep.

As the usual time to go searching for Tommy approached, Emmaline looked over at Sukey, breathing heavily, finally motionless, one hand clutching the coverlet fiercely, and decided she couldn't leave. Instead, she went into the kitchen and started the fire, laying out the breakfast dishes and the tray for Master Thorn –

Sukey's jobs. *Would this have been the morning I'd have found Tommy?* She hated to think of the few lost hours of searching.

Thomas came out of his room. "Not going out this morning, then?" he asked.

Emmaline shook her head. "Sukey's poorly. I thought I'd help her out a bit before I start in the laundry," she told him.

He nodded. From the look on his face, Emmaline suspected that Thomas knew about the baby.

When she and Maggie came in for their dinner, Sukey was standing at the table, looking down at the food as if in a trance. Her face reflected the yellow sheen of her cotton nankeen collar.

"Are you feeling better?" Emmaline asked, although it was clear how terrible Sukey felt after drinking most of the bottle of rum the night before.

"A little," Sukey answered, meeting her eyes briefly and then glancing at Cook, as if warning Emmaline.

"With so much less laundry, I expect we'll finish up early today, won't we, Maggie?" Emmaline said.

"I expect so," Maggie agreed, eagerly reaching for a thick slick of mutton.

"So I could give you a hand later, Sukey," Emmaline suggested.

"That would be right helpful. I'm to polish the grates with blacklead today," Sukey said.

"Do you want me to make up a bran poultice?" Cook asked.

Sukey shook her head.

"I think you should get yourself upstairs right now, and put your feet up for a few minutes," Cook said. "The house is quiet, without His Majesty about. And I've called for the physician."

"No!" Sukey cried.

"Not for you," Cook said. "It's time Master Thorn is properly looked at. He won't be happy with me, but someone's got to take a stand. So get on upstairs, Sukey, and take a bit of a rest."

Sukey nodded. "Thank you, Cook. And you too, Emmaline." She got up from her chair, wincing. She walked up the back stairs, her palms flat against the walls on either side for balance.

POOR UNWANTED THING

ukey stayed upstairs the rest of the day. Emmaline rushed through all the work – in the laundry, and then Sukey's, stopping midafternoon to read to Master Thorn. The physician had just left, and the old man was weak from a bloodletting. But he kindly patted Emmaline's hand when she fussed over him, arranging his blankets and holding a cup of weak tea to his lips.

"Don't worry about an old man, my dear," he said. "It will do me a world of good just to hear your voice for the next while."

"I think we should read something lighthearted today, Sir," she said, partly for Master Thorn's sake, and partly for her own.

"Whatever you like, Emmaline," Master Thorn said, and Emmaline went to one of the shelves in the library and took out *A Midsummer Night's Dream*.

By the end of the hour Master Thorn was feeling better, sipping the cold tea on his own and giving an occasional laugh that sounded like dry twigs snapping.

After supper Emmaline carried a plate of buttered bread and a chunk of cheese up the stairs in case Sukey was hungry.

She found the girl sitting on the bed, her hands in her lap. She was very still and so, so pale that her skin was almost transparent. A cold wave washed over Emmaline as she lowered herself beside Sukey. "I brought you something to eat," she said.

Sukey looked at the plate on Emmaline's lap. "It didn't work," she told her. "You were right. It must have been only rum." She talked to the cheese. "I pray every night, and extra hard on Sundays. I pray and pray for an answer. And He hasn't given me one."

Emmaline sat, silent.

"I don't know what to do. About . . ." Sukey put one hand on her stomach. "This." She moved her hand away. "Master Eugene treated me so nice at first, Emmaline. I never knew what it was like to be treated so. He made me laugh, and told me I were pretty. No one never told me I were pretty before."

Emmaline looked at Sukey's thick hair and broad face. When Sukey smiled, her face shone; the smile brought something to her eyes that changed them, lightened them. Emmaline could imagine what it would have meant to Sukey to have the attention of a good-looking young man like Master Eugene.

"I thought . . . oh, Emmaline. I were a fool. I really thought he fancied me. And then . . ." Her hand strayed back to her stomach, her fingers opening and closing on the fabric of her uniform. "And then I realized I weren't nothing to him after all. I've been the oldest kind of fool. I prayed that Master Eugene would look at me in the way he had for a time. Tell me he fancied me again, even though I knew it were only a fool's dream. People like Master Eugene never really fancy a girl like me."

Her hand stopped its stroking.

Emmaline swallowed. "Does Master Eugene know? About . . ." She couldn't bring herself to say *the baby. Poor unwanted thing.* She felt she might cry if she did.

Sukey's mouth was a grim line. "Oh, he knows all right."

"Will he not . . . help, in some way?"

One side of Sukey's mouth turned up in the parody of a smile. "Oh, he's already been right helpful. Told me as long as I said nothing about it, I could stay on until it started to show, and then I'd have to be gone. And expected me to thank him for giving me a few months, for not throwing me out on the spot. And then he told me, only a few weeks ago, that he'd had a change of heart."

"A change of heart? But that was good news, wasn't it?"

Sukey laughed, a sound as harsh as Master Thorn's cough. "His change of heart were that if I . . . if I got rid of it, that I could stay." She shook her head. "So I were trying, last night, Emmaline." She bit at her thumbnail. "I think Cook is starting to suspect, eyeing me oddlike. Soon – another month, maybe – I won't be able to hide it. Thomas knows," she added, unexpectedly.

"Thomas knows?" So she'd been right.

"He said he'd try and help me, although we haven't figured out yet what I should do. But he were real nice about it, and didn't judge me none. In fact, he told me it were what happened to his own mother. She were caught, like me. He never knew who his father was, and when he were a young lad his mother was finally forced out of town, back in Ireland, because of the disgrace. She took Thomas and came to where nobody would know her shame." Sukey suddenly looked up at Emmaline. "I didn't mean to tell you. He told me he'd never told no one that before."

"I would never say anything to him about it, Sukey."

A heavy silence fell over the room.

"Is that what you want, Sukey? To get rid of it? Of him, or her?" Emmaline asked, finally.

"I can't let myself think of it as a real thing. If I think of it as a wee babe, how can I think to harm it? But with an outside child, there's nothing ahead for me. I'll lose my place here, and be out on the street, and have to go into a poorhouse. Them places is worse than the street. I just want another chance. I feel sorrow for it, the thing inside me, but I wish it had never started."

She looked toward the window. "I knows some girls what have just thrown their mistakes in the privy, or left 'em in the gutter. But I couldn't do that. I have no choice but to be put into a poorhouse along with the babe. I'll never get another proper place. I'm so afraid, Emmaline."

Emmaline put her arm around the other girl. The plate slipped to the floor, the food spilling. "I know."

Sukey straightened her shoulders, and wiped her eyes with her sleeve. "You know, before all this business with Master Eugene, I dreamed of staying on here, and maybe someday taking over Cook's position. She's got a lot of aches and pains, and says herself it won't be long before she won't be able to stay on her feet all day. And I'm turning into a right smart hand in the kitchen myself. Cook learnt me good. I had that to look forward to," she said, but she didn't sound very convincing.

"Oh, Sukey," Emmaline said, aching for Sukey, forgetting, for those few minutes, the ache for her own brother.

Sukey lay down and curled into a ball, one hand under her cheek, her back to Emmaline. Eventually Emmaline lay down, curving herself behind Sukey so that she could put her arm around her. She watched the long shadows on the cracked walls behind Sukey blend, until they formed darkness.

WATCHING THEM WORK

mmaline tried to carry on normally. One morning, after she'd been out searching, as she sat down at the table to start her breakfast, there was a sudden clattering at the back door. Thomas appeared with two boys carrying burlap sacks.

Emmaline jumped up, her mouth opening, but Thomas held out his hand, stopping her before she spoke. "I'm sorry, Emmaline. They're just here to clean the chimneys. Because Cook doesn't have to use the fireplace for these next few days, with Master Thorn not wanting any big meals and Master Eugene not here, she decided we should have the kitchen fireplace cleaned properly. I should have told you they were coming."

Emmaline watched them set to work.

The smaller one tucked a brush under his arm and, using only his bare knees and elbows, hoisted himself up inside the narrow brick chimney. A dusty rain of soot fell as he brushed at the bricks, and the older boy stood back.

"Are yis goin'?" he called up, once, and when there was no answer, crouched in the chimney opening. Craning his neck, he shielded his eyes from falling cinders and soot with one hand. Emmaline saw him put his other hand into his pocket and pull out a long, sharp-looking pin. He reached up with it, and in the next instant Emmaline heard the smaller boy give a tiny wail.

"Ow!" he cried. "It's narrow. I'm trying me best."

"Does yis need to slant?"

"Aye," came the faint reply.

Emmaline closed her eyes, imagining Tommy working his way up the tiny, dark flu passage, his elbows and knees rubbed raw from scraping against the rough brick, and being poked from below by the prodder.

Cook came into the kitchen, tying her apron. "Are they near done?" she asked Thomas, and he nodded.

Eventually the little boy called down the chimney. "All up," he cried, finished, climbing out on the roof. Emmaline heard him scrambling down a rain pipe, and then he came back in the kitchen. The other boy had swept all the fallen soot into the burlap bags.

Cook put her hands on her hips. "Get out to the courtyard. Sukey, take them out a pail of water. You two imps, wash your hands and faces, and then get back in here and I'll give you a bowl of porridge. But only if you're not so filthy that we have to wash down the kitchen after you're gone."

The boys disappeared, reappearing in a moment, drying their faces and hands on the sacking Sukey had given them. They stood in the kitchen doorway, naked except for their torn trousers, arms crossed over their scrawny chests and shivering in the spring breeze.

Emmaline could hardly stand looking at them. It had been one thing to stop them on the streets. It was another to watch them work.

"Sit yourselves down," Cook said, placing a bowl of oatmeal in front of each boy. They dived into the hot mush, their elbows crooked high, awkwardly in the air, shoveling the spoonfuls in so fast that by the time Cook had made her way back to the sink, the bowls were empty. Emmaline took them to refill them.

"Nay, lass, all they get is one bowlful," Cook said. "There won't be enough for the rest of us otherwise."

"They can have mine," Emmaline said. She didn't feel she'd ever be able to eat again after seeing the sweeps at work. The boys, especially the little one, brought Tommy's image back in an aching rush. She wanted to put her arms around him, pretend, for the briefest moment, that it was her Tommy she was holding.

"I've already had a bun," Thomas said, in the next second.

"I'm not hungry," Sukey added.

Cook shook her head. "You'll only have them expecting to be fed this way elsewhere, and maybe they'll get nothing but a cuff 'round the ear," she said. "But suit yourself."

Emmaline filled the bowls, and, when Cook wasn't looking, crumbled grains off the sugarloaf and sprinkled them over the top of the porridge.

The boys didn't eat quite as quickly this time.

"What are your names?" Emmaline asked.

The smaller boy looked at the older one, who gave a slight nod and said, "I'm Tip."

"An' I'm Barker," the little one said around a mouthful of sweetened oatmeal.

"Parker?" Emmaline asked.

"Nah. Barker. Cos o' me cough." To demonstrate, he gave a series of short hacking barks that cackled like distant gunshots. Emmaline saw that there was a faint shine of pinkish spittle on his lips. "I can keep up me barkin' all night," he announced, "can't I, Tip?"

"Aye," the other boy agreed. "Don't let none of us get any sleep some nights."

Emmaline glanced at Cook, who had her back to them, then took two jam buns from the basket on the end of the table, and pushed one toward each boy. "Do you know a sweep named Tommy?" she asked. "He's my brother."

Tip snatched his bun and held it against his chest. "I knowed a Tommy once," he said. "But he growed too big for climbin'. Ain't seen him since." He put the bun to his mouth and licked the crusty, buttered top.

"This Tommy can't hear, or talk," Emmaline said, her eyes never leaving the older boy's face.

"Nah," he said. "Don't know none such as that."

"I does," Barker said, swallowing. He'd stuffed his whole bun into his mouth, and jam squished out onto his lips.

Emmaline gave him another bun, moving slowly, afraid that if she made any sudden movement the boys might be off. "You do? You know a boy named Tommy that can't hear or speak?"

Barker took another big bite, and as he swallowed too quickly, choked and started to cough. Wet bits of the yeasty bun flew across the table. Cook made a sound of disgust in her throat, and Barker's head swiveled toward the door, as if gauging the distance if he had to run for it.

"It's all right," Emmaline said. She smelled the brassy odor of blood on the boy's breath. "Never mind that. I'll clean it up in a minute. Tell me where I can find him, the boy Tommy."

Barker shrugged. "Don' know. I just seed him yestiday. Up on Little Cherry Road. You seed him too, Tip."

Emmaline stood, unaware that she was doing so, her heart hammering.

"Nah," Tip said, shaking his head, putting out his tongue to touch the top of the bun again. "That ain't Tommy. It's just Toby. An' he can hear n'all, but he gots the harelip, so he can't talk so good. Does I get another bun, too?"

Emmaline sat down again. There was a thudding in her temples. She gave Tip another bun.

"All right, lads. Off you go, now," Cook said, holding out a few coins to the boys. "Pick up your bags from the court."

"Will you have us back?" Barker asked, his eyes on the remaining buns.

"Not if you expect to be fed like kings," Cook said, snatching up the basket and holding it against her round belly, as if the boys might grab it and run. "You're doing them no favor by spoiling them, Emmaline," she said.

"If you see someone like the climber I told you about," Emmaline said, following the boys into the courtyard, "will you come back and tell me? I'll give you each a tuppence, if you do."

Tip eyed her solemnly. "I'll look out for him," he said. "You should go over to the May Day parade wot comes down through here in a few weeks."

"Why?" Emmaline asked, as the boy stood looking up at her, the two buns still cradled tenderly against his dirty chest.

"There's a Jack-in-the-Green, and the sweeps and milkmaids from all over follow him. Maybe you'll see your bruvver there. Now hoist both bags, Barker. I got me buns to carry," he said, importantly.

The smaller boy managed to get both bags of soot up onto his shoulders, and together they straggled out of the courtyard.

Emmaline heard the loud clang of the gate behind them.

BRANDY JACK

here's a smell of rain," Emmaline said, raising her nose, eyeing the clouds.

"Anytime now, I suspect," Thomas said, leaning on his fork.

Emmaline was working beside Thomas in the garden. They were forking over a hard patch to plant some herbs that Thomas had bought in a stall in the Haymarket. There was a gust of fresh wind, and the rain started – just tiny spits at first, but quickly growing stronger. Emmaline ducked inside the potting shed, and Thomas followed. "It should blow over soon," he said.

"Do you want some?" Emmaline asked, opening a wrapped package of the supper she'd brought out to the potting shed with her: hard biscuits and dried apricots and almonds, and a thick slice of cake, solid with fruit.

Thomas shook his head.

Emmaline ate a few apricots and then folded up the rest of the food into the small square of cotton and put it on a shelf beside a collection of rusted garden forks. On the potting table were wire and twine, and a pot of nasturtium seeds hard as gravel. The sound of the rain grew louder, beating against the wooden roof in staccato bursts. The wind blew in through the open door, sliding under Thomas's loosened shirt and teasing his hair.

"How is it you come to read, Thomas?" Emmaline asked, running her fingers through the nasturtium seeds.

"My mother taught me. You said your father taught you?"

"Yes. I learned a bit in the Sunday school in our village, but it was mainly my father. We read together all the time. He died, when I was ten." She wasn't sure why she added that. She wanted to hear about Thomas's family, but didn't want to pry. "But my mother's back in Tibbing," she told him. The seeds left a silty dust on her dirty fingers. She wiped her hands on her apron.

"I sometimes dream that I'm still a boy at the workhouse, and my mother's come back for me," Thomas said, picking up the broken, jagged end of a hoe and holding it out in the rain.

"She's alive, then?"

Thomas shrugged, studying the wet splintered wood. "Maybe. When she left me at the workhouse, she said she'd be back. I was to stay there, because then she'd know where to look for me. But after about a year, I knew she wasn't coming."

Silence stretched. The rain grew stronger, and with it came the smell of wet, freshly turned soil from the garden. It smelled like the fields behind the shop. Emmaline hadn't smelled it for all those years in Tibbing, where there was only brick and cobblestones, the dark smoke from the factory chimneys coating everyone's nostrils. Now the scent from the tiny patch of garden filled her with yearning.

"You can only wait for someone so long," Thomas said. "Then you know it's time to move ahead."

Emmaline saw the glisten of moisture tracing the silken lines of a spiderweb in the corner beside the doorway. "A year is a long time. Tommy's only been gone a few months."

Thomas swung the hoe harder. "I wasn't talking about your brother," he said.

"Did you ever think you might . . . well, make inquiries? Maybe your mother did go back, and when you were gone, she didn't know where to look. Maybe it's your turn to go and search for her."

Emmaline saw the tips of his ears grow a dull red. She wanted to take it back, reel in the words like a kite on a string.

Thomas turned to face her, and she saw that the color was spreading now, scalding his face and neck. "Like you've done? Is that what you're really saying? That she shouldn't have just left me there, that I shouldn't have let her, that I should have looked for her? Are you telling me I'm a coward? That I'm not as brave as you?"

She took a step toward him. "Of course not. I'm sorry, Thomas. It's a completely different situation. I —"

Thomas hurled the hoe with startling strength out into the rain, into an elderberry bush growing beside the shed. A tiny hidden lark flew straight up in alarm, and then, small wings fluttering, dipped low and disappeared, darting this way and that as if looking for a path through the raindrops.

Thomas walked away from the potting shed, and Emmaline.

"Please come back," Emmaline called. "I said I was sorry. Please. I didn't mean anything by it."

But Thomas disappeared around the side of the house that led to the street. His white shirt, Emmaline saw, just as he turned the corner, was already soaked through, so that it clung to the strong curve of his shoulders.

The next Sunday afternoon in Steeplemount, Emmaline saw a climbing boy crouched on the broad stone steps of a church. As she approached him, the doors of the church opened, and a man and woman, the woman carrying a small nosegay of violets, emerged. A handful of people followed them. They were all chattering happily.

Emmaline realized the couple must have just been married. Cook had told her at dinnertime that there would be a number of weddings that afternoon, for during certain times of the year – Advent and Easter – some parishes would marry poor couples without a fee.

The climbing boy rushed to the bride and groom, bowing low in front of them. The bride kissed her own fingertips and then touched the boy's head, while the groom gingerly shook the boy's hand. Then the man reached into his pocket and gave the boy a coin. As the climbing boy turned to leave, a small tight grin on his face as he looked down at the copper on his palm, Emmaline stepped in front of him, holding out a raisin tart. She'd learned that food was the only way to get close to a climbing boy.

The boy looked at the tart, then at Emmaline, his fist closing on the money he'd just earned by letting the newly married couple wish on him for good luck.

"If you'd like this tart, you have to answer my questions," Emmaline said to him.

The boy shoved his coin into his pocket. He glanced over his shoulder nervously, looked back at the tart, and then up at her.

"I'm looking for my little brother, Tommy. He's very small."

"All climbing boys is small." The boy's voice was raspy, as if he had something lodged in his throat. He stepped closer to the tart. Emmaline saw him sniffing for a whiff of the treacle and raisins.

"I know. But Tommy's really quite tiny. And he can't hear – he's deaf."

The boy's eyebrows knotted. "Well, I knows of a boy what can't hear nuthin. Climbs for Brandy Jack."

Emmaline reached out to clutch the boy's knobby shoulder. "Is his hair almost white? Lots of curls?"

"Can't tell from hair color," the boy said, hunching his shoulder slightly, as if the pressure of Emmaline's hand hurt his bones. "Us all got us hair shaved off, so's it don't get caught."

"I know. I just thought –"

"But it ain't him. His name ain't Tommy," the boy told her, and disappointment, sharp as a hot pointed stick, plunged through her chest in one quick clean stroke.

"Are you sure? How many deaf climbing boys would there be?" she asked. Without waiting for an answer, she repeated her question, just to make absolutely certain. "You're sure that – what did you say he was called? Brandy Jack? You're sure his deaf boy's name isn't Tom, or Tommy? Thomas?"

"I told you, it ain't him," the boy insisted, squirming under her grip. "Gimme the tart. I answered yer questions."

Emmaline opened her hand, seeing that her palm and the undersides of her fingers, where she'd held the boy's shoulder, were smudged with oily soot. She gave him the tart.

Balancing it carefully in his hand, the boy backed away from her, his eyes never leaving her face, as if afraid she might try to grab him again. "His name weren't none of those. It's Moony. At least we calls him Moony."

"Why?"

"Cause all we knows is his name starts with *M*."

"*M*? The letter *M*?"

The boy shook his head, scattering a dirty halo of gray dust around his shaved skull. "Don't know me letters. But he's crazy after lookin' at the moon, and at first, when we tried to figger wot he was called, evertime someone asked him anything, all he'd say was *M*."

Unexpectedly he turned and darted away. Emmaline stood as if rooted to the spot, seeing, from the back, the wings of the boy's small shoulder blades, and the way one of his bare feet turned out at a sharp angle, putting the weight on his heel, as if it hurt to put it down flat.

"Wait!" she cried, running after him. "Wait! That's him. It's Tommy, my brother. Take me to where I can find him."

The boy didn't turn his head, but kept running.

"It's him," Emmaline called, her breath coming in short gasps. "It's Tommy."

The deaf climbing boy wasn't saying the letter *M*. He was saying *her* name – Em, and he was watching the moon, the way Emmaline had taught him.

"Please. Take me to him," Emmaline yelled as she turned a corner after the boy. Finding herself on a street thronged with people and horses and carts, she ran in circles around the square block of buildings, but the boy had disappeared, like a puff of smoke.

As the light began to fade, Emmaline walked home slowly. *Brandy Jack.* At least she had something now.

I'LL DO AS I PLEASE

ater that week, as Cook, Sukey, Thomas, and Emmaline sat in the kitchen having their midday meal, Eugene stormed in. He had returned a few days earlier. Cook jumped up in alarm, her fork clattering to the floor.

"Master Eugene! Is something amiss with your father?"

"Yes, something's very wrong. And I'll tell you what it is, shall I, Cook? It's that someone from down here has been reading to him, wasting work hours sitting in the comfort of my father's bedroom, reading to him. He told me so himself, although he wouldn't tell me who. Getting paid for hard work, and instead reading. Reading!" He spit out the word. "Is it you, Paddy? Or is there someone else, besides the Irish, who can read?" he demanded, slurring.

Sukey widened her eyes at Emmaline, warning her to say nothing. Emmaline ignored her. "I can, Sir," she said, rising to stand beside Cook. "And it's me who's been reading to your father. At his request."

"What's this house coming to?" Eugene shouted. "First a dirty Irish, and now the scullion? What about you, Sukey? Can you read, too?"

Sukey shook her head. "I can spell my name, and Emmaline and Thomas's. I learnt that lately. But other than that, no. I might be a fast learner at some things, Master Eugene, but reading ain't one of 'em."

Eugene ignored her. "Is it that there's some new movement underground that I don't know about? Are the masses becoming educated, now?" He clumsily ripped out the printed cravat that had been tucked inside his open-necked shirt, throwing it on the table. "You should concern yourself only with your hands. All it brings is trouble if you attempt to use your head for anything more than directing your hands. As for you," he said, suddenly reaching forward and pulling Thomas up by the collar, "you'll watch yourself around my father as well."

Before Thomas could make a sound, Emmaline said, "But I told you, it's me who's reading to your father. Thomas has nothing to do with it." She heard her own voice, high and thin, like glass. "So there's no reason to take up with Thomas. And since Master Thorn is the true master in this house, and he wants me to . . ."

Eugene's face boiled scarlet, and in the next instant, he swung his fist and punched Thomas squarely in the face. Thomas fell to the ground, his hand over his nose. Blood poured through his fingers as he scrambled to get to his feet.

"Now what do you think of your outspoken little tart?" Eugene sneered. "Need a girl to stand up for you? We'll see about that. I've ways to take her down a notch or two."

Thomas straightened his shoulders, moving his hand away from his face. Blood poured over his lips and down his neck, pooling along his collar. "I wouldn't touch Emmaline, or Sukey again, if I were you, Sir," he said, his voice muffled by the blood in his throat.

Eugene gave a haughty laugh. "I'll do as I please, boy, and there's nothing you can do about it. All I have to do is this," he snapped his fingers, "and you're out on the street."

"I believe Cook speaks to your father about the staff, Sir," Thomas said, moving closer, so that he was face-to-face with Eugene, who was a good two inches shorter. "I'll say it again, Sir. You can express your anger to me, but I'd prefer it if you left the girls alone." Even though his words were controlled, there was a tight anger in his voice.

Emmaline saw Eugene swallow, his Adam's apple moving in his throat like a sharp plum. That one tiny movement made her swell with hope and pride. Eugene was afraid of Thomas.

"My father is old and sick," Eugene said, quietly now, through clenched teeth. "And when he's gone, I'll be the one master here. Then we'll see how this house runs."

Thomas stayed where he was, and Eugene stepped back, glancing at Emmaline. "Laundry drudges and kitchen scullions are ten a penny, and she'll be the first to go. Until then, which, mark my words, will be any day now, I won't bother wasting my time down here," Eugene said then. "You're all useless. Useless," he repeated, then stormed to the side door, stumbling on the step, and up into the courtyard.

The kitchen seemed larger with him gone.

"Dear, oh deary me," Cook said, into the quiet room, while Sukey helped Thomas, mopping at his bleeding face with Eugene's cravat.

Emmaline thought about Master Thorn, knowing that what Eugene had said was true. He wouldn't last much longer, not with the bloody cough and wasting body. And then, as Master Eugene had said, he'd be in charge.

But Emmaline knew she was close to finding Tommy, now that she had discovered the true name of the man he worked for. She just needed a few more mornings. And then she'd have Tommy and be gone – far from Thorn House, and from Master Eugene's threats.

But she'd also be leaving old Master Thorn, with his kindly ways, and Sukey, who was starting to show definite signs of the baby she was carrying.

And she'd be leaving Thomas.

That night Emmaline awoke with a start. She'd been dreaming of Master Eugene, his hands covered with blood, although whose blood she didn't know. She sat straight up in her bed.

Sukey was asleep. Emmaline used the edge of the soft coverlet to wipe her forehead and neck, slick with sweat from the night terror. Then she lay back down, staring at the outline of her uniform on its nail on the back of the door. Soon she became aware that there were no snores coming through the wall from Cook's room. She got out of bed and put her ear to the wall, but could hear only a very soft murmuring. *Is Cook all right?* There had never been a night, except for those first two after she'd arrived at Thorn House, when she was so deep in sleep that probably even the ceiling falling in wouldn't have woken her, when she hadn't been aware of Cook's throaty rumble.

Rising, she opened the door and stepped out into the hall. Cook's door was partly open, throwing a slender triangle of candlelight onto the floor. Emmaline moved closer, listening to the murmur that she'd heard through the wall.

She took another step, and through the narrow opening between the door and the jamb, she could see Cook sitting on her bed, her unwound braids hanging in two long, thin gray plaits over the front of her nightdress. She wasn't alone.

Master Eugene was sitting on the floor at Cook's feet, his head in her lap. Cook ran her fingers through his hair, slowly, in a comforting way, as a mother might to a small child. She patted his shoulder, and whispered, "Now, now, I know."

Emmaline watched, her mouth open.

Eugene lifted his head, saying, "You're the only one who ever understood me, Cookie." He wiped his eyes on his arm. "I'm too old for this nonsense," he said. "It was one thing to come to you when I was a child, but –"

"None of us are too old for a spot of mothering," Cook said, and continued to stroke Eugene's hair.

Emmaline slowly backed away to her own room, closed the door and got into bed, pulling the covers to her chin. She tried to remember the last time her own mother had touched her as tenderly as Cook had Eugene.

A VISIT FROM THE SOLICITOR

Emmaline was almost caught by Cook the next morning. She had been so determined to find Brandy Jack that she had ignored the chiming of the bells until it had gone almost seven. She tore back to Thorn House, rushing into the kitchen. The table was set and the food sat on it.

Sukey was soaking cleaning rags in borax in the scullery sink, and didn't greet her. Thomas was intently sharpening a small kitchen knife with a whetstone.

Cook glowered at her. "Just where have you been?" she demanded. "We're waiting to start morning prayers. Our breakfast has gone cold."

"I . . . I went out for a walk," Emmaline answered.

"Don't let me catch you leaving this house without permission again. Is that clear?"

"Yes, Cook," Emmaline said, thinking, *I won't let you catch me. I won't let myself forget the time again.*

Later that morning Sukey opened the laundry door. "Emmaline! You're to come into the kitchen. Cook needs you. Maggie, you're to dismiss Emmaline for an hour."

Maggie frowned as she shook out a clean bedsheet. The heavy cotton made the sound of snapping wings. "So now she's to leave for an hour in the morning, as well as the afternoon? How am I to manage on my own?"

"Come, Emmaline," Sukey said.

"What is it?" Emmaline asked, wringing her wet apron as they hurried across the courtyard.

"There's company coming." Sukey's cheeks had high color. "It's the first time in . . . oh, must be over two years now. Master Thorn told Cook that he'll be needing service in the sitting room, and he wants you there. Thomas is helping him dress right now."

"What does he want me for?"

"I don't know. All I know is what Cook told me."

As they hurried inside, Cook arranged an assortment of small cakes on a silver tray. "Run upstairs and put on your Sunday dress. You look a right treat in it," Cook said. "And comb through your hair. Don't you have a hair ribbon you can lend her, Sukey?"

"I do, Cook."

"Then get it for her. Now go on, both of you."

"Yes, Cook," Emmaline and Sukey said.

"And hurry back, Emmaline. You'll have to be in the sitting room in ten minutes. Sukey, you open the windows and air it out." As the girls left the kitchen, they heard her talking to herself: "Goodness. If I'd only had some warning. We should have had fresh flowers. I wonder if we should have a small fire? No, 'tis too warm for that. When were those curtains last taken down and given a good beating? Dear me. Should I add more cakes?"

Eight minutes later Emmaline was on her way through the foyer to the sitting room. She had changed into her good dress, and dipped the end of the scarlet ribbon Sukey had loaned her into the water jug. She used the damp ribbon to rub some extra color into her cheeks and lips. Thomas was standing by the front door, ready to open it. He had on a footman's livery: a white shirt covered by a short black jacket with a braided trim, dark green velvet knee breeches, and white silk stockings. Emmaline had never seen him wearing anything so grand. She was taken aback to see how handsome Thomas was, in well-fitting clothes.

"Where's Master Eugene?" Emmaline whispered.

"He's away until tonight," Thomas whispered back. "Master Thorn told me to inform him the next time the young master would be gone for the day. As soon as I reported to him about Master Eugene's plans, he sent me running with a note, to an office on Evenside Road, telling me to wait for an answer. When I brought it back, he started all this preparation."

Emmaline said, "You're looking quite fine, Thomas." Without giving him a chance to reply, she slipped into the sitting room.

"Good morning, Master Thorn," she said.

"Good morning to you, Emmaline," Master Thorn answered, turning his dark glasses in her direction. He was wearing a deep blue morning coat and black pants. He had been freshly shaved, and Thomas had brushed his thick white hair. Even though Thomas had obviously done his best, Master Thorn's face appeared to be sinking inward, and his skull showed clearly under the thin ashen skin. Emmaline had to look away. "You appear well today, Sir," she lied.

Master Thorn turned his head toward her, and his lips attempted a smile. "Not a word of the truth. Nothing shy about you, is there, girl?"

"I believe praise does no good without being spoken," Emmaline told him. "My father always said that."

"Well, I can't see you well enough to return the compliment, but if I go by your voice, I'm sure you're looking quite a picture yourself," the old man said. Without warning, he coughed so sharply that Emmaline's lungs ached. Then he fumbled in his pocket for a handkerchief, and wiped his mouth with it. As he pulled it away, Emmaline saw a shock of brilliant red on the cloth. There was also blood smeared on his chin.

"Let me help you, Sir," she said, and took the handkerchief from him and gently wiped his chin. Then she folded the handkerchief so that blood was hidden, and tucked it back into his pocket.

"Please, sit beside me," he said, patting the seat of the chair to his right.

"Thank you, Sir," Emmaline answered, and then sat, her ankles neatly crossed, and her hands folded in her lap. She looked around the faded but attractive sitting room, and, knowing Master Thorn couldn't see, let what she considered to be a gracious smile hover on her lips.

Before long Thomas brought a man into the sitting room.

"Mr. Paltron, Sir," he announced, then stepped back out, shutting the door.

"Come in, come in, Donald," Master Thorn said, half rising and extending one hand. His other hand gripped the armrest, white and trembling violently with the effort of trying to stand.

Mr. Paltron shook Master Thorn's hand. "Good to see you again, Anthony," he said.

"And you. This is Emmaline Roke," Master Thorn said, heavily lowering himself back to the seat. "My assistant for today. She'll do any reading for me, and act as witness to my signature."

Emmaline knew she should rise and curtsy, as was custom for anyone from below stairs, but something made her stay in her seat. She extended her hand to Mr. Paltron as Master Thorn had. "Miss Emmaline Roke," she repeated, unnecessarily.

Mr. Paltron took her hand in his and bowed over it.

Emmaline held her lips together tightly. She knew if she let out even the smallest smile, it would turn into a huge grin. A gentleman bowing over her hand!

"Mr. Paltron is my solicitor," Master Thorn said, turning his head in Emmaline's direction. "He's here to straighten out a bit of business."

"Shall we get started?" the lawyer said. He sat at the kneehole desk and put a flat leather case on it, opened it, and sorted through his papers.

"Ring for tea, would you, Emmaline?" Master Thorn asked, and Emmaline went to the braided silk rope hanging beside the door and pulled it.

"I've brought the papers you indicated, Anthony," the solicitor said, as Emmaline returned to her seat. "It will be a small matter to make the changes and have them witnessed."

The sitting room door opened. Emmaline was surprised that Sukey would have arrived so quickly with the tea tray.

But it was Eugene.

"What's all this?" he said, taking in the scene.

"Eugene? I thought you wouldn't be home until tonight," Master Thorn said, frowning.

"Obviously. I changed my mind. Good day to you, Mr. Paltron. Is there some business afoot that I've not been made aware of?" His eyes flicked in Emmaline's direction. "And is there a reason that the laundry drudge is all trumped up and sitting in Mother's chair?"

Emmaline got to her feet. "I'm sorry. I wasn't told about the chair. I –"

Eugene interrupted. "The matter of the chair isn't important. The fact that you are here, with my father and his solicitor, is what is distressing."

"She's being my eyes," Master Thorn said. "She can read, and understands what she reads. I needed someone to help me."

Eugene crossed the room to stand in front of his father. "What is it that you need help with? Could you not have waited for me to return?"

Mr. Paltron noiselessly set a paper over the one on the desk in front of him, but Eugene caught the movement from the corner of his eye, and turned back to the solicitor.

"Mr. Paltron? Is there something here that I should be aware of? Are you hiding something from me?"

Donald Paltron didn't answer.

"You know that he doesn't have all his wits," Eugene continued, as if his father weren't in the room with them. "Quite mad, at times. I wouldn't take into consideration anything he might have to say to you."

Mr. Paltron stood. "Perhaps we'll finish this another day, Anthony," he said to the old man.

"Now see here," Eugene said, pushing his chest forward and stepping up to Mr. Paltron. Emmaline recognized the same threatening stance and tone he'd used with Thomas in the kitchen. Except now she knew it was a bluff. "As my father's sole offspring and heir apparent, I'm entitled to know what the old man's up to. You can't let him make any decisions without my approval, for he can't be held accountable."

"That will do, Eugene," Master Thorn said, attempting to rise from his chair. Emmaline put her hand under his elbow, helping him up. "Although you may not consider me of sound mind and body, I can assure you that most days I'm quite aware of everything that goes on in this house. Everything," he added, emphasizing the word. Then the coughing started.

The impact of the deep coughs forced him to slump back into his chair, and Emmaline tried to thump his back the way she had many times before, but it didn't seem to help this time. He coughed and coughed, with terrible, choking sounds, managing to get his handkerchief up to his mouth to catch the blood that surged out.

"Shall I send for the physician?" Donald Paltron asked, wringing his hands.

"No need for that," Eugene called, not moving from his spot. "Come now, Father, that's enough. Take deep breaths. For God's sake, girl, get him to his room. You should never have allowed him out of bed. Have you no sense at all?" He turned and charged through the sitting room door, bumping into Sukey with her full tea tray. "Look out, you fool," he bellowed, jumping back so milk slopping out of the pitcher wouldn't wet his clothes. In the next instant, the front door slammed.

Sukey set the tray on the nearest table, and rushed to help Emmaline with Master Thorn. Thomas joined them, and between the three of them, with Donald Paltron following anxiously, they got Master Thorn upstairs and propped against pillows on his bed. Emmaline held a glass of Madeira to his blue-tinged lips, and the old man swallowed a few sips, but immediately brought it up with the next round of coughing.

Blood and Madeira splattered the front of Emmaline's dress. She ignored it, wiping Master Thorn's face with the damp rag Sukey handed her.

Eventually Master Thorn grew calm, and he waved his hand weakly. "Thank you, my child. Thank you for your patience with an old man. I expect I'll be all right now. Where did Donald get to?"

"I'm still here, Anthony," Mr. Paltron said, a worried look on his face. "You need immediate medical treatment, old friend. I'm going to send for the physician. I insist."

"Fine, fine," Master Thorn said. "But first, we need to finish this business."

"Surely not now, Anthony. I'll come another –"

But Anthony Thorn cut him off. "We'll do it now, Donald. Have you the papers from downstairs? It's important, and I won't chance not getting it done before . . ."

He didn't finish the sentence. "Emmaline, you stay and witness my signature," he added.

Sukey and Emmaline exchanged a glance, and Sukey left.

"Do you think he'll die soon, Sukey?" Emmaline asked later, when she'd come down to the kitchen.

Sukey shrugged. "We all has our time to die, Emmaline. It does seem Master Thorn's is coming. Let's hope he hangs on for a bit, although it appears to me that his heavenly future with his lady and son is a sight more sweet than what he's got now. It's our future wot I'm worried about, for it won't go well on any of us once the old man is in his eternal rest."

Emmaline thought of Eugene's words in the kitchen only a few days earlier, then went upstairs to change out of her soiled dress.

YELLOW FOG

he fog was thick as wool, a still, yellowy mist creating an eerie calm as she strained to see. Even the solemn ringing of the church bells was muted. The damp air filled Emmaline with an unnerving sense of danger. Every person that came toward her was menacing as a mythical serpent or dragon, slowly undulating, dreamlike. She turned around and retraced her steps back to Thorn House, knowing any further searching would be impossible.

She was waiting for the pot of tea to steep, disappointed and frustrated, when Cook came in. Surprised to see her, as it was still a good half hour before even Sukey would come downstairs, Emmaline was glad she'd come home from her search before the usual time. "You're down early," she said. "Is Sukey ill?"

"No," Cook said, dabbing at her eyes with a handkerchief. She pulled out a chair and lowered herself heavily. Emmaline saw that her uniform was buttoned unevenly, one edge of her collar tucked in.

"What's wrong, Cook? Why are you crying?"

"It's the old master," Cook said. "He's gone."

"Gone?"

"Passed on, not more than half an hour since. Thomas and I were with him; he rang the bell in the middle of the night, and Thomas went to see what he needed. He fetched me when he saw the state of the poor fellow. We spent his last few hours with him, although he wasn't aware of us, I'm sure. Thomas is still there."

Tears spilled out of her small eyes, running down her plump, wrinkled cheeks. "I knew, when Thomas woke me, that this fog was a bad omen. It's unnatural for this time of year, to be so thick – and this odd yellow – with May nearly upon us. And I went over all funny just before I went to bed last night. At first I thought maybe it was only my lumbago, starting up." She mopped her face with her apron. "He was a good man," she murmured.

Emmaline's own eyes were smarting. She was glad she had slipped into Master Thorn's room before she went to bed, saying good night to him and making sure he was warm enough. As she smoothed his blanket over his chest, he had given her a small smile and weakly laid his hand over hers.

She poured Cook a cup of tea and set it in front of her.

"A good man," Cook repeated, putting her hands around the cup. "Eugene will take this hard."

"What do you mean?" Emmaline asked, askance. "Eugene? He doesn't seem to care about anyone but himself."

Cook shook her head. "I see that you've no pity for him, and I can understand why. But he's lonely, Emmaline. He drinks and carries on because he feels useless. He was never good at school, and couldn't hope to go into law like his father – another disappointment to Master Thorn. He learned to use his charm to get what he wants, but when his charm doesn't work he turns nasty, and has got into the habit of taking what he wants by force."

Emmaline longed to tell Cook about Sukey at that moment, but before she had enough time to decide if it would hurt or help, Cook stood up. "Now let's both get to work. There'll be much to do, with a funeral. And idle hands don't help the troubled mind."

The moment passed.

The day after the funeral Emmaline stayed with Cook after breakfast. She was restless, picking up dishes and setting them down, looking out the window, twisting her hair. She'd been close, so close to finding Tommy before her search had been disturbed – first by the fog, the day of Master Thorn's death, and then the days following, when Cook had them all up early to cook and clean and run errands in preparation for the funeral. Emmaline hadn't dared to take the chance of being caught by Cook again.

Her head ached from frustration at not being able to search for Tommy and from the tears she'd shed over Master Thorn the day before, both at the funeral and later, by herself, out in the potting shed. Thomas had found her there, and without a word put his arms around her. The beating of his heart against Emmaline's cheek grew stronger, faster, and his arms tightened.

She wanted to stand that way forever, not thinking, not worrying. But the image of Tommy wouldn't leave her. "I don't think I can bear it much longer," she'd said to him, her voice muffled against his shirt.

"Bear what?" he'd asked, reluctantly pulling away to look into her face.

"I almost have Tommy. I can feel it, Thomas. All I need is another day or two, and I'll find him."

Thomas's face lost something, some color, or expression, although Emmaline couldn't put her finger on it. "And then you can leave," he said.

Emmaline had nodded, opening her mouth to say more, wanting Thomas to put his arms around her again, because something about the way he said it – *And then you can leave* – sent a rush of coldness through her. But before she had a word out he turned and left her there, among the cobwebs and rusted garden tools and broken pots, her mouth hanging open like a fool. He hadn't looked at her again since.

"Cook?" Emmaline said now.

"Aye, lass?"

"I know this isn't a good time, but –"

"I know." Cook went to a drawer in the kitchen and took out a locked box. Using a key she carried on a string around her neck, she unlocked it and fished out some coins, giving them to Emmaline. "Thirtieth of April. Here you are. Your monthly wages."

Emmaline took them, putting them into her apron pocket. "Thank you. But that wasn't what I was about to ask you."

"Spit it out, my girl," Cook said, locking the box and returning it to the drawer, then going back to the steak and kidney pie she had been making.

"Well, tomorrow is May Day." Emmaline hadn't forgotten what Tip had told her, about the sweeps at the May Day parade.

Cook finished placing pastry over the top of the pie. "Why, so it is. What with all that's been going on, I haven't given it a thought. And what does May Day have to do with you?"

"I was hoping . . . I wanted to go to the parade."

Cook's eyebrows knotted, and she crimped the edges of the pastry all around. "First of May. It is a joyous day."

"So I was wondering if I could get an hour or two off. You can dock my pay."

"I was once crowned Queen of the May," Cook said, brushing the top of the pie with beaten egg. "Not here, but in my own town. You wouldn't dream it now, would you, but I was quite a looker in my day. Had young men lining up to court me, after I was presented with my hawthorn crown."

Emmaline tried to imagine the heavyset old woman, with the thick prickle of hair on her upper lip and jiggling triple chin, as a young woman – eyes shining, a full mouth of teeth – looking forward to what was to come.

Cook leaned on her elbows on the floury table and gazed toward the window. Seeing her dreamy expression reminded Emmaline of her mother, when she talked about better days. *I won't let this happen to me*, Emmaline thought. *Not just memories of a few glory days, and the rest of my life nothing but hard work and resentment. I'll never be like Cook, or like mother. I'll make better things happen.*

Emmaline touched Cook's arm. "Could I have an hour or two off, then, Cook?"

The old woman started. "Yes, I suppose so. I've given Maggie tomorrow off, partly in mourning, and partly for the holiday. So there'll be no work in the laundry, and the house is still clean after the preparation for the funeral guests. My. The old man did love May Day, in past times," she said. "He'd take Master Wallace, and later, Master Eugene, out to watch the parade every year."

As Emmaline left the kitchen, Cook was muttering quietly to herself.

ACCUSATIONS

he next morning, as Emmaline helped with the breakfast dishes, Cook told Sukey she would be serving an early dinner in the formal dining room. "It's Mr. Paltron coming. Master Eugene told me last night," she said, "and he wants a proper meal for the two of them. Thomas, you'll act as footman. Make sure your uniform is ready."

Thomas nodded.

Emmaline scrubbed at the copper bottom of the oatmeal pan. "But I'll still be on my way in the afternoon, Cook," she said. "Remember? You said I could go to the May Day parade this afternoon."

"Yes, yes, you can go once you've helped Sukey clean up from Master Eugene's dinner. But be back sharp, mind," she said. "Soon as it's over. No loitering about." She looked over at Sukey. "I expect you'll be wanting to go, as well."

Sukey shook her head. "No, thank you, Cook. I'll stay on here, as usual." She undid the neck button of her uniform, as if it were choking her. Emmaline saw that Sukey's face was puffy, and she knew the young woman's uniform was growing too tight.

Emmaline worked with Cook and Sukey to get the fancy meal of many courses prepared: cream of mushroom and leek soup, followed by red mullet with Cardinal sauce, and then a joint of roast beef basted with apple, sloe, and rosehip jelly, with side dishes of asparagus and peas. Next came plovers' eggs in aspic, and finally dessert, with a choice of chocolate cream or a marvelously rich syllabub.

While Sukey served, Emmaline scrubbed cooking and baking pans. She washed and dried the dishes from each course as Sukey brought them down and took up the next serving tray. She kept glancing toward the window, longing to be out of the scullery, afraid she'd miss part of the parade if the meal didn't end soon.

Finally the last of the dishes and silver were washed and dried and put away. Leaving Sukey and Cook in the kitchen, she went upstairs to put on her purple poplin and was sitting on her bed, slitting open the hem of her old dress. She planned to take the five pounds, hoping against hope that she would be able to use it this day.

The door banged open with a crash.

It was Eugene, his face a stiff mask of fury.

Emmaline jumped up, the old dress falling to the floor. "What is it, Master Eugene?"

"You sneaky little wench," he said, striding to her and grabbing her wrist. He twisted it, and Emmaline involuntarily whimpered. "Think you're smart, don't you?" he said, his face so close to hers that she could see his pupils dilate. There was a vein pulsing in his temple. Emmaline tried to remind herself that his father had just died, but try as she might, she couldn't summon an ounce of pity.

"What have I done?" she asked, but he twisted her wrist harder, and she squeezed her eyes with the pain.

"You know damn well what you've done, worming your way in here, stirring things up, changing the routine of the house. You had it all planned, didn't you?"

"Planned? I don't –"

Eugene dropped her wrist with a shove, and Emmaline was thrown off balance, coming down awkwardly on the edge of the bed.

"I might have known," Eugene said. "Thieving as well." He stooped and picked up her old dress from where it had fallen. One of the pound notes was exposed in the opened hem. He ripped the hem and pulled out the other four.

"What else have you stolen?" he said, his voice fierce.

"No. No, that's my money," Emmaline said.

"Five pounds? That's well over a year's wages for you. You wouldn't be working as a laundry drudge with five pounds to your name. You've crept into my room, and stolen it."

"No. No, Master Eugene. It's my money, to buy my brother back, from out of sweep service. I brought it with me."

Eugene's top lip curled in disgust. "I don't want to hear any more of your lies. What else have you stolen?" He pushed her aside and ripped back the coverlet, pulling the sheet off the mattress with such viciousness that the worn cotton ripped down the middle. Then he took her uniform off the nail and ran it through his hands, stopping to finger the hem of the dress and the apron.

Finding nothing, he looked around wildly, grabbing the two books that Mrs. Stanley had given her as she was leaving Tibbing off the washstand. The violence of his movements made the empty water pitcher teeter, and Emmaline instinctively grabbed for it, catching it before it hit the floor.

"These as well," Eugene said, triumphantly, holding up the slender volumes. "Probably stealing more of my father's books, and selling them."

"More? What do you mean?"

But Eugene pulled open the one drawer of the washstand with a rattle, and stared down at the coins Cook had given her that day, as well as those from March. He snatched them up.

"Those are my wages, Sir," Emmaline said, her voice firm and quiet. Her thumb traced the design on the handle of the heavy pitcher.

"Wages? You think you deserve wages, after all you've stolen from me?"

"I've stolen nothing," Emmaline said, never changing her tone.

"You liar," Eugene roared. "You know exactly what you've stolen," and he raised his open palm in the air.

But before he had the chance to strike her, Emmaline put her other hand around the pitcher, and with a force that she didn't know she possessed, smashed it into Eugene's face.

And then she ran.

JACK-IN-THE-GREEN

he raced for blocks and blocks, not thinking, just wanting to get away from Master Eugene, his eyes staring into hers like shards of pointed glass. And then, her chest burning and a cramp pulling in her left side, she let herself slow to a walk. The enormity of what she had done sank in, and the shaking started. She trembled so violently that she had to sit on the curb to calm herself. Now she had nothing – not a single penny, not even her shawl or two books. And she could never go back, for who knows what Master Eugene might get into his head to do to her.

What had brought him to her room in such a rage, and why did he go on about what she had stolen? *I can never go back.*

She thought of Sukey's sad smile, and her predicament. And she thought of Thomas, and the look on his face when he'd first seen her in her Aunt Phoebe's dress, and the quiet strength of him as he stood up to Master Eugene for her. She thought of him as a small boy, waiting, his eyes glowing as he watched and hoped for his mother to return to the workhouse to get him, and the glow fading with time and disappointment. She thought of his clean smell, and the way his arms had tightened around her in the potting shed, and the racing beat of his heart beneath her cheek.

And then she thought of Tommy.

Even though she no longer had any money, she still had to find him. To see him, and know he was alive. Once she found him, she would worry about how to get him back. Her only chance was the May Day parade.

She hurried to the High Street and joined the crush of people milling about to see the parade. She watched as three men suspended a set of hoops, wreathed and ornamented with an odd but eye-catching assortment of colorful ribbons, threaded flowers, cheap sparkling necklaces with broken clasps, dented and bent silver spoons, embroidered handkerchiefs, and all manner of cast-off finery, at a considerable height above the road. The hoops were secured by ropes tied to second floor drainpipes and window boxes of houses on opposite sides of the street. Emmaline watched as children attempted to throw balls over the hoops, trying not to hit the dangling objects, begging pennies from the watching crowd for the highest, cleanest throw. She smelled orange and spice from the cakes being sold by wandering merchants.

Suddenly there was a roar of mingled voices, and all heads turned to look up the street. The May Day parade was coming.

At the front of the procession was a girl about Emmaline's age, a milkmaid dressed all in white, her shining hair a beautiful red-gold. On her head was a crown of flowers woven into a slender looped branch of hawthorn in full bloom. She was Queen of the May, and her waves and smiles were met with male bellows of approval, and clapping and cheers from everyone.

Emmaline pushed her way to the front of the rows of spectators. There were all sorts of adults in costume in the procession, some as lords and ladies, some as fools or clowns. There were men carrying money boxes, and others blowing pipes and flutes. Dancers were dressed in clothes streaming with ribbons, so as they twirled they created bright fluttering wheels of color. Around them all scampered children, doing handstands or cartwheels, always landing on their feet with a hand toward the onlookers, hoping for a few pence to spend on a festive meal or bags of sweets to finish off the day in grand style.

The whole parade, Emmaline realized, was a form of begging from the crowd; she saw that many of those watching carried small purses of coins, which they gave out freely.

The parade continued, and finally, in the midst of all the music and shouts and laughter, Emmaline heard a high-pitched voice from near her elbow. "Here he comes!" the voice screeched, and she looked down to see the small boy beside her pointing up the street. "It's Jack-in-the-Green!"

A chorus of other children joined in, chanting, "Jack-in-the-Green, Jack-in-the-Green." As Emmaline watched, a tall leafy shape emerged from the middle of the crowd of paraders. It appeared to be a high wickerwork cage smothered in green branches, leaves, and flowers.

"What is it?" she shouted into the ear of the woman beside her.

"He's playing at being Summer," the woman yelled back. "Summer is brought in by Jack-in-the-Green every May Day."

As the strange spectacle drew nearer, Emmaline could see a pair of eyes, barely visible through a hole in the front of the cage, and, when she looked down, there were a pair of booted feet at the very bottom of the cage, walking along briskly. Following the Jack-in-the-Green were a whole gaggle of milkmaids and sweeps — the milkmaids clean and neat, all in white; the sweeps, in tattered black pants and shirts and dirty faces.

Emmaline stepped forward at the sight of the first sweep. But they were moving so fast, and there were so many of them, all with their hands out, darting in and out of the crowd, hoping for a penny here and there. Many were beating their brushes and tools, adding to the uproar. She couldn't see the ones on the other side of the Jack-in-the-Green, hidden by his bulk of greenery. She pushed right into the crowd of milkmaids and sweeps, trying to see the boys' faces, for there was no other way of recognizing any of them. From even a few feet away, they all looked the same.

"Tommy!" she shrieked, fully aware that even if he was here, he wouldn't hear her. "Tommy!" she called, pulling at little arms and tugging shoulders to turn one boy or another around. Would she even recognize him? He could have been any one of these boys with their shaved heads, their eyes too big and crusty in narrow faces. She stopped in the middle of the road, letting the children pass by her, one hand at her mouth.

And then she saw him. He was a good distance up the street, surrounded by other sweeps, and he must have been on the other side of the Jack-in-the-Green, or in the crowd begging, when he passed her. All she could see was the back of him, from the waist up, but she knew. She hadn't forgotten what he looked like at all, hadn't forgotten the length of his neck, the way one ear folded slightly in against his head, how he swung his left arm more than his right when he walked. She hadn't forgotten.

She struggled to make her way toward him. But at that moment, from behind her, came a swoop of little girls, the girls who sold matches and oranges and bootlaces on the streets. They were running, waving ribbons high over their heads, singing and shouting at the top of their lungs. She was swamped by them, and she had to make her way to the side of the street, or be knocked over.

"Wait!" she called, one arm stretched toward the spot in the street she had last seen Tommy. "Stop him! That boy," she screamed, although she knew no one could hear her in all the pandemonium.

The parade danced on, farther and farther up the street, with the spectators filing in to follow the performers and participants, forming another tight mass of bodies, blocking Emmaline's path even more.

She'd had her one chance to get her brother back, and she hadn't been quick or clever enough to grab him. After all this time, she'd finally seen him, and somehow had let him pass right by her.

And now he was gone again. Gone, just as he'd been gone that day, over two months ago, when she'd come home to the millworkers' row on Milk Court.

NOT A DREAM

mmaline ran down empty side streets, trying to stay parallel to the crowd, following its cacophony. Shouts of laughter and echoes of songs and the bleat of horns ebbed and flowed, and she kept going, trailing the sounds. But eventually they grew weaker, and afraid she had taken a wrong turn and was losing the parade, Emmaline stood still, her ears straining. She was bathed in sweat and her head was pounding. Light swam dizzily in front of her eyes, and she leaned over, trying to catch her breath.

There was a sudden high burst of laughter, followed by giggling. Emmaline raised her head, listening, then followed the sound. She came upon two young orange sellers, counting the coins they held in their hands. Hearing Emmaline's footsteps, they curled their fingers tightly over their money.

"Where has the parade gone?" Emmaline panted. "Which way did it go?"

"Oh, they've all gone 'ere and there," one of the girls answered cautiously, eyeing Emmaline and edging closer to her friend.

"It's over? Everyone from the parade has gone?" Emmaline cried.

"Aye," she said.

"Even the sweeps, all the little climbing boys?"

"We told you. They've all gone off," the girl answered, frowning.

"They might have gone over to Ashley Square," the other girl said. "You know, Bess. How that lady gives them climbers a feast on her lawn on a May Day? I seen it last year; you too. You was with me. Smashing, it looked. Food and drink for all them what's sweeps."

Emmaline drew a deep breath. "Where is Ashley Square?"

"Just down this street a ways," the girl told her, pointing, "then up to Chapel Lane, and turn toward the church. There's a graveyard, and the square is near to that."

"Thank you, thank you," Emmaline said, starting to run in the direction the girl had pointed.

"Ain't you got a penny for us, then, Miss?" one of the girls called after her.

"I'm sorry," Emmaline answered, over her shoulder, and kept going. She found Chapel Lane, running past a tall, spired church and a huge, quiet graveyard surrounded by a stone fence. From there she found Ashley Square. It was easy to spot the home of the woman supplying the meal to the sweeps. It was a tall grand house, the gates flung open, and there were dozens and dozens of climbing boys, more than a hundred, supervised by a clutch of men in black coattails and tall black hats. To Emmaline the master sweeps appeared to be a murder of crows, heads bobbing and tails twitching. She hated them all.

They were drinking from tall mugs, their laughter loud, while the boys were quietly stuffing themselves with jam sandwiches and small cakes. There were three men creating merry tunes with a squeezebox and fiddle and kettledrum, while a plump, smiling, middle-aged woman stood beside the tables laden with food, pouring what looked to be lemonade into tin cups and handing it out to the children.

Emmaline hurried through the gates. She realized how conspicuous she would be rushing into the middle of the boys, so she moved along the side of the high fence, stepping between hedges, her eyes anxiously scanning every small body. *If only they'd stop moving*, she thought. It was as if she were staring at a sea of small black swimming animals.

Then her heart stopped. He was standing by himself, near a flower bed, hurriedly packing a thick sandwich into his mouth, clenching a second in his other hand. As he chewed, he studied a gillyflower, its pink blossom swaying near eye level.

For a moment Emmaline couldn't move or breathe; it was as if her body were frozen. And then panic – the fear of losing him again – shivered down the length of her backbone. She made her way around the lawn so she could be even nearer, never taking her eyes off him. When she was as close as she could get without going right to him, she stood in the shadow of a sturdy oak, her back against its rough trunk. Eventually Tommy turned his head slightly, and she knew she was in his line of vision. She raised both arms over her head and waved.

The movement caught his attention. He turned his head in her direction and looked at her for a long moment. She made the *come* sign to him. He stopped chewing, the second sandwich falling from his fingers.

She made the sign again. Still clutching his half-eaten sandwich, he started toward her, slowly.

Sister? she saw him sign as he drew nearer, and she held out her arms. And then he dropped the sandwich and was running, crying, in his creaky little unused voice, "Em! Em!" He threw himself against her with such force that if she hadn't had the tree behind her, she would have fallen backwards.

Dream? he signed, pulling away from her suddenly and looking into her face. *Tommy dream more?*

He had been dreaming of her as she dreamed of him, night after night. *No*, she shook her head. "No, no, no, Tommy. You're not dreaming again. It's not a dream. It's me. I've come to get you," she whispered, leaning down to put her mouth against his ear, blowing into it the way she always had when she wanted to make him smile. His stubbled skull was bony and bristly against her cheek.

And then his arms twined around her neck so tightly that she could hardly breathe, and under her own arms she could feel his spine like a row of hard little buttons. He felt smaller and thinner than the last time she'd held him, back in Tibbing, even though he was months older. Now she could feel his body racked with violent shaking, and she knew he was weeping, as she was. They stayed that way for a long time, in the middle of the music and yelling and shouts of laughter of the master sweeps, and the boys' bodies milling about in front of them. Finally Tommy took his arms away and pulled back so he could see her face. He reached up and gently stroked her wet cheek. "Em," he whispered.

She nodded. *Fast*, she signed. *We go*, and holding his hand, she started back toward the gates, along the edge of the lawn, trying to keep them inconspicuous between the shrubs, the same way she'd come in. She was pulling Tommy behind her, walking quickly, not wanting to run and attract attention. The gate was ten feet away when she felt Tommy's hand stiffen in hers.

"Hoi! Hoi, you there, girl! Where'dya fink you're going with my boy?"

CAN YOU NOT HELP US?

he man was short and bowlegged. His wrinkled black coat and pants were shiny with wear. His face was shadowed with day-old whiskers, and Emmaline saw that he had only a few teeth.

"You're Brandy Jack?" Emmaline asked, keeping her voice steady.

"I might be. And who might you be?"

"I'm Tommy's sister. And I'm taking him with me," Emmaline said, thrusting her chin forward. "He was taken away under false pretenses."

Brandy Jack crossed his arms over his chest. "Is that so, now?" he said, grinning horribly at Emmaline, the remaining teeth little more than brown stubs. "And you're thinkin' you'll just walk off wiv him?"

Emmaline hesitated. "Well, no. I mean, I was going to buy him back."

Brandy Jack laughed, shooting flecks of saliva in Emmaline's face. "Buy him back? Buy the boy back?" he repeated, hooting hoarsely. "That's a good joke. Do you expect to hand me a few shillings and take a 'prentice with a number of good years left in him off me hands?"

"No. I had the five pounds that was paid for him."

"Five quid? It would be double that, for he's been profession-ally trained, and this lad has proved hisself right valuable. But I'll take your five pound in payment, and when you has the uvver five you could bring it round, and take the boy then." He put out his thick hand, the smile never leaving his face. "Aye. I suppose I could be persuaded to let him go for ten pound, five pound now." But Emmaline knew that even if she still had her money, and gave it to him, Brandy Jack would make sure she'd never find Tommy again.

"Well? Give it here," Brandy Jack said. "An' I'll see to it that your bruvver gets an extra rasher wiv his breakfast each morn." He gave her a bold wink.

"I don't believe you," Emmaline said, pulling Tommy against her.

"I knowed you didn't have no five quid," Brandy Jack said, and yanked Tommy's arm so hard that the boy's head jerked on his neck. "So you just shut yer pie-hole and get off wiv ya."

"NO!" Emmaline cried, grabbing the arm that held Tommy, and shaking it as hard as she could.

Brandy Jack didn't budge, looking down at her fingers grip-ping the sleeve of his coat. His face registered surprise, and then grew dark with anger. "Don't you get on yer high horse wiv me," he growled, and then gave her one hard swift cut across the chest with his other arm. Emmaline dropped to the ground, the air knocked out of her.

"What's this? What's going on?" Emmaline heard, and saw the woman who had been at the table hurrying across the lawn towards them. "There'll be no violence on my grounds. Heavens. Get up, my child. Up. Are you hurt? What's the trouble?"

Emmaline struggled to her feet. She opened her mouth to speak, but nothing came out except gasps.

"How do, Missus Freeman," Brandy Jack said, raising his hat, uncovering his balding, freckled head. "I'd like to report a disturbance, with this here girl. She's made me the victim, Missus Freeman," he went on, resettling his hat. "Yes. This young lady would steal away one of my best climbing boys. You should have her arrested, Missus, so you should."

In the fuss Tommy had been able to break away from Brandy Jack, and now he clung to Emmaline, his arms around her waist, his face buried in her skirt. She put her arms around his back, enclosing him.

Mrs. Freeman looked at the way Emmaline and Tommy were holding on to each other. "What is going on, young lady?" she asked.

Emmaline took a shaky lungful of air, breathing around the tightness. "He's my brother, Mrs. Freeman," she said. "He was taken from us, and I'm just getting him back."

"He was paid for right fair, with a signed contract," the man growled.

"Is this true, dear?" Mrs. Freeman asked.

"Well, yes, my mother signed a paper, but she couldn't read it. And she . . . she wasn't fit when she did it. She didn't understand what it was about, and that she was selling Tommy for five years, to be a climbing boy."

Mrs. Freeman shook her head. "I'm sorry, child. But I can't really demand that this . . . this *person*," she said, the word coming off her tongue as if it contained acid, "give the child back. It's not my place. But what I can do is contact the Child Labor Authority. They've created new rules about this form of deed – this entrapment – of very young children. I can take down your name, and that of your brother, and go down to their offices tomorrow, and start some form of action." Her tone changed, hardening, as she turned to Brandy Jack. "And I'm sure you're very aware of the more recent rules involving the age and treatment of sweeps, are you not, Mr. . . . ?"

The man ducked his head. "Just call me Hillis, Missus Freeman. I'm Master Sweep Hillis. And I don't know about no authority. I only does what I'm told, by those higher up." He put his hand around Tommy's arm and tried to drag him away from Emmaline. "I'll be thankin' ye kindly for givin' me boys a treat today, Missus," he said. "But it's time they were off. There's still light for a few more hours' work," he added.

Tommy clung to Emmaline, and she attempted to pry Brandy Jack's unwieldy fingers off her brother's scrawny arm. "Let him go," she cried. "Please, Mrs. Freeman, can you not help us? By tomorrow I'll never find him again. It's taken me months. Please," she repeated.

Watching Emmaline's face, Tommy let go of her and reached out and took Mrs. Freeman's plump white hand in his own small black one, beseeching her to help in the only way he could. With his other hand he made the sign for *please*, putting the back of his thumb against his lips. Emmaline was afraid Mrs. Freeman would pull her hand away in disgust, but instead she kindly covered Tommy's small cold hand with her own.

"He can't speak," Emmaline told her. "He's saying *please*. There, his thumb against his mouth, that's how he says *please*."

"I'm sorry, my child," Mrs. Freeman said to Tommy, shaking her head, and Emmaline saw tears in the woman's faded brown eyes. "I wish I could send you on home with your sister, back to your mother and father. I'm sure they would be so happy to see you, safely home at last." She gently disentangled her hand from his, even though Tommy had started a steady beat with his thumb against his lips. *Please. Please please please.*

Emmaline watched, aware that she was nodding in time with Tommy's thumb, but it was as if she were a puppet, with someone behind her pulling the strings in her neck to make her head move up and down. She didn't bother to correct Mrs. Freeman, to tell her that they had no father, and as for their mother – all Emmaline could see in her memory was the haggard, drugged look of her mother's face when she had stood forlornly in the middle of Aunt Phoebe's elegant bedchamber, her plaid shawl knotted carelessly across her chest.

Do we even have a mother now? And we'll never have a home together again, Emmaline thought.

Home, Tommy signaled to Emmaline, putting the fingers of both hands together and making a steeple. *Home*, he signed, as if picking up her thoughts, leaning against her skirt again. *Home*, he signaled one more time, watching his own hands, not looking up at Emmaline any longer. He sighed as he did it, a slow, stifled sigh, as if it pained his chest.

"So I'll just be taking my boy and rounding up the rest of 'em," Brandy Jack said, reaching toward Tommy again.

"Oh," Mrs. Freeman said suddenly, stepping closer, positioning herself in front of Brandy Jack, so that Tommy and Emmaline and the open gate were behind her. "I've just remembered something, Mr. Hillis. I believe I've forgotten to get out the whiskey I had put aside for the master sweeps today."

"Whiskey, you say?" Emmaline heard Brandy Jack echo.

"Yes. I know the ale kegs you gentlemen have been working on must be almost empty, and as an added treat I thought I'd bring out my husband's aged whiskey, from the cellar. Now look. Isn't that master sweep over there, no, the one near the table," she pointed, turning Brandy Jack by the shoulder, "isn't he tipping the last of the kegs? It's surely time for –"

And then Emmaline and Tommy were gone, running faster than they'd ever run, out through the gates.

SOULS OF THE DEAD

s Emmaline and Tommy turned the corner of the square onto Chapel Lane, only seconds from Mrs. Freeman's gates, she heard Brandy Jack's angry shouts. Emmaline and Tommy were running alongside the stone wall of the church graveyard. The street stretched out, empty, in front of them, and Emmaline knew that any second, if she turned and looked behind her, Brandy Jack, with perhaps his henchmen, would come around the corner and catch up with them with their long strides. Instinctively she snatched Tommy up and, not knowing where the strength came from, threw him over the chest-high wall. She heard a thud and the *whoosh* of his breath as he landed in the shrubs on the other side, and then she scrambled over, painfully scraping her shins. She crouched, hidden in the scratchy shrubs behind the wall, holding Tommy against her, and listened as two or three sets of heavy footsteps thundered by.

"They won't get far," one man's voice panted, and the minute the sound of the footsteps grew fainter, Emmaline grabbed

Tommy's hand and ran, staying low and zigzagging through the tall stone markers and towering, dark yew trees, farther and farther from the wall and street beyond. The treed graveyard was immense, row after row of old graves, some with crosses leaning crookedly, others with pitted headstones crowned with moss-stained angels and lambs and praying hands. As she ran, Emmaline spotted a row of stone mausoleums, miniature houses holding the tombs of dead family members. A number were overgrown with trailing woodbine, and didn't look as if they'd been stepped into in years. She headed toward them. She couldn't hear anything but her own breathing, so loud that it blotted out any other sound, and all she could feel was Tommy's small damp hand in her own, and the jolt of her feet hitting the ground under the long grass. She ran as if in a dream, her legs pumping, overcome with the dreadful thought that she was moving in slow motion. When they reached the first mausoleum, she saw a thick padlock on the door. She kept going, past each door, seeing a similar locked padlock on each one. They were all locked. Almost all. The second last one had the padlock hanging undone, and she pushed against its door. With a burst of hope that gave her added strength, she felt it give, and pushed harder, Tommy helping her. The door huffed along the stone floor, just enough to let her and Tommy slip inside, into a dark coldness. She forced the door shut with a loud rasp as it grated against the floor. Then she leaned against it, slowly sliding to the floor, aware of the door's heavy coolness against her back, and her arm around Tommy.

Time passed, although whether minutes or perhaps half an hour, Emmaline couldn't tell. All she knew was that Tommy was beside her, and there was no sound from outside. She closed her eyes.

She'd been asleep, she thought, although perhaps not, more like in a dazed state of exhaustion and fear. Something had brought her back to awareness – some small persistent sound. It was dark in the crypt, dark and fusty, the chilled miasma of mold and decay all around her. The only light was a tiny circle on the floor in front of her outstretched legs, coming from a matching tiny circle of a window above the door. The circle of fading light and another dim glow. From a narrow stone ledge in front of the row of tombs, each carved with a name and dates, was an almost extinguished taper, sputtering and wavering. Beside it lay a small nosegay of fresh violets. It was the sputtering of the candle that she'd heard.

Someone had been in the mausoleum earlier, leaving flowers, lighting a prayer candle for a deceased loved one. Emmaline sent out a silent thank you to that person, who, perhaps in their grief, had neglected to secure the door as they left.

She looked down at Tommy, although all she could make out was his profile. He was asleep, his breathing short and rapid, his skin, when she put her hand on his forehead, clammy. But they were safe. She twisted her neck to look up at the miniature round window, seeing that the light was almost gone. Evening was falling. They would stay here until morning. By tomorrow Brandy Jack would be gone for good, back at work with the rest of his sad little tribe of climbers, and then, in the bright light of a new day, she would think of what they could do next.

With one swift sly whisper, the candle went out.

Emmaline and Tommy were alone, in the darkness of the silent mausoleum. Around them were only the souls of the dead.

Emmaline moved Tommy so that his head was in her lap, and took slow, even breaths, trying to will herself into sleep. She would need sleep to face tomorrow.

The dead can't hurt us, she told herself. *It's the living we have to fear.*

SISTER HERE

he night was terrible. The events of the day kept running through Emmaline's head in fragmented and frightening images: the fight with Master Eugene, the whirling confusion of the parade, the flight from Brandy Jack. Unsettling half-pictures swarmed behind her eyes, dropping her, with a startled jerk, back into consciousness whenever she felt herself drifting in the direction of sleep. The stone floor was cold and oozed a dank moistness that seeped through her skirt, chilling her bones. She pulled Tommy up into her lap, and in his sleep he curled against her, his bare arms and legs warmed by her body.

She didn't move from the door, in case someone should try to open it. Tommy barely stirred, although once he sat up suddenly, making small distressed mewing sounds, and in the complete darkness she put her hands on his, and signed into them, *Sister, Sister here.* He pushed hard against her, as if reassuring himself that she was really there, and in a few minutes she felt his body soften. She knew he was easing back to sleep.

The smell in the crypt was hard and black, and at times Emmaline felt as if she were drowning in a cold dry sea. There were noises above and below and all around her – small sharp claws on rock, the rustle and sigh of powdery wings. She felt something move across her boot and drew a deep breath but didn't move, concentrating on repeating her favorite stanza from Wordsworth's *Lucy* that she'd read to Master Thorn more than once.

In one of those sweet dreams I slept,
Kind Nature's gentlest boon!
And all the while my eyes I kept
On the descending moon.

She thought of her father, laughing, with the crown of moonflowers on his head, whispering the stanza over and over, until she fell into a kind of trance.

And finally it was morning; somehow they had survived the night in the crypt. A tiny beam of light grew like a lengthening finger from the circle above the door, and Tommy seemed to feel the light, too – even in his sleep – stirring and cautiously moving his tightly curled legs. Emmaline watched him open his eyes, and saw a moment of fright in them. She imagined this was what he would have felt every morning that he and the other boys were shaken awake by Brandy Jack in some dark cellar after a night of shivering sleep on bags of soot.

But the fear was washed away by joy as he looked at her. He smiled. *Sister here*, he signed.

Emmaline got to her feet, trying to shake the blood back into her toes, feeling aches from her ankles to her neck. She shivered as she looked around the small rectangle of the mausoleum, knowing that behind each of the square stones on one wall were decaying flesh and bones.

But the tomb had kept her and Tommy safe, hidden from Brandy Jack.

Now they could leave, although where they would go she didn't yet know.

Emmaline got Tommy away from Chapel Lane as fast as she could, hurrying down alleys and cautiously peeking around corners, just in case Brandy Jack was still in the area.

Soon Tommy pulled on her hand. *Drink*, he signed. *Hungry, drink*, Tommy signed again, then *home, Sister and Tommy*. Emmaline saw that his lips were cracked and blistered, his eyes dull.

We have no home, Emmaline thought, *and I don't know how I'm going to feed you*, but she gripped his hand tighter, squared her shoulders, and put her feet down more firmly with each step, purposefully, so as to not let Tommy realize she didn't know what to do next.

Down the next alley Emmaline spotted a lid from a pot sitting under a drainpipe. It had a few inches of water in it; she tasted it, and it was tinny but fresh. Holding the lid to Tommy's mouth, she let him drink until he had enough, and then finished what was left.

Hungry, Tommy signed again.

She remembered, now, where there was food. But dare she go back to the potting shed and take out the small packet of biscuits and cake and dried fruit and nuts that she'd left there when she and Thomas had worked in the garden? It would hold him for at least today. And what choice did they have? They could pass near to Thorn House on their way out of London, back to the north road that led to Tibbing.

The important thing right now was that she had Tommy. She told herself it was all that mattered – Tommy safe. She knew that her dream of living a free life in a village, as she had with her father and mother, was just that – a dream. The quicker she put it out of her mind, the quicker she could stop letting herself believe she could make it come true. If they got back to Tibbing, Tommy would be with Cat, and she –

Tommy tugged on her skirt, and she looked down at him. *Never go away*, he signed. *Tommy always with Sister.* "Em," he said, when his hands stopped.

And she would be with Aunt Phoebe in the fine house on Mosely Road, and never see Tommy. Emmaline gave him a small smile and ran her hand over his bristled skull. Then she took his hand and they started walking again.

As they approached Thorn House, Emmaline knew that it was too early for anybody in the house to be up and about. But to be safe, she took Tommy around into the lane at the back. At a spot in the high fence that Emmaline knew wasn't visible from the courtyard, she clambered up, and reaching down for Tommy, dragged him up with her. She lowered him onto the hard dirt behind the potting shed. Jumping down lightly, she winced as her foot landed on a dry stray stick from the pile of debris she and Thomas had raked out of the garden and stacked behind the small sloped building. The crack of the stick seemed shockingly loud, and she stood still for a moment, listening, but there was no other sound – no footsteps nor voices. She crept into the potting shed, then dropped Tommy's hand in surprise at what she saw.

Thomas was sitting on a pile of sacks, leaning against the wall. There was a knotted bundle at his side. One hand held a sharp hoe. His eyes were closed and his head was tilted uncomfortably to one side. At the scrape of Emmaline's boot on the threshold, he opened his eyes and leapt up in alarm, brandishing the hoe in Tommy and Emmaline's direction. And then, seeing Emmaline, he threw it down with a clatter.

In three swift steps he crossed the floor, and she reached her arms out to him, and his eyes shone as if a candle had been lit behind them. He put his face into her hair with a small sound that Emmaline had never heard before.

SOMETHING THAT BELONGS TO YOU

"hat are you doing here?" Emmaline asked quietly when they finally stepped away from each other. She glanced behind her toward the courtyard, then closed the door of the potting shed.

"You've found your brother?" Thomas tore his eyes from Emmaline and looked Tommy up and down. "Poor mite," he said, shaking his head.

"Yes," she said, rooting on the shelf while Tommy held her skirt with one hand, eyeing Thomas. On top of the packet of food she had left was an unfamiliar square package, wrapped in a piece of coarse bleached cloth. Her name had been written on the cloth with what looked like a charred stick. Putting the packet on the low potting table in front of her, she pulled out the food, unwrapped it, and gave it to Tommy. He sat on the floor, cross-legged, and ate quickly, watching Emmaline and Thomas.

"What were you doing, sleeping here?" Emmaline asked Thomas a second time.

"I daren't go back in the house," he said. "And I was waiting for you."

"Waiting for me? How did you know I'd be back?"

"I didn't. I hoped you would. I was going to stay until tomorrow, and then I'd have to leave. This – the potting shed – was the only place I could think of that you might come back to if you were desperate for shelter. Sukey told me there'd been some kind of commotion, and I knew you must have run off. I was out on the streets of Steeplemount, looking for you, until a few hours ago, but . . ." He stopped. "I know he did something to you." By the way he said *he*, his voice going so hard, Emmaline knew he meant Eugene. "Did he hurt you?"

She shook her head. "No. But I hurt *him*. I gave him a good clout, square in the face, Thomas, with a wash jug. So I had to run. I only came back to get this bit of food for Tommy. I took a chance that Eugene wouldn't catch me."

She looked at Tommy. The brindle cat had slunk out from somewhere, and now Tommy was petting it, his small dirty hand gently smoothing the sleek fur. He offered it an almond. The cat sniffed at it, uninterested, and Tommy popped it into his own mouth.

Thomas gave a low chuckle. "Good for you," he said, admiration in his voice. "I wondered about his face – the plaster over his nose and the blackening eyes. However hard you hit him, he deserved more. Anyway, he sacked me and Sukey. Threw me out yesterday, and told Sukey to be gone by the end of the week. I've got my things here with me." He gestured toward the bundle.

"But why? What have you done? He's got it into his head that I was stealing from the house, money and something else – I don't know what — but why has he given you the shove? How will he run the house?"

"He's hiring new staff. He says he's going to run Thorn House the way it should be run. Wants a fresh start, with proper help, he says — no riffraff from the workhouse. Especially no *Irish* riffraff, which, of course, is the worst kind." He smiled again, but it was a sad, slow smile.

"What about Cook?"

"He let her stay on."

Emmaline nodded. She ran two fingers over her name on the wrapped package. Black smeared onto her fingertips. "And you and Sukey? What will you do?"

"I'll be all right. I can find something, although it won't be domestic, not without a letter. I've managed to save a few shillings; I shared them with Sukey, but what I have will tide me over until something turns up. There's always day work, loading wagons or hauling boxes. And there are the mines, up north, if all else fails."

"Mines? Never, Thomas."

"I'll do what I have to," he said. "But Sukey . . ." Suddenly his chin trembled, and he put his hand on it to still it. Emmaline saw him as he must have looked as a small boy, turning to Sukey for help in the workhouse. "I don't know what will become of her." His voice trailed off, and in the silence Emmaline knew that Sukey would have no choice but to return to the workhouse until she had her child. And it would kill her, Emmaline knew, if she was forced to leave her baby there. But she wouldn't be able to get work with a newborn baby in her arms. "I told her I'd slip back, once I knew where I was going, to say a proper good-bye," Thomas said.

Tommy had finished the food and was twirling a piece of broken crockery on the floor for the cat, who was watching it attentively. Tommy glanced from Emmaline to Thomas and back to Emmaline from under his long lashes.

"And what about you? Where will you go?" Thomas asked.

Emmaline busied herself brushing her hand down her skirt, as if trying to rid the fabric of a stain. "Oh, now that I have my brother, I'll go on home again – back to Tibbing," she said, not wanting to let him see the anxiety that she knew was in her face. She concentrated on the dark stain, rubbing briskly. Then she looked up at Thomas as she saw his hands lift the wrapped square with her name on it.

"This is something that belongs to you. It's part of the reason I don't want Master Eugene to find me, either, for he'll know by now that it's missing, and that it was me who took it." He put the package into Emmaline's hands.

She unwrapped it. It was two books, their covers soft morocco, the pages gilt-edged. They looked old, but well cared for. One was a copy of Jonathan Swift's *Gulliver's Travels*, the other *The Vicar of Wakefield*, by Oliver Goldsmith. She looked at Thomas. "I don't understand."

"It was in the will, according to Mr. Paltron. I let him into the study at dinner yesterday, and afterwards he read the old master's will out to Master Eugene. I listened from the hallway because I wanted to know what our future would be. And while Master Thorn left the house to Master Eugene, there's not a lot of money. He left a good deal of his savings to charities and poorhouses, and Master Eugene was furious. I take it he had thought that he would fall into a large inheritance, and could live in high style.

But it appears that he'll definitely have to lower his standards."

"But these books . . ." Emmaline hugged them to her chest, thinking of the old man's almost sightless eyes turned in her direction as she read to him.

"He must have wanted you to have them."

"Well, I'll certainly remember him, whenever I read them."

"Emmaline? You can keep them, if you like. They're yours to do with as you please. But they're quite valuable. The most valuable ones he owned, I take it. That's why Master Eugene was so furious. I heard Mr. Paltron tell Master Eugene that he should inform you that he could easily find a buyer for them. Master Eugene said he would contest the will, all of it, but Mr. Paltron said he had no grounds to do this, that Anthony Thorn made his decisions in a clear mind, and that he – Mr. Paltron – would attest to that. He said Master Thorn's decisions would be honored in a court of law."

Emmaline's hands caressed the cover of the top book. "They're worth money? These old books?"

"A lot of money, according to Mr. Paltron. They've been signed by the authors. I can take you to Mr. Paltron, right away, if you like. He'll tell you what to do, Emmaline."

There were sudden voices in the courtyard, and Thomas stepped in front of Emmaline and Tommy, picking up the hoe and facing the door. But Emmaline put her hand on his arm. "It's only Maggie and Peg," she whispered. "They'll never come in here."

Thomas looked down at her hand, then back into her face.

"Will you take me to Mr. Paltron, Thomas?"

"I will," he answered.

A SOLID PROPOSAL

iss Roke? Would you all care to step inside my office, please?" Mr. Paltron said, removing his hat as he entered the waiting room, where Thomas and Emmaline and Tommy had been sitting on stiff horsehair chairs. "Have you been offered refreshments?" he asked, stopping at his office door.

"Yes," Emmaline answered. "We were given a light meal. Thank you."

"I'm sorry to have been so long. You've had quite a wait – much of the day – I realize. The transaction took longer than I had expected. But it went well. Now, come along, if you will."

Emmaline and Tommy and Thomas followed Mr. Paltron into his office.

"It's growing dark," Mr. Paltron said. "Let me light the lamps. Please, have a seat."

Thomas sat in a brocade chair beside Emmaline. She balanced Tommy on her lap. The little boy wore patched but clean clothes – pants, a shirt, and jacket. There were shoes on his feet, and a small cap covered his head.

Mr. Paltron's assistant, after instructions from his employer, had shown Emmaline and Tommy into a small chamber, where Emmaline did her best to clean Tommy with warm water and cloths. Thomas had disappeared, returning with the used items he'd bought from a street vendor, and the assistant had gingerly carried away the ragged, filthy clothes.

"Now," Mr. Paltron said, sitting across from them, "the dealer in antique books was quite pleased by what I had to show him. He has a number of collectors who will jump at the chance to bid on the books. He's an honest man, and I know the offer he made was a fair one, and so I took it. I trust you'll be pleased." He gave Emmaline a square brown envelope. "The receipt is enclosed as well."

She opened the envelope and took out a pile of banknotes. She'd never seen so much money at one time. "It's a fortune," she breathed.

Mr. Paltron smiled. "No, my dear. It's not a fortune, but it will do you nicely for some time to come, if you use it sensibly. Do you have plans for it? You mustn't just carry it around; you might lose it, or be tempted to make an unwise decision. Or of course fall prey to thieves."

Emmaline gently touched the stack of notes with one finger.

"Would this be enough to buy . . . a place?"

"A place? What kind of place?"

"A small one," Emmaline told him, leaning over Tommy's shoulder. "In a village. Perhaps a cottage, where I could open a shop."

"Oh, it's more than would be needed for something like that. What kind of shop are you thinking of?" Mr. Paltron asked, a smile on his lips.

"I'm not entirely sure." Emmaline glanced sideways at Thomas. "Perhaps a sewing shop. Perhaps." Now she held her hands together, tightly over Tommy's chest.

"A seamstress shop, in a village? There's no question it would do. Yes, certainly it would be enough to purchase the building, and for initial supplies. What has given you this idea?" He saw that her eyes were shining.

Emmaline smiled. "It's always been my dream," she said.

"Well, you'll be able to make a nice little living, if you work hard, I expect," Mr. Paltron said, distracted by a sudden crash, and then shouts, from the street. He got up and went to the window, saying, over his shoulder to Emmaline, "You strike me as someone who isn't afraid of hard work. Anthony must have seen something in you, as well, to include you in his will." Tommy jumped down off Emmaline's lap and followed Mr. Paltron to the window.

"Silly fool down there," he commented. "Turned over his wagon of day-old bread coming 'round the corner. And here come the children, to help themselves before he can load it back up again."

Then he turned back to Emmaline, studying her. "You're very young," he said. "You intend to run this business on your own?"

Emmaline blinked, as if she had been lost in thought. "Oh, no, Sir. There'll be others, others to help in all manner of ways. My family – my mother and my brother here. And I have two friends I'd like to join me. If they're willing." She felt Thomas's hand rest on her shoulder then, lightly.

Mr. Paltron nodded at Thomas's hand. "I see. Well, it sounds like a solid proposal." He went to his desk and worked at straightening the mess of papers on top.

Tommy was looking out the window, now, his fingers moving.

"What's he saying?" Thomas asked. He had watched Emmaline and Tommy talk to each other with their hands throughout the day.

Emmaline crossed the room to her brother. "He sees the moon," she told Thomas. "Come and look. Tommy says no more dark; he sees the moon."

As Thomas came to stand behind her, Emmaline said to Tommy, "No more dark. Soon you'll be able to see the moon the way I always told you." She signed to him again, and Tommy smiled and put his hand on his chest. Emmaline nodded. *Yes. Mama, too.* Then Tommy touched his chin, made a circle with his hands, and put them on his head.

Yes. Our father was the Moon King, Emmaline signed. *And I am the Moon King's daughter.*

The three of them stood at the window, watching the moon.

"Thomas? Do you suppose Sukey has ever seen the way the moon looks in a country sky?" Emmaline asked, looking at her own reflection in the window, with Tommy's image in front of her and Thomas's over her shoulder.

"She's never been out of London."

"She'll like it, don't you think?"

"Yes," he agreed. "I know she will. I remember it. From when I was a boy myself, back in County Clare." His breath was warm against the back of Emmaline's neck. "I remember that the moon is so much bigger, and brighter, in the country sky."

"Yes," Emmaline said. "Yes, it is."

And they stood together, watching the pearly orb rise between the chimneys of the London rooftops.

The End

AUTHOR'S NOTE

The locations where Emmaline Roke lived and worked – Maidenfern Village and Tibbing in Lancashire County, and the area of London where she searched for Tommy – Steeplemount Way – exist only in my imagination. They are, however, based on in-depth research of specific areas; the names were fictionalized to avoid misrepresentation.

Greatly assisting me on historical accuracy of life in England in this era of the Industrial Revolution were a number of nonfiction books. Most notably I referred to *Mayhew's London* and *London's Underground*, by Henry Mayhew; *A History of Everyday Things in England 1733–1851*, by Marjorie and C.H.B. Quennell; *Chimney Sweeps Yesterday and Today*, by James Cross Giblin; *What Jane Austen Ate and Charles Dickens Knew*, by Daniel Pool; and others too numerous to name.

ACKNOWLEDGMENTS

Thank you, as always, to Kathy Lowinger for her astute suggestions and challenging questions and always, always for her gift of insight; and to Sue Tate, for her wonderful attention to detail and her unbelievably keen eye during copyediting.

Also by Linda Holeman

RASPBERRY HOUSE BLUES

Selected for the BOOKS FOR THE TEEN AGE by the New York Public Library.

"An appealing book with a host of unusual characters that will worm their way into readers' hearts."

School Library Journal

Poppy is on an odyssey. Her adoptive mother has taken off for the summer to find herself, so Poppy decides to live with her adoptive father, his new wife, Calypso, and their toddler, Sandeep, in a ramshackle raspberry-colored house that seems like a throwback to the sixties. At first Poppy can't stand the household with its incense, granola, and the endless blues records her father plays – on a record player! But the raspberry house becomes a jumping-off point for her search for her birth mother, a search in which Poppy discovers a great many things. But will she find the mother who gave her up so many years ago, and the acceptance she craves?

Also by Linda Holeman

MERCY'S BIRDS

Selected for the BOOKS FOR THE TEEN AGE by the New York Public Library.

"Eloquent and impacting, Mercy's story is an engrossing one, charged with emotional depth."

Booklist (starred review)

Mercy lives with her mother and her aunt, and her small family is spinning out of control. Her mother is holed up in her bedroom and seems to be shrinking because she's depressed and can't eat. Her Aunt Moo is taking refuge in alcohol and tarot cards and she can't do anything *but* eat. And any day now, Moo's creepy boyfriend Barry is coming back to live with them. Mercy is holding on – just barely – with a job she likes in a flower shop and a sort-of friend, but she knows the problems in her household are too much for her. When help arrives from an unexpected source, will she accept it?

Also by Linda Holeman

PROMISE SONG

Selected for the BOOKS FOR THE TEEN AGE by the New York Public Library.

" . . . this novel will engage readers . . . Rosetta's pluck and determination make her an admirable heroine, and the story is exciting."
School Library Journal

The year is 1900, and like many thousands of children before them, fourteen-year-old Rosetta and her small sister Flora have been sent across the sea from an English orphanage to make their home in a new country. But when they arrive, their dream of a family vanishes. Instead, small pretty Flora is adopted by strangers and Rosetta is sent off to work on a farm. The hardships Rosetta faces are greater than she had ever imagined – and so are the rewards – as she learns the true meaning of sisterhood.